BORDERLANDS

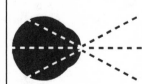

AN INSPECTOR DEVLIN MYSTERY

BORDERLANDS

BRIAN MCGILLOWAY

THORNDIKE PRESS
A part of Gale, Cengage Learning

GALE
CENGAGE Learning

Detroit • New York • San Francisco • New Haven, Conn • Waterville, Maine • London

GALE
CENGAGE Learning™

LIBRARY OF CONGRESS CATALOGING-IN-PUBLICATION DATA

McGilloway, Brian, 1974–
    Borderlands : an Inspector Devlin mystery / by Brian McGilloway.
        p. cm. — (Thorndike press large print mystery)
        ISBN-13: 978-1-4104-1135-8 (hardcover : alk. paper)
        ISBN-10: 1-4104-1135-4 (hardcover : alk. paper)
        1. Police—Ireland—Fiction. 2. Murder—Investigation—Fiction. 3. Teenage girls—Crimes against—Fiction. 4. Ireland—Fiction. 5. Large type books. I. Title.
PR6113.C4755B67 2008b
823'.92—dc22   2008035378

Published in 2008 by arrangement with St. Martin's Press, LLC.

Printed in the United States of America
1 2 3 4 5 6 7 12 11 10 09 08

For Tanya, Ben and Tom,
and for my parents

■ ■ ■ ■

ANGELA CASHELL

■ ■ ■ ■

CHAPTER ONE

Saturday, 21st December 2002

It was not beyond reason that Angela Cashell's final resting place should straddle the border. Presumably, neither those who dumped her corpse, nor, indeed, those who had created the border between the North and South of Ireland in 1920, could understand the vagaries that meant that her body lay half in one country and half in another, in an area known as the borderlands.

The peculiarities of the Irish border are famous. Eighty years ago it was drawn through fields, farms and rivers by civil servants who knew little more about the area than that which they'd learnt from a map. Now, people live with the consequences, owning houses where TV licences are bought in the North and the electricity needed to run them is paid for in the South.

When a crime occurs in an area not clearly in one jurisdiction or another, both the Irish

Republic's An Garda Siochana and the Police Service of Northern Ireland work together, each offering all the practical help and advice they can, the lead detective determined generally by either the location of the body or the nationality of the victim.

Consequently then, I stood with my colleagues from An Garda facing our northern counterparts through the snow-heavy wind which came running up the river. The sky above us, bruised purple and yellow in the dying sun, promised no reprieve.

We shook hands, exchanged greetings and moved to where the girl lay, prone but for one hand, which was turned towards the sky. The medical examiner, a local doctor named John Mulrooney, was kneeling beside the girl's naked body, testing her muscles for signs of rigor mortis. Her head rested at his knees. Her hair was blonde at the ends, but honey-coloured closer to her scalp, her skin white and clean except for thin scratches across her back and legs caused by the brambles through which her body had fallen. A SOCO leaned in close to her, examining the cuts as the medical examiner pointed them out, and took photographs.

We watched as three or four Gardai moved in to help turn her over. I stepped back and stared across the water to the northern side, where the arthritic limbs of the trees stretched towards the snow clouds, the black branches rattling in the winter wind.

"Do you recognize her, sir?" one of the northerners asked, and I turned back to the girl, whose face was now exposed. My vision blurred momentarily as a breeze shivered across the river's surface. Then my sight cleared and I moved over and knelt beside her, suppressing the urge to take off my jacket and cover her with it, at least until the Scene of Crime Officers were finished.

"That's Johnny Cashell's girl," a uniformed Garda said, "from Clipton Place."

I nodded my agreement. "He's right," I said, turning to the northern Inspector, a man called Jim Hendry, whose rank was the same as mine but whose experience was vastly greater. "She's ours, I'm afraid."

He nodded without looking at me. Hendry was at least a head taller than me, well over six feet, with a wiry frame and dirty, fair hair. He sported a thin, sandy moustache at which he tugged when under stress; he did so now. "Poor girl," he said.

Her face was fresh and young; she was fifteen or sixteen at most. She wore make-up in a way that reminded me of my own daughter, Penny, when she played at being a grown-up with my wife's cosmetics. The blue eye-shadow was too heavily applied, contrasting with the redness of her eyes where the veins had burst in her final moments. Her whole face had assumed a light-blue hue. Her mouth was partially opened in a rictus of pain; the bright red lipstick she had so carefully applied was smeared across her face in streaks.

Her small breasts carried purple bruises the size and shape of a man's hands. One bruise, smaller and darker than the others, resembled a love bite. Snowflakes settled on her body as gently as kisses and did not melt.

Her trunk and thighs were ivory white, though her arms and the lower parts of her legs were tanned with cosmetics, the streaks and misapplication clear now against her pallor. A pinkish colour was forming on her legs and chest. She wore plain white cotton pants which were inside out.

"Well, Doc?" I asked the ME, "what do you think?"

He stood up and peeled off the rubber gloves he had been wearing. Then he stepped away from the body and took a cigarette offered to him by a Garda officer. "Hard to say. The body is fairly stiff, but it was a cold night so I can't really give you time of death. More than six hours, no more than twelve. You'll know better when the autopsy's done. Cause of death — I can't be totally sure either, but I'd say the bruising on her chest is significant. That blue tinting of the face is caused by smothering or crushing of the chest. That, and the chest bruising, would suggest suffocation, but that's an educated guess. Lividity indicates she was moved after she died, though you hardly need me to tell you that. Naked women don't just appear in the middle of fields."

"Signs of struggle?" Hendry asked.

"Signs of something. Her fingernails are bitten so close I doubt you'll get anything from under them. Sorry I can't be more help, Ben," he said to me. "I can tell you that she's dead, and that someone killed her and dumped her here, so it's over to you now. The state pathologist will be here as soon as possible."

"Presumably this was sexual," I said.

"Don't know for sure. The pathologist will take swabs as a matter of course. Personally, I'd say fairly likely. Good luck, Ben. Take it easy." With that he dropped the gloves into his case, lifted it and walked up the embankment to his car, barely looking at the body as he passed it.

I looked again at the girl. Her hands rested

on the leaves beneath her, the bright red nail polish a little incongruous on fingers so small and on nails bitten so near to the quick. There was a little dirt around her nails, and soon enough a SOCO wrapped her hands in plastic bags which he secured at her wrist. I noticed that, on her right hand, she wore a gold ring set with some type of stone. It looked too old-fashioned for a girl of her age; a family heirloom, a gift from a parent or grandparent, perhaps. The stone was tinted green, like a moonstone, and surrounded by diamonds. I asked the photographer to take a shot of it. As he did so, the flash illuminated an engraving on the band.

"Looks like something's written on it, sir," he said, crouching right down and holding the camera in one hand as he angled her hand slightly with his other. Then he focused the camera tight on the ring. "I think it says AC, sir: her initials."

I nodded for no particular reason and turned again to the group of northerners.

"Shitty enough one to get the week before Christmas, Devlin. Good luck to you," Hendry said, nipping off the end of his cigarette, then putting the butt in his pocket so as not to contaminate the crime scene. That was a bit of a joke. Our resources in the arse-end of Donegal are hardly FBI quality and, besides a dozen or so policemen and the waiting ambulance crew and the group of poachers who had discovered the body, God only knew how many other people had tramped back and forth past the body and along the roadway where those who dumped it must have stopped.

We would look for distinctive tyre treads, footprints, and so on, and try to find whatever forensics we could, but the spot where this body had been abandoned, though secluded, was only a few hundred yards behind the local Cineplex. On weekend nights this whole stretch of lane was lined with cars, each respecting the other's space, obeying an unspoken rule of privacy to which I had myself subscribed when younger, when I was finally allowed to take my father's car to collect my girlfriend. The makes of cars had changed since then — and I tell myself, in moments of righteous indignation (though I accept that it's probably not true), that the kind of activities in which the couples engage has probably changed too. However, the place remained the same — as dark and furtive as any of the clumsy embraces which take place on back seats there at night. Indeed, it was possible that Angela Cashell had met her death in such a car.

"They might have been from your side," I said to Hendry, motioning towards the top of the embankment, where those who had left her must have stood.

"They possibly are," he agreed, "but this one's yours. This must be your first murder since —"

"1883," replied one of ours. "And he was hung!"

"Rightly bloody so," agreed another northerner.

"Oh, there's been more since," I said. "We just haven't found all the bodies yet."

Hendry laughed. "We'll help any way we can, Devlin, but you're the lead on this." He looked at Angela one last time. "She was a lovely-looking girl. I'd hate to have to tell her parents."

"Jesus, don't talk," I replied. "You don't know her father, Johnny Cashell."

"Oh, I know enough," Hendry replied darkly and winked. "British Intelligence isn't totally down the drain yet." With that, we shook hands and he walked off towards his own side, steadying himself against the thick buffets of air carrying the smell of the water across the borderlands.

Johnny Cashell was known to all the Gardai

in Lifford on a first-name basis, having spent many nights in the holding cell of the small police station in the centre of our village. In fact, when the county council recently gave the whole village a facelift, putting new lamps and hanging-baskets all around the cobbled square and benches along the main roads, we named the bench outside the station "Sadie's", in recognition of the amount of time spent on it by Cashell's wife while she waited for him to be released in the morning from the drunk-tank.

Johnny Cashell was an obdurate man with a chip against anyone better educated than himself. He would hold court in the local bars, boasting of all he had achieved despite having left school at fourteen. In reality, he was a petty criminal, stealing from phone boxes and charity tins, and pissing it against the wall of the Military Post as he staggered past on his way home.

No matter how low Johnny sank, Sadie was always waiting for him, even when he stole his mother-in-law's pension book. However, we all had to reconsider Sadie's loyalty to Johnny when he got out after serving nine months for that. Three months later she gave birth to a baby girl, the only member of the Cashell family who didn't have Johnny's bright copper colouring but a head washed in wisps of white-blonde. They called the girl Angela, and Johnny cared for her as if she were his own, as far as anyone knew never questioning her parentage. We all suspected that secretly it hurt him — the bright blonde so obviously at odds with the fiery reds of her siblings. In weaker moments, when Johnny shouted profanities from the holding cells until we couldn't take it any more, we taunted him about his blonde-haired daughter and how she was the prettiest of the bunch. The slightest comment was enough to silence him and ensure a full night's sleep for whoever was stuck on duty because of him.

The snow ceased as the assistant state pathologist arrived, black medical bag in hand. I stood by the river as she worked, wondering what to say to Johnny Cashell, and watched the sun exploding low over the horizon, turning the ribs of the clouds first pink, then purple and orange.

Cashell was a barrel-chested, red-faced man with thick, curly red hair that he kept tied back in a ponytail. He dressed as if from a charity shop and his clothes had a musty, damp odour. He was more particular about his feet, and I never met him wearing the same pair of trainers twice: they were always new and always a brand label. When you spoke to him he looked at the ground, scrunching up his toes so you could see the movements through the white leather of his shoes. When he spoke it was not to your face but to a spot just to the left, as though someone else waited at your shoulder for his words. All his children had developed the same habit, which their social worker had thought of as rude until she got to know them.

As we stood at his doorway, he stared at his shoes while I told him of his daughter's death and invited him to identify her. Then he looked past me, his eyes flickering with grief or anger. He exhaled a breath which he seemed to have been holding since I arrived, and I thought I could smell drink under the cigarette smoke.

"It's her," he said. "I know it's her. Sh'ain't been home these two days. Went out to Strabane on Thursday." He leaned back a little, as though steadying himself against the door jamb, the sunlight burnishing to gold the red curls on the back of his hands.

Sadie Cashell appeared behind him, face ashen, seemingly having overheard our conversation. She was drying her hands on a dishcloth. "What is it, Johnny?" she asked

19

with suspicion.

"They've gone and found Angela. They think she's dead, Ma!" he said. And with that his lips softened and his face crumpled.

He spluttered rather than cried, spit and tears dribbling down his chin. His eyes stopped flickering as the final rays of sunlight stole from the sky and the world darkened almost imperceptibly.

"How?" Sadie demanded, her jaw muscles quivering.

"We . . . we don't know yet, Sadie," I said. "We think someone has killed her, I'm afraid."

"There's been some mistake," she said, her voice rising hysterically, her grip tightening on her husband's arm until her knuckles whitened. "You're wrong."

"I'm sorry, Sadie," I said. "I'll . . . we'll do what we can. I promise." She stared at me, as if waiting for me to say something else, then turned and went inside.

Johnny Cashell snuffed through his nose, his face turned towards Strabane. I guessed that Sadie had broken the news to their children, for I could hear the cries of girls begin from inside the house, the sound building quickly to a crescendo.

"We need you to come to the morgue, Mr Cashell. To identify her. If you don't mind."

"She needn't be there now. Bring her home," he said.

"Mr Cashell, we have things we have to do, sir, to find out what happened to her. You mightn't get her back for a day or two, I'm afraid."

He took a tin from his pocket and removed a rolled cigarette from it, put it in his mouth and lit it. Then he spat a piece of tobacco from his tongue and looked once more in my direction, just beyond my shoulder. "I know what happened to her. I'll deal with it," he said.

"What do you mean? What do you think happened, Mr Cashell?" I asked.

"Never mind," he said, still not looking at me.

His wife reappeared at the door. "Where's my girl, John?" she asked her husband. He pointed to me with his thumb.

"He says we can't have her yet. She ain't ready to come home, he says."

"Who did it?" she demanded.

"I . . . we don't know, Mrs Cashell," I said, glancing at her husband. "We're working on it."

"You're fast enough to pick up on innocent people in the street, maybe has a drink. Now you're slow all of a sudden. Some rich girl, you'd be faster, I'd say."

"Mrs Cashell," I said, "I promise we will deal with this as quickly as possible. Can I speak with your other daughters, please?"

Sadie looked first at me, then at her husband, who shrugged his shoulders and walked away from the door, still smoking. Then she allowed me in.

Angela's three sisters were seated around a table in the kitchen. They looked remarkably similar. A baby, dressed only in a nappy, clung to the chest of one of them, bunching up her white blouse in his fist.

I sat at the table and took out my cigarettes.

"No smoking around my wee'un," said the young mother, tapping her own cigarette ash onto the linoleum floor.

I did not put the cigarette away, nor did I light it. The youngest daughter was still crying, but the other girls stared at me, one red-eyed, one vaguely defiant, as if unwilling to show emotions in front of a Guard.

"I need some help in finding out what happened to Angela," I said. "Perhaps you could tell me people she was with, boyfriends, that sort of thing."

The youngest girl opened her mouth as though to speak but was interrupted by the one holding the baby, whose name I seemed to remember was Christine.

"We don't know nothing, *Inspector.*" She pronounced each syllable of the title deliberately and with as much disdain as she could muster. I noticed that she alone, of all the sisters, had not cried since she had heard the news. Her eyes were clear and white. Aware of my gaze, she looked down at her baby instead, her head tilted slightly to one side.

I turned to the youngest girl. "Were you going to tell me something?" I said. "To help me?"

She glanced furtively at her sister, then lowered her head and stared at her hands, which were joined in her lap. She looked undernourished, her bony pink hands like baby birds in a nest.

Christine spoke again. "Like I already told you", she said, "we don't know nothing." With that, she lifted her baby's bottle and began to feed him, holding the cigarette in her mouth and squinting through the smoke.

I asked Sadie if I could see Angela's room. She led me up the stairs in silence, pushed open one of the bedroom doors and waited for me to go in. I was a little surprised to find the room so tidy, and at the same time a little ashamed at the unworthiness of the thought. A window dominated the far wall, facing onto the backyard.

The room looked freshly painted, a lavender tint; the carpet and bed linen were light green. A poster of someone called Orlando Bloom had been tacked carefully to the wall behind the bed. The wardrobe was packed with clothes, neatly arranged and hung according to type and size. I spotted the corner of a paperback on the floor, peeping out from the overhanging bedspread. I recognized the author as one whom my wife Debbie read. Flicking through the pages absentmindedly as I looked around the room, I noticed that Angela had been using a strip of passport photographs as a bookmark. The strip showed the half-faces of two girls, grinning in from the white border on either side. One of them was Angela. In the final picture their faces touched lightly and Angela was no longer smiling, yet seemed all the more content. It saddened me to see her so alive. I held the pictures up to Sadie and asked her who the other girl was, but she simply shrugged her shoulders and asked if I was finished. I replaced the strip of pictures, careful not to lose the page, before I realized the futility of the gesture.

In the corner of the room there was an old CD player and a plastic rack with a dozen or so discs sitting under a freestanding mirror. Most of the bands I either did not know or had heard of only from Penny. Strangely, I noticed in the middle a CD by the Divine Comedy, whom I had seen perform in Dublin a few years previously. It seemed a little incongruous amongst all the boy bands. I asked Sadie about the CD. Again she shrugged and moved into the hallway, making it clear that she did not wish for me to remain in her daughter's bedroom. I thanked her and offered my condolences again as I made my way downstairs and outside to arrange for Johnny Cashell to identify the body.

He was still standing in his front yard when I left the house, picking the last remaining deadheads off a florabunda rose bush. The heads themselves were heavy and brown, hanging low. He broke them off with his hand, clasping fists full of dead petals.

"I am sorry, Mr Cashell." I said, shaking his free hand. "There is one other thing. Can you tell me what Angela was wearing when last you saw her?"

"Jeans, probably. A blue hooded thing her ma bought her for her birthday, I think. 'Twere only last month. Why? Don't you know what she's wearing?"

As a father myself, I could not deprive him

of his assumption that his daughter had retained some vestige of dignity in death. I opened my mouth to speak, but the air between us was brittle and sharp with the scent of decaying leaves and I could think of nothing adequate to say.

When I returned to the station, Burgess, our Desk Sergeant, told me that I was wanted immediately by the Superintendent. Costello — or Elvis to everyone who spoke of him (though not to his face) — was famous in Lifford, having served here, in and out of uniform, for almost thirty years. It was suspected that he knew many of the family secrets that most people preferred to keep buried. It meant that, in the village, he was universally admired but secretly mistrusted. However, he never knowingly used the information he had gathered unless absolutely necessary, and he excused many ancient crimes on the grounds that if they had not merited punishment at the time, how could they do so now? By rights he should have been stationed in Letterkenny, which is the centre of the Donegal division, but following his wife Emily's mastectomy several years earlier, he had requested and been granted permission to use Lifford as his headquarters.

His nickname came not only from his surname, but also his Christian name, Olly; more than once, Gardai called to public-order disturbances had been greeted with a drunken chorus of "Oliver's Army", despite the fact that his name was actually Alphonsus. The name stuck to the force in Lifford in much the same way that Elvis stuck with Costello. He never said it, but I think he was secretly pleased by the nickname, taking it as a tacit sign of affection, recognition of his position as an institution of sorts.

"Cashell is a Cork man," he said now, straightening his tie in the mirror hung behind his office door. His position meant that he was the only person in the station to have his own office, while the rest of us shared rooms. In fairness, Elvis had been careful not to rub our faces in his perks: the furnishing was perfunctory, not expensive.

"Really?" I asked, unsure of his point.

"Yes. Moved here when he was three. A lot of us suspected at the time that they were travellers, but his family rented out towards St Johnston. He got placed in Clipton Place after he got Sadie pregnant the first time. Didn't fit in too well to begin with."

"Apparently not," I said. "Drove the neighbours on one side out with the noise, drove the neighbours on the other side out with a claw hammer."

"For which he was cautioned. Still, this is a terrible thing to happen. How did he take it?"

"As you would expect. He seemed shattered. I thought one of the daughters was going to tell me something, but the rest of the family closed tight."

"Years of mistrust, Benedict, learnt at the dinner table." Costello is also the only person I know who refers to me by my full Christian name, as if it would be unmannerly of him to do otherwise. "Leave them a day or two and try again. Maybe when fewer of them are about."

"Yes, sir."

"Have you a jacket?" he asked, nodding at the informality of my jeans and jumper — one of the few perks of being a Detective.

"Not with me."

"Nip home and get changed. You're doing a press conference at five. RTE'll be here, and the northern stations, so look sharp." I had reached the door when he added, "They haven't found her clothes yet, Benedict. I've requested the Water Unit to search the river in the morning. The PSNI have said they'll help. It'll be an early start."

■ ■ ■ ■

The press conference was the first that I had done and, while probably quite low-key in comparison with other such events, it was daunting to face the banks of lights, cameras and microphones. Costello read a prepared statement, then invited questions. My role, I had been told, was to sit there so he could identify me for the cameras. That way, justice would not be faceless, he said, without a hint of irony. I was also to handle any operational questions which Costello couldn't answer, though I was told not to go into specifics. It was strange hearing our voices echo back at us with a slight delay, almost mocking the fact that, despite all that we said to reassure the public, we had no idea who had killed Angela Cashell, how she had been killed or, more worryingly, why someone would kill a fifteen-year-old girl and dump her naked body on a river bank.

Penny and Shane were granted a maternal dispensation to stay up past bedtime to watch Daddy on TV. They almost fell asleep, though, during the main report, which was on the US President's announcement that

50,000 troops were to be sent to supplement the 60,000 already stationed in the Middle East.

When the brief article on the Cashell murder was finally aired, it was sandwiched between a report on the rising price of housing and a story about a drug trafficker who had been murdered in Dublin. The newscasters expressed more sincere concern about the house prices than the death of the unnamed dealer.

As I placed Shane in his cot, I heard a knock on the door, and a few seconds later the sound of Debbie inviting a visitor in. I peered out through our bedroom window and saw our neighbour Mark Anderson's pick-up truck parked in the driveway. Mark actually lived over half a mile away, but he owned all the land bordering our house, fields in which he grazed his sheep and cattle. He was an odd, socially awkward man, and I was surprised to see him. The only time he had called on us before was to appeal for leniency after I arrested his son, Malachy, who had been caught peeping in Sharon Kennedy's bedroom window from the tree outside her house. Her husband had felled the tree that same evening.

When I came back downstairs Anderson was sitting in the living room, perched so close to the edge of the sofa he looked as though he would fall off. He stood up when I came in and I smiled and extended my hand. "Happy Christmas, Mark," I said. "Good to see you."

He did not reciprocate my smile or greeting but said simply, "Your dog's been annoying my sheep."

"Excuse me," I said, moving over to where Debbie was sitting.

"Your dog's been worrying my sheep. I saw it."

Our dog is a six-year-old basset-hound called Frank, which I bought for Debbie on our fifth wedding anniversary when it seemed we could not have children. Four months after we bought him, Debbie found out she was pregnant with Penny, and so Frank became very much my dog. Now that Penny was older, she too had become attached to him. At night we kept him locked in a shed we built for him, and I told Anderson as much.

"I know what I seen," he said. "Anything happens to any of my sheep, I'll put a bullet in the mutt. I've warned you."

Penny, who had stopped watching the TV at the start of the conversation, now stared up at Anderson open-mouthed and panic-stricken.

"There's no need for threats, Mark. Frank's a good dog and I don't think he'd be annoying your sheep. I'm sure you're mistaken, but we'll keep an extra careful eye on him." I winked at Penny conspiratorially. She tried to smile back, but did so without confidence.

"Well, don't say I didn't warn you. If that dog's in my field, I'll kill it," he repeated, then nodded, as though we had had a conversation about the weather, and bade us a happy Christmas.

When he left, Penny sidled over to me and tugged on my trouser leg. "Is he gonna hurt Frank, Daddy?" Her voice cracked as she spoke and her eyes reddened.

"No, sweetie," Debbie said, and came over and lifted her in her arms. "Daddy'll make sure that Frank stays inside every night, then nothing will happen to him. Isn't that right, Daddy?" she said, looking at me while hugging Penny into her and swaying lightly from side to side.

"That's right, sweetheart," I said. "Frank will be alright."

Chapter Two

Sunday, 22nd December

The following morning I took Debbie and the children to early Mass, where Penny insisted we say a special prayer for Frank, and the entire congregation prayed for the repose of the soul of Angela Cashell and for comfort for her family in their tragedy. Yesterday's snow flurries had cleared and the sky was fresh as water, the wind sharp, the bright winter sun deceptively warm-looking as we sat in church, staring out. Strangely, the roses in the gardens at the front of the church were budding again despite the lateness of the year. As I stopped to admire them on our way out, Thomas Powell Jr approached me.

Powell was someone I had known when I was young, at school in Derry. He was my age, but where I was stocky and carrying extra weight around the gut, Powell was lean and tanned and carried only the aura of good health, achieved and maintained through prosperity. He was the husband of a girl I had also known when younger, and the only son of one of the richest men in Donegal, Thomas Sr. The old man had been a highly influential politician in his time, and rumour had it that the son would soon follow suit. It was about the father that Thomas wished to see me.

"Devlin. Anything on the old man?" he asked, shaking my hand in both of his, a gesture which was strikingly disingenuous.

"What old man?" I asked.

"My father, of course. I'd assumed you'd know." He smiled with some bewilderment.

"Sorry, Thomas. Did something happen to your father?"

He seemed irritated. "I thought they'd have told you. I phoned your station this morning. About the intruder."

"I haven't heard, Thomas. Where was this?"

"His room in the home: Finnside. He woke in the middle of the night, Wednesday, and swore there was someone in his room. Look, we told the guy who answered the phone. He said it would be investigated."

"I'm sure it will, Thomas. We're a bit up to our eyes with this Cashell girl's death. Was your father hurt?"

"No."

"Was anything taken?"

"No. But that's not the point. Someone was in his room."

I could see Powell beginning to get annoyed so, having promised to follow it up at the earliest opportunity, I excused myself.

As I turned to leave, I caught sight of his wife, Miriam, standing in the vestibule of the church, talking to Father Brennan but looking over at us, seemingly distracted. Her eyes caught mine and something shivered inside me and settled uneasily in my stomach. She smiled lightly and returned her attentions to the priest.

As there were only three days till Christmas, I had promised Penny a trip to Santa's grotto and I wanted to get on the road to Derry as soon as possible. The events of the day before had made me all the more resolved to spend time with my children; I couldn't help seeing their faces when I thought of Angela. Although it was my day off, I had my mobile phone with me and as we drove from the churchyard its urgent ringing startled me.

It was Jim Hendry. He was calling to tell me that Strabane police were holding Johnny Cashell for attempted murder. As I drove across the bridge to Strabane in the beautiful December sunshine, I was able to look down and see frogmen from both sides of the border taking turns at searching the murk for anything that might help us catch his daughter's killer.

On the northern side of the border, a local government agency, tired of traveller encampments clogging up car parks and industrial estates, decided to provide the travellers with their own area. The agency chose a site off the main road and miles away from any other housing developments and then, showing a severe lack of understanding of the term "itinerant", built twenty houses for the traveller families to live in. Needless to say, the travellers parked outside the houses and lived in their caravans as they always had. However, someone systematically stripped the brand new houses of anything that could be sold, making a neat profit and leaving the estate looking like a terrorist training ground. For several months afterwards, the less reputable local builders made a huge and completely illegal profit, buying cut-price piping and slates and putting them into new houses.

It was unusual, Inspector Hendry told me, when I drove over to Strabane that morning, for the police to have to go into the camp — the travellers normally resolved disputes in their own ways. That morning had been different, apparently.

From what could be gleaned from various witnesses, it seemed that Johnny Cashell and his three brothers had walked from his home to Daly's Filling Station in Lifford at 11 p.m. the previous evening, just as the nightshift staff came on, and there they each filled ten-litre jerry cans with petrol. The four of them then sat in McElroy's Bar until 2.30 in the morning, drinking Guinness and Powers whiskey. While most of the other drinkers in the bar smelt the fumes coming off the four jerry cans in the corner, no one asked about them or reacted in any way to imply that such an occurrence was unusual; not even when Brendan Cashell went to the bar and bought a single packet of John Player cigarettes and four disposable lighters. Many of the regulars looked at Johnny with a mixture of pity and suspicion. No one mentioned Angela's name, though some patted him on the shoulder as they passed by, and a few, including the publican, stood him a drink. Others were more circumspect, perhaps wary of being seen to take sides, in case at a later date it transpired that Johnny himself had been involved in some way in the murder of the blonde-haired child.

The Cashell brothers walked the half-mile to Strabane from Lifford, each carrying a can of petrol, and were spotted around 3.30 a.m. crossing the bridge above the point where the rivers Finn and Mourne merge into the Foyle. What they did for the next hour is unclear, but they entered the traveller camp at 5 a.m., just as the first tendrils of grey crept into the pre-dawn sky.

Once there, they doused as many of the houses and caravans as they could with petrol, then they each took out cigarettes and disposable lighters, lit their smokes, and then the houses and caravans around them. The four brothers did not run away, but rather sat on the massive boulders which had been placed at the mouth of the encampment to prevent any more caravans from entering. Johnny listened dispassionately as screams began to shudder through the flimsy metal of the burning caravans.

A passing taxi driver radioed for the police and fire engines and watched while Johnny and his brothers cheered as one traveller family after another stumbled from the burning caravans, screaming and crying. Then Johnny spotted one person in particular — a thin boy who looked no more than twelve or thirteen, with hair so blond it was almost white. Johnny was seen shouting at him. Then he and his brothers ran after the boy, who scuttled like a rabbit through the bushes behind the encampment and across the fields beyond, his bare back luminous in the moonlight.

It was not clear who realized the Cashells' culpability first, but by the time the police arrived, someone had beaten Johnny's brothers so badly that they were unidentifiable. The youngest, Diarmuid, had been rushed to Altnagelvin hospital. A female taxi-driver had described how she had watched two of the travellers, barefoot and bare-chested, yet seemingly oblivious to the winter night (or, perhaps, heated by the flames and the adrenaline of the situation) grab Diarmuid by his straggled hair and throw him to the ground. As he cowered against the boulders blocking the entrance to the estate, they took turns kicking and stomping on him with enough force to shatter his teeth and his jawbone, which soon hung loose and useless as a dead man's.

Frankie Cashell was dragged to the ground by the jacket his wife had made him wear and, though he cursed her when it gave the travellers something to grab, the padding buffered most of the kicks he received to his trunk so that, although his skull was fractured, his ribs were only bruised.

The third Cashell brother, Brendan, was set upon by a number of women, one of whom bit off one of his ears. By the time the police found it later that day, spat into the bushes beyond the smouldering wreck of a caravan, it was beyond saving.

Johnny himself, bleeding profusely, had been found lying in the field across which he had reportedly pursued the traveller boy. The boy had turned on Johnny, pulling a knife on him. Only when Johnny was in the ambulance did it become clear that he had received only a superficial wound, and so he was arrested as soon as he was discharged from hospital and taken to Strabane. Hendry had heard all about it that morning when he arrived for work. Recognizing the name from our exchange the day before, he contacted me.

Johnny sat on the metal frame which doubled as a bench and bed in the holding cell, his fingers exploring under the bandage which had been taped around his abdomen. He looked up when he saw me enter the cell, but went back to his work, testing the wound for tenderness and inspecting the dressing for blood.

"Well, Johnny. Do you feel better now?"

"Piss off, Devlin. You're not allowed in the North. You shouldn't be here."

"Neither should you, Johnny. I'm off duty. This is a social call. What were you playing at, taking on the travellers?" I asked, but his attention remained focused on his dressing. Hendry kicked at Johnny's foot when he still didn't look up.

"I've nothing to say," Johnny muttered. "Have you a fag?"

"Aye," I said, taking the cigarette packet out of my pocket. "But I've forgot my lighter. Have you got one?"

"Ha, ha! Stick it up your arse, Devlin."

"Oi! Mind your mouth, son, you're not in the South now," Hendry said. "Jesus, Devlin, what class of criminal are you lot breeding over there?"

I squatted down beside Cashell, hoping to get his attention. "What had this to do with Angela, Johnny?" I asked, and saw, for a second, the slightest glimpse of recognition. "It *was* Angela, wasn't it, Johnny? You see, that's why Inspector Hendry here has contacted me — on account of what happened to Angela. But this won't bring her back, Johnny." I didn't intend to sound as patronizing as I did.

41

He looked up at me fiercely, anger and pride defiant in his face. "And you will, will ye Devlin? Fucking resurrect her? Is that it? You couldn't catch cold in a snow storm. You're a joke. Fuck you." He grew more animated as he spoke, getting angrier and angrier until he almost spat in my face, "Fuck the lot of you!" Then in the silence that followed, his venom spent, he sank back onto the metal frame again. He buried his face in his hands, as would any grieving father who has vented his anger and frustration at the person nearest him because of his failure to do so at those who actually deserved it.

"The boy he was seen chasing was Whitey McKelvey. His real name's Liam or something, but everyone calls him Whitey. A bad wee bugger, too," Hendry told me as he walked me back to my car, where Debbie and the children were waiting for me. "He looks about ten but he's nearer eighteen. Undernourished. Some of the lads here reckon it's deliberate so he can slip through windows more easily when he's robbing a place. Whitey's been in and out of detention centres. He hasn't done anything yet to do real time for, but it'll happen soon enough. Wouldn't surprise me if he's involved in the girl's death. Knives are his thing, mind you.

I don't know if he'd be strong enough to lift a body, either. He's wiry but fairly weak. Vicious rather than strong, you know."

"I know him," I said. "He's popped up once or twice on our side too. White-blond hair, FA Cup ears? Let us know if you lift him. Cashell obviously thinks he knows something."

We shook hands. "Surely," Hendry said, "though I hope you get him first. Last time we lifted Whitey, he left the place in a right mess."

Later that evening Superintendent Costello arrived at our house. He does this fairly frequently; part of his personable, policing-the-community bit. He squeezed into the armchair in the corner furthest from the TV and held in his hand the teacup and saucer Debbie had given to Penny to bring him. The coffee table upon which a plate of biscuits sat was just a little beyond his reach and the effort required to set down and pick up the cup was evidently too much to make it worthwhile. The cup looked tiny in his hand and he seemed awkward drinking from it.

"Quite a good response from the RTE thing," he said, holding the cup just below jaw-level, his third and fourth fingers jutting out, the handle of his cup too small to accommodate them. "Twenty-three calls. Twelve nutcases."

For the press conference we had decided not to mention that Angela's body had been dumped naked but for her underwear, nor the ring which she had been wearing, in an attempt to weed out the cranks from those with genuine information.

"A few promising leads though," Costello continued, stirring the tea now to give him something to do with his hands and the cup. "A mention of a traveller boy, presumably Whitey McKelvey. The two of them were seen together on Thursday night, at a disco in Strabane. Drugs were mentioned too." I nodded, unsurprised. "In connection with her — not him, Benedict."

"Might be worth asking for toxicology reports from the state pathologist," I suggested, though I suspected Costello had already done so.

"I spoke to her earlier," he said, trying to place the spoon back on the saucer as gently as possible. "The manager of the Cineplex saw Angela there on Friday afternoon with her sisters. They bought tickets for a children's matinée but went to some horror thing. They were thrown out at about four o'clock." The spoon clattered off the side of the cup and fell to the ground. Penny scurried over on all fours and retrieved it with a smile.

"On Friday?" I repeated. "Are you sure? Cashell said she left the house on Thursday."

"Best check it out in the morning," Costello replied. "Preliminary findings are through from the pathologist as well. They put time of death at somewhere between 11 p.m. Friday night and 1 a.m. Saturday morning." As he spoke, he lifted a cream-coloured folder out of the bag he had brought with him. He passed it over to me and turned his attention to Shane, who was sitting on his sheepskin rug, watching Costello with open mouth, a rusk held aloft in his hand, his face smeared with soggy biscuit. He grinned, showing off his two teeth, and gurgled with satisfaction.

I skimmed through all the technical jargon. In short, Angela had been engaged in sexual activity before she died — more than likely consensual and most definitely using contraception; the lubricant found in swabs taken from her suggested Mates condoms, and precluded any possibility of finding DNA evidence, unless hairs could be found on her body.

Stomach contents seemed to verify that she had indeed been at the cinema on the day of her death: there was no doubt that Angela had eaten popcorn, chocolate and, at a later stage in the day, burger and chips. The pathologist also noted a partially decomposed tablet of some sort, speckled brown and yellow. Toxicology would identify the exact constituents.

The level of lactic acid in Angela's muscles — all her muscles — when she died was massive, suggesting that they had been in vigorous use at the moment of her death. The pathologist suggested that this was probably not consistent with regular activity. It was more likely that Angela had suffered some kind of seizure. She had died through asphyxiation. The bruising on her chest and other bruising, discovered around her mouth when the lipstick was removed, suggested that someone fairly small had sat or, more likely, knelt on her chest and covered her mouth, perhaps while she thrashed beneath them in a fit. Eventually the lack of oxygen and massive electrical activity in her brain became too much.

"Someone knelt on her?" I said, breaking my own rule of never discussing such things in front of my children.

"Someone small," Costello said, "and s-e-x-u-a-l-l-y active," he added, mouthing the letters, while motioning with his head towards my children, who sat pretending to watch TV but were listening to the exchange. I decided not to tell him that Penny is top of her class in spelling — though I trusted they had not reached polysyllables like that in Primary Two.

"Outside, kids," I said and waited until Penny pulled the door quietly shut behind her, hefting Shane in her other arm. "What do you reckon with the tablet? E?"

"Could well be. We'll find out soon enough. Check with the family about drugs history. Check about epilepsy as well. If she'd never had a fit before, 'twould fairly much guarantee that it's drug-related in some way."

I nodded. "Still, this mention of someone small would seem to suggest Whitey McKelvey."

"Looks that way, Benedict," Costello agreed. "I'll put out a description, see if we can't pick him up. Either that or hope the northerners get him before Cashell's extended family go out and buy more petrol."

CHAPTER THREE

Monday, 23rd December

On Monday morning I stopped off at the station early and was informed by Burgess, the Desk Sergeant, about Tommy Powell's father, who had reported seeing an intruder in his room at Finnside Nursing Home. Neither Burgess nor I felt it warranted much of an investigation: a seventy-five-year-old man, placed in a home because he suffers from dementia, claims someone was in his room, in a place where the nurses check on the patients every hour or so, night and day. It seemed like a no-brainer. On the other hand, Powell was not only very rich, but also influential, with a mouthy son who would think nothing of going to the local papers about how Garda carelessness left his poor father prone to intruders in his own bedroom. I told Burgess I would follow it up myself when I got the chance, just to keep Powell Jr quiet.

I phoned ahead to the cinema to make sure that Martin, the manager, was there, then drove round and took his statement, which simply confirmed all that Costello had told me. Martin knew the Cashell girls; he'd recognized Angela because of her blonde hair, and her two sisters — one older, one much younger. Better still, he was able to show me the CCTV recording for that afternoon.

We sat in the back office of the cinema, the building strange in daylight without the smell of heating popcorn. Martin fast-forwarded the video until 2.45 p.m. and we watched. A few minutes later a group entered the shot, coming into the cinema. But the girl who should have been Angela was not wearing the jeans and blue hooded top her father had described. In fact, she was wearing a short skirt and a red coat. It was difficult to identify her for certain because of the graininess of the shot, but Martin was convinced.

"That's them," he said, pointing to the group.

"Are you sure? That's not what we were told she was wearing."

He sighed and looked at me as though I had disappointed him. "I'm telling you, that was them. I served them myself; I remember

Angela Cashell. My wife calls that thing she's wearing a greyhound skirt."

"Why?"

" 'Cause they're just behind the hare." He laughed at his joke.

He forwarded further through the tape, seeming to know where to stop and I suspected that he had gone over it a few times already in preparation for a visit from the Guards. At 4.03 p.m. Angela Cashell walked out of the cinema with her sisters. Despite the graininess of the footage, I think she laughed as she spoke to the other girls. I hope she did.

"The younger one was the problem," he explained: "why we asked them to leave. The older two could watch the horror movie, but not the young girl. It would give her nightmares."

I nodded and silently considered that the murder of her sister might have a more lasting impact on her than a horror film.

Before getting back into my car, I walked the few hundred yards from the cinema to the spot where Angela Cashell had been found. The grass was well-trodden now and some locals had left bunches of flowers lying just beyond the spot where she had lain. Blue and white crime-scene tape fluttered in the breeze and tangled in the branches of the old hawthorn tree to which it had been tied.

I went over to the bouquets at the base of the tree, reading the cards attached with grim curiosity. There was a bunch left by the Cashell girls. Sadie had left an old battered teddy bear with "From Mummy and Daddy with love" written on a piece of foolscap tucked into the ribbon around its neck. The whole thing reminded me of the fairy trees people used to talk about in the west of Donegal. Locals would tie talismans of some sort around the tree and, in return, the fairies would bless them. The base of this tree was covered with Mass cards and rosary beads, sympathy cards and flowers. Among them I saw a photograph, clearly taken decades earlier. In it, a young woman was sitting on a set of concrete steps. Behind her, I could see children playing on a beach. I assumed the woman was a grandmother of Angela's and replaced the photograph, tucking it behind a vine of ivy that snaked up around the trunk of the tree. I read a few more of the messages, laying each card gently onto the bed of damp moss at the tree's base.

Days later I would still feel saddened by the simplicity of Sadie's message; what else could adequately convey a parental emotion so instinctive it could barely be expressed?

When I arrived at her house, Sadie was sitting on a wooden kitchen chair on her front door-step, smoking a cigarette and talking to her neighbour, who leaned across the hedge that divided their two houses. The neighbour, Jim something-or-other, nodded towards me as I got out of the car and I heard him say, "Hey Sadie, someone's brought home the bacon."

I wanted to tell him to screw himself, but nodded politely and smiled. Sadie stood up as I approached and walked into the house, leaving the door open, which I took to be as close to a sign of hospitality as I was going to get.

The two younger daughters were sitting at the kitchen table, almost exactly as I had last seen them and, I noticed, in the same clothes. Both looked up from their play when I came in, then returned to their dolls. Sadie was standing at the stove, removing a fresh cigarette from the packet on the work-top beside her.

"Have I not enough to be bothering me? What do you want?"

She leaned over the stove, removing a pot from a gas ring and lighting her cigarette from the flame. She had to drag at it several times to get it lit, billows of smoke mingling with the steam from the pots which left her face damp and flushed.

"I've a few questions, Sadie. About Angela. If you're feeling up to it."

"The fuck you care if I'm up to it. That bastard's gone and got himself nicked again. Two days shy of Christmas. What am I meant to do? Eh?" She sat down, a tacit recognition that, try as she might to blame me, she knew I was not the architect of her misfortunes. I sat opposite her, studying her face.

She had always been a fairly heavy woman, her chestnut brown hair tied back from her face. It had lost its lustre now, and the deep brown, which once had resembled a mare's mane, was streaked with white and dirty grey. Her skin was weathered as leather, peppered with burst blood vessels. In another life, with another husband perhaps, she could have been attractive in a way, but life with Johnny Cashell had taken its toll on her. She looked significantly older than her forty-seven years. I had never seen her look more dejected in my life. I opened my wallet and took out three 50 euro notes that I had withdrawn from the bank machine that morning in order to buy Debbie's Christmas present. Sadie watched me with open suspicion.

"Sadie, we had a whip-round at the station, seeing as all that's happened the past week to you. Take this to tide you over Christmas."

Her initial response was indignation and anger, though I assured her that it was not charity as such, but simply a contribution to help her over a bad patch. Slowly, and without thanks, she took the money, folded the notes once and slipped them under the fruit bowl. Then she gestured towards me without discernible reason, which I assumed to be a sign of her assent to the interview. I looked at the two girls, not wishing to speak in front of them, but Sadie, wafting the smoke from in front of her face, said, "It's okay. They don't understand anyway."

"Sadie," I began, still glancing at the girls uncomfortably, "we think Angela took a fit of some kind —"

"Is that what killed her? A fit?"

"We don't know. We're fairly certain that at some time before she died she went into a seizure. Was she epileptic? Did she take fits?"

"Never. But then, if she had a fit, she weren't murdered. A fit's not murder, is it?" For a moment a spark of hope seemed to flicker in her eyes, as though the means of

Angela's death could somehow alter the final outcome.

"We don't know, Sadie. She never took fits?"

"Never."

"Was she on medication of any kind?"

"No. She were on iron for a while, months back, but not now."

"What did her iron tablets look like Sadie — in case maybe she took some recently and you didn't know?"

"Why? What difference do iron tablets have to make?"

"Just clearing some things up. Can I see her tablets?"

"Muire, run up and fetch them tablets from the bathroom, love," Sadie said, and the younger of the two girls — the girl whom I had thought was going to speak on my last visit — ran up the stairs, her footfalls thudding across the ceiling above us.

While I waited for her to return, I promised Sadie that we would bring Angela to them as soon as possible. "And her belongings, Sadie. You'll want that gold ring back, I'm sure," I said, remembering the ring Angela had been wearing.

"What gold ring? She didn't wear no gold rings."

"Are you sure? She was wearing a gold

ring with some kind of stone in it. It looked expensive."

She paused for a fraction of a second too long before responding. "Oh, right. Aye. That ring. Aye. I forgot about that. Bought it herself, she did."

But I knew she was lying. Angela didn't wear a gold ring and Sadie was chancing her arm for a piece of jewellery she didn't own.

A more important issue, though, was where, then, the ring had come from. A boyfriend or lover perhaps? The lover who had had sex with her before she died and who was, presumably, the last person to see her alive and, logically, therefore, her killer?

Muire returned with the tablets. They were red and green in a plastic coating and looked nothing like the description of the tablet discovered in Angela's stomach.

"Sadie, could you ask the girls to leave? I have one or two more questions," I said.

"Go'on out and play wi' yourselves," she said and the two girls left with their dolls.

"Did Angela have a boyfriend?" I asked.

"Probably. She were a lovely looking girl."

"You don't know any names, Sadie?"

"No."

"What about Whitey McKelvey?"

"Are you joking? You're as bad as that

ignoramus I married. She wouldn't have spat on McKelvey if he was on fire." She paused briefly as she realized how inappropriate her choice of words had been.

"Then why did Johnny go after him? They were seen together. Might she have been seeing him without you knowing?"

"I'm telling you. Whatever she was meeting McKelvey for, it weren't boyfriend stuff."

"Do you know where she stayed on Thursday night? Johnny said he hadn't seen her since Thursday, yet we know she was with your girls on Friday at the cinema. I'm a little confused, Sadie."

Sadie paused and I sensed there was something she didn't want to get drawn on. "She stayed with one of her friends; I don't know who. Then she met the girls at the cinema on Friday and that's that."

"Where did she go after the cinema?"

"A friend's, I suppose. Is this not what you're meant to be finding out yourself?"

"Why did she stay away on Thursday night?"

"Girls do these things. Wanted to visit her friend and have one of those American things — sleep-over things." She knew as well as I did that the answer was a weak one.

"Why did Johnny say he hadn't seen her since Thursday? Did he not know that the girls were with her on Friday?"

"They had a row, that's all. Same as any family. He didn't need to know she was taking the girls to the pictures. He wasn't lying; he didn't know any better and none told him otherwise."

"What was the row about Sadie?"

"None of your business. It was about family stuff — nothing to do with what happened to her."

"What about Angela and drugs, Sadie? Any chance Angela was taking drugs? Was the row about drugs?"

"You lot are all the same. Always thinking the worst of people." But again, despite her indignation, it didn't have any conviction. "Kids'll be kids, Inspector. You know that. Or do your wee'uns not shite like the rest of us?"

Muire was playing in the garden by herself as I was leaving. I stopped and watched her. If she was aware of my presence, she did not show it.

"What's your dolly called?" I asked.

"Angela," she replied without looking up.

"Angela was very special to you, wasn't she?" I sat on the edge of the chair where

Sadie had been when I arrived. The girl nodded, but still did not look up. "Did she take you to the pictures on Friday?"

"Some scary thing. It was rotten!" She pulled a face, finally looking at me.

"Where did you go after that?"

"Home."

"Angela too?"

"No. She went to see her friend, I think."

"Whitey?"

"No."

"Who, Muire? Think. It's really important."

"I dunno. She never said."

"Did she say where her friend lived?"

A shake of the head.

"Which direction did she go in when you came out of the cinema?" She bit her bottom lip and frowned in concentration, but again couldn't answer me. "The bus stop, just. We left her at the bus stop."

"Good girl, Muire. That's going to be very helpful," I said trying to sound sincere. "One other thing, Muire, and then I'll go. Did Angela have a fight with someone the day before? On Thursday? Did she row with your Mum?"

Muire shook her head, but would not look at me again and busied herself with her dolls.

"Was it your dad she rowed with?" Again a shake of the head, but this time in pantomime fashion, as a child does when trying too hard to appear truthful; my own daughter had done just such a thing many times before. "What did she row about with your dad?" Nothing. I squatted down right beside her, pretending to play with her doll. "What happened, Muire? It's really important if I'm going to catch the man who hurt Angela."

She looked up at me and tears began to well in her eyes. "Angela said Daddy was watching her."

"Watching her?"

She nodded solemnly. "In the house. Watching her when she went to bed." The tears began to run down her face but she did nothing to stop them.

"Is that what you were going to tell me the last day?" I asked and she nodded at me shyly. Then her expression changed and her line of vision shifted to above and behind me.

"Don't talk to strangers, Muire!" Sadie said. Shoving past me and grabbing the girl by the wrist, she pulled her to her feet. She slapped her sharply across the tops of her legs, the girl's dress cushioning most of the blow. "Now, get into the house."

Sadie marched behind her and left me standing alone in the garden. I looked round to see the neighbour from earlier, still standing at the hedge, smiling over at me. "Can I help you, sir?" I asked.

He shook his head, still smiling. "No. I'm just enjoying the entertainment."

"Would you enjoy it more down the station?"

"Piss off, prick," he said, then went into his own house.

When I returned to the station, I learnt that Costello had assigned two uniformed officers to assist me full-time in the investigation, while others in the station could be co-opted when needed. This he explained to me while the two sat outside his office door. I knew both of them fairly well.

The more senior was Sergeant Caroline Williams, a native of Lifford, who had been a Guard for eight years and had recently been promoted. Costello suggested that she might be useful if the case involved a sexual crime, which was looking increasingly likely. I liked Caroline. She was straight-talking and had a good manner with members of the public. Luckily none of those people had seen her, as I had, baton into submission a six-foot-two rocker who had caused a public-order disturbance after he tried to break into his ex-girlfriend's house. He would probably have sued for GBH had it not entailed publicly admitting that a woman of five-foot-five had left him crying in a doorway with a broken nose.

And yet, while Williams was meting out such punishments to woman-abusers and wife-beaters by day, she was herself, for many years, being beaten nightly by her husband, an insipid salesman frustrated in his life and content in venting his frustration on the woman who had borne him a son for whom he had little regard. Caroline Williams told no one about it, but one of the sergeants noticed bruising on her arms and neck and, in the bar some nights later, we put together the pieces. Foolishly, that same night, fuelled by the courage a few pints can bring, four of us visited her house and taught Simon Williams a salutary lesson in how Gardai stick up for each other and how it feels to be on the receiving end of things. The following morning, while we congratulated ourselves on our fraternal actions, Caroline Williams covered with make-up the two black eyes her husband had given her in the belief that she had set us upon him. We did not get involved in the affairs of the Williams family again.

Then, one night Caroline and her young son, Peter, arrived in the station and slept in the holding cell to escape Simon's latest rage. Costello visited him the next morning and, though no one knows what passed between them, by the following weekend Simon Williams had left Lifford and moved to Galway.

The second assignee was Jason Holmes, an officer who had moved to Letterkenny from Dublin about eighteen months earlier. In Dublin he had been involved with the drugs squad and had gained considerable kudos for helping bring down a dealer whose name was linked with the murder of a leading lawyer. Holmes moved from Dublin soon after, partly for his protection from reprisals and also, as he told me later, because he had grown sick of city living. It was a fair enough reason. Holmes was quiet, bringing a reputation from Dublin which circumstance had not allowed him to cement. Again, Costello had a reason for including Holmes: following the discovery of the tablet in Angela's stomach, his knowledge of drugs might be useful.

Costello called the two of them into his office and asked me to bring them up to date on what we had gathered so far. It was useful to reconsider what we had learned as

I jotted down key times and events on the small easel blackboard Costello had had placed in the corner of the room.

"So, Angela is seen in the company of Whitey McKelvey, known petty criminal. On Thursday, she has an argument with her father, when she accuses him, I think, of spying on her getting undressed. She leaves home on Thursday, and stays somewhere overnight where she gets a change of clothes. Both those clothes and the clothes she wore on Thursday are still unaccounted for." Williams nodded.

"Friday afternoon," I continued, "she takes her sisters to the cinema. Leaves just after four. Probably at the bus stop by 4.15 p.m., from where, I think, she is going to meet someone, possibly a boyfriend. At some point late that night, we think, she suffers a seizure and dies — possibly after taking drugs. Her body is dumped behind the cinema that night and is discovered the next morning. She is wearing only her underwear, inside out, and a gold ring which I suspect her family didn't know she owned. McKelvey has been linked with her, but I don't take him for a murderer. In his favour, so to speak, the drugs link would seem to suggest him, as would his size in terms of being small enough to kneel on

64

her chest. On the other hand, if this was a sexual crime — which it seems to have been, to some extent — we know that her father, no stranger to our cells before this, might have had more than simple fatherly love for his girl."

"Especially if she wasn't his girl," Costello said, nodding sagely, happy to have made a contribution. "Though I would never have taken Johnny Cashell for a paedophile."

"A couple more months and he wouldn't have been though, technically, would he?" Holmes said, and smirked.

I saw a flash of something in Caroline Williams's eyes, and then her face softened and became unreadable. "It's still his daughter, though. Biological or not."

"So," I said, "the questions are: where did she spend Thursday night? Who was she with on Friday night? Who gave her the change of clothes? Where are they now? Who gave her the ring? I don't think she bought it; it looked very good quality, a family heirloom."

Williams spoke first. "Might be worth checking pawn shops, local second-hand jewellers and so on to see if any of them sold it."

"Check lists of stolen goods too," I replied. "This might have been part of a stash.

Someone lifted it and gave it to her. It's a safe bet her boyfriend, whoever he was, didn't *buy* it for her."

"The whole ring thing might be a little tenuous, Inspector," Costello suggested. "Might be best to follow up the drugs angle too."

"What about clubs?" Holmes said. "If drugs were involved, she got them somewhere. She was spotted clubbing on Thursday night; chances are she was out again on Friday. Maybe we could find out who she was with."

"Good," I said. "This is all good. If you each want to take your own suggestion and follow it. Caroline, ask Burgess on the front desk to pull you up lists of stolen goods for the past six months, say. Jason, start with the Strabane clubs and move onto Letterkenny. We meet everyday at 9.30 a.m. and 4.30 p.m. to review status. Okay?"

Costello wished us success from behind his desk, and then we were dispatched to our new office. It was actually a storeroom whose contents — mostly cleaning products — had been removed. Two desks had been set facing each other, each furnished with a phone and a plastic chair. Behind one of the desks, a corkboard had been nailed. I was busying myself with pinning up crime-scene photographs and a timeline for the case when Burgess phoned through from the front desk, despite the fact that it was only fifty feet away.

"Detective Devlin," he said, with a formality designed only to impress the public, "there's a lady here to see you."

I stuck my head out the doorway of the office and saw, standing beyond Burgess's desk, Miriam Powell, wife of Thomas Powell Jr. I said earlier that I had known him when we were younger, but it was not the whole truth. I knew Powell because, when we were eighteen, he had started dating Miriam Kelly, unbeknown to me, despite the fact that I was her boyfriend at the time. In fact, they had been dating for four months before she told me.

We were parked below the waterworks station, along the back road to Strabane, lying on the back seat of my father's car. She had returned from holiday and her skin was tanned. It seemed to radiate with heat and light, even in the darkness of the car, and I could smell and taste coconut off her shoulders and neck as I kissed them, pushing off her blouse and fumbling with the clasp of her bra until she reached back and opened it for me. She unbuttoned my shirt and ran her hand down my chest. Her breath fluttered in my ear and tickled against the soft skin at the back of my neck, which affected me in ways I could not express.

Less than ten minutes later we were driving out onto the main road again. She did not look at me as I apologised for my lack of control. Nor, indeed, did she look at me as she smoked the cigarette that I gave her and told me why she did not wish to see me anymore and that she wanted me to run her home. As I watched her walk up the driveway to her father's house, I was disturbed by the notion that she had provided for me out of pity, a last charitable act which caused her no more thought than the cigarette butt she flicked onto the driveway.

Three nights later, at a local dance that my brothers had forced me to attend, I watched her dance close to Thomas Powell with an ease that only intimacy can achieve. She pressed her stomach against him while they swayed under the flashing lights, and I watched her hand slide into his pocket as his slid onto her buttocks. She whispered something to Powell and he looked over at me watching them. Then, the two of them laughed at a shared secret, which I was sure involved me and the incident in the back seat of the car. Consequently, I can never meet Powell without seeing his smiling face in my memory. Likewise, I can never see his wife without the same, overshadowed by the memory of the urgency of her breath, hot against my neck, and the scent of coconut from sun-kissed skin.

Burgess pointed to me and I watched her now walk down towards our storeroom office, deftly swaying from side to side to avoid the corners of desks and filing cabinets which cluttered up the main working area of the station. She wore a linen suit to accentuate a tan achieved despite the fact that it would be Christmas in two days. Her brown hair was cut short and slightly spiked. She held a small handbag under her arm and held out a perfectly manicured hand to me. Unsure whether to kiss it or shake it, I opted for the latter and invited her to sit. She did so and crossed her legs in a languid manner, straightening the right leg of her trousers to ensure the crease fell properly. She wore sandals even though it was freezing outside. I noticed she had a tiny gold ring on her little toe.

"Benedict. Lovely to see you. How's . . . your wife?" Miriam had attended college with Debbie and they had lived together for a year, around the time when Debbie and I started dating. Although she still invited us for drinks every so often and sincerely promised to meet soon for dinner when we bumped into each other coming out of Mass on an occasional Sunday morning, we all knew that the polite invitations were just that, formalities which both sides hoped the other would not insist upon honouring. "Deborah, that's right."

"Debbie's great, Miriam. It's good to see you, too. How can I help you?" I tried to avoid eye contact, but I believe that Miriam sensed my discomfort.

"Thomas told me that he saw you at Mass yesterday. I believe he behaved deplorably towards you, Benedict, and I wish to apologise. He's very upset about his father, you see. Sometimes Thomas has difficulty in telling his friends from . . ." She faltered mid-sentence, flicking open her handbag as though it might contain the words she wanted.

"His enemies?"

She laughed gaily, dismissing the word with the slightest wave of her hand. "We're all terribly worried about Tommy Senior, Benedict. Especially after this scare, when he saw someone in his room."

"What do you want from me, Miriam?"

"Thomas is afraid that, after his behaviour yesterday, there might be some . . .

animosity between you that would hamper your willingness to investigate what happened with his father. That's all." She paused, but when it became clear that I was not going to speak, she continued. "Tommy Senior did a lot for this county. He was a great TD in his time. A great advocate for this area. Thomas wants to ensure that his father is afforded the best treatment he can get. In all things."

Tommy Powell Sr had indeed been a TD, a member of the Dail, the Irish government, right through the worst of the Troubles. He had remained resolutely independent, switching allegiances between Fianna Fail and Fine Gael, depending on which promised him most for Donegal. He had secured a number of large textile factories for the area, bringing with them several hundred jobs and a boost to the economy. On the negative side, most of them set up along rivers and pumped effluent into the water, leading to some high-profile environmental protests. In every case Tommy Powell Sr appeared in the local media and decried the types of liberals who would put fish before people and seaweed before food on the table. His earthy, common-man rhetoric made him immensely popular, and even those who personally disliked the man —

and there were many — had to admire the charisma he brought to the job. He had retired two years earlier, after suffering a minor stroke, and rumours were circulating that, in the next election, Thomas Powell Jr would follow in his father's footsteps and enter the world of politics. Certainly he had the wealth and media savvy to undertake such a venture as a vanity project, regardless of his sincerity or likely success.

"I'll see what I can do, Miriam," I said, and smiled, I hoped sincerely. She toyed with the top button of her linen jacket, perhaps inadvertently drawing my vision to the lace decorating the top of the white satin camisole she wore underneath. Perhaps. She looked down at it, then looked quickly at me, following my gaze away from it, a smile dancing on her lips.

"We'd appreciate anything you can do, Benedict, what with this terrible business about the young girl. Say, why don't you and Debbie call for drinks over Christmas? We could catch up on old times; recall our wild youth." As she spoke, she widened her eyes in mock promise for a second and smiled lightly.

I returned the smile. "Perhaps we will, Miriam, but with the baby and so on, it's difficult to get out."

She stood. "Merry Christmas then," she said and leaned toward me, placing her hand lightly on my shoulder and offering her cheek, which I kissed awkwardly, feeling all the more clumsy as she kissed the air beside my own cheek. I caught the scent of coconut and it would linger in my memory almost as long as the sensation of her cheek on mine, her breath fluttering against my skin.

I watched her as she walked back through the main room of the station and out past Burgess, noticing that a number of the other male staff in the room were doing likewise.

Caroline Williams's face appeared in my line of vision. "Your wife is on the phone, sir. Shall I tell her you're busy?" she asked, and walked away before I could answer.

Chapter Four

Monday, 23rd December

Strabane and Lifford straddle the banks of two rivers, the Finn and the Mourne, which join the Foyle midway between the town in the North and our village in the South, which are separated by a distance of half a mile. The Foyle then flows for miles through Derry and on to Lough Foyle, where it joins the Atlantic. A bridge spans the point where the three rivers meet and, traditionally, lies in unclaimed territory, several hundred yards from where the British Army checkpoint used to be during the Troubles and several hundred yards before the Irish customs post. It was in this area of the borderlands that Angela Cashell was found. Just at the customs hut, a sharp left turn brings you to Lifford Community Hospital and, tucked behind but separate from it, Finnside Nursing Home.

I sat in my car, smoking. Overlooking the

river, I could see, on the curve of the embankment further down, the crime-scene tape, still fluttering in the breeze. I wondered about the Cashell girl's death. And I wondered why, when that investigation was in need of much work, I was about to waste time on the ramblings of a senile old man. I told myself it was out of respect for all Powell had done for Donegal; I told myself it was to stop his son making public complaints about Garda disinterest; I told myself it *wasn't* because, in a strange way, it brought me back into the circle of Miriam Powell.

The home was fairly nice — or as nice as these places can be. The walls were painted neutral colours, white and magnolia predominating. The carpet was dark red. The scented candles and oil burners burning at various points in the reception area failed to cover the unmistakable smell of disinfectant and the faint hint of urine. The owner of the home, Mrs McGowan, waved at me from her office and gestured towards the mobile phone into which she was speaking. I went over and waited for her to finish her phone call.

"Ben, come in," she said when she was done. "Sorry about that — my daughter is cooking for her in-laws and wants to know how to cook beef. I tell you, I don't know where I failed!" She laughed, a soft tinkling laugh that she probably reserved for children of her patients, as if their parent's incapacity were but a trifle.

"I'm here to see Tommy Powell, Mrs McGowan. I believe he had an intruder."

"So he says," she replied and I could tell from her expression that Powell was probably not her favourite patient. "Of course he had someone in his room. The staff here check on him every two or three hours. It's part of our service. You're welcome to see him, but it's a waste of time, Ben. Next week someone will be trying to poison his dinner. Wait and see."

The door to his room was ajar and I could see Tommy Powell, sitting up in his bed, being spoon-fed creamed rice by a young nurse in a pink uniform. I watched in wonder as she fed him, scraping the dribbled food off his chin and chatting to him about her night out, her future plans, anything to fill the silence and prevent her listening to his laboured, rasping breath or the soft grunting noise he made as he ate. Her hair was bunched up under her hat, though I could see the roots were dark. Her neck was slender, the skin soft and white as lily petals.

I knocked softly on the door and, when she became aware of my presence, she blushed slightly. Something about her seemed very familiar, though I didn't recognize her. I assumed she thought the same, because she stood before me as if to speak. "I'm here to see Mr Powell," I explained, pointing towards the bed.

"Oh, okay," she said, smiling a little, then disappeared out through the doorway before I could say any more.

Tommy Powell watched me, moving only his eyes. His head rested against a pillow, his mouth slightly open. One side of his face was frozen, as though he had just come from the dentist and I noticed a dribble of food just to the left of his mouth. As I considered his loss of dignity, I saw again the unbidden image of Angela Cashell, lying naked in a field, decaying leaves cushioning her head as her blood ran cold.

"Mr Powell, my name is Inspector Devlin. I'm here about the intruder in your room last Wednesday."

"Deblin," he said, "who Deblin? Who your fader?"

"Joe Devlin, sir."

"Furniture man?"

"That's right, sir." My father is still known

as a French polisher, though he has not practised this in years. Powell's speech may have been affected, but his memory certainly had not.

"What . . . want?" he said, visibly straining to complete even so short a sentence. This was going to be a dull conversation unless I cut it short, I thought. I rebuked myself inwardly for my lack of charity and decided on brevity anyway.

"I'm here about the intruder on Wednesday night. Do you remember that?"

"Not stupid son . . . sick."

"Of course, sir. Your son told me what happened. I was wondering if you'd anything to add. Anything else you remember?"

"Could . . . be woman . . . boy."

"Excuse me?"

He rasped, breathing heavily through the patrician nose; his teeth were clenched in exasperation and he struggled to straighten himself in the bed. His pyjama jacket was unbuttoned revealing a chest, matted with wispy grey hairs, which looked shrunken and collapsed. I could see his pulse vibrating in the wattles of skin hanging at the sides of his throat. "Might've . . . been . . . a gir . . . girl," he said. "Or a boy. Small."

He dropped back against his pillow and turned his head towards the wall, not looking at me again. His jawline flexed momentarily with anger or resentment that I should see him so weakened. I started to ask a further question, simply to engage him, but he waved me away with a hand so wizened and bony it could have belonged to a woman.

On the way out I did not see again the nurse who had been feeding Powell, nor could I place where I had seen her face before. I stopped Mrs MacGowan and asked her name.

"Is she in trouble?"

"No, no," I said. "I know her face from somewhere."

"She's here on probation for a month before I make her permanent. If she's in trouble with the law, Inspector, she's out on her ear. We have to trust our staff completely, what with old people's money and belongings lying around."

"No, she's not in trouble. It's nothing important; I just can't place her face. I've seen her somewhere recently. Kind of like déjà vu," I lied.

"Yvonne Coyle. She's from Strabane: Glennside, I think."

"Right. Maybe I've seen her round the town or something. It'll come to me eventually."

I thought of driving out to Powell's house to tell Miriam that I had spoken to her father-in-law, despite the fact that I knew that she and her husband would once again make me the object of some new private joke. In fact, I made it as far as the house, a massive Victorian manse which Powell Sr had bought from the Anglican Church after their minister moved out to Raphoe from Lifford in the early '60s. Oaks and sycamore, trunks heavy with vines and ivy, surrounded the house. The wall around their two-acre estate was added maybe forty years ago, built, I remember being told by my father, from bricks from the old jailhouse that had been demolished in 1907. They were unidentifiable now under the thick, wet moss that cushioned the coping stone and had broken off layers of the brick, which lay shattered on the pavement beneath.

I sat opposite their driveway gates and peered beyond to where Miriam had parked her BMW next to the Land Rover that her husband drove, as befitted one of the landed gentry. Powell Jr lived off the rent collected from his father's various properties — wealth to which, as far as anyone knew, he added very little. The jailhouse bricks were typical of Powell Sr: an extravagance that no one would notice, so that he retained his image as one of the common men, while the rumours of opulence added to his enigmatic status. The Land Rover, meanwhile, was indicative of his son, adding to the image of ostentation he had created for himself.

I debated whether or not to go in, then decided against, partly because Powell Jr would be there. As I shifted into gear I couldn't help but feel that I was being watched.

I was washing up the dinner dishes that evening, while Debbie cleared the table. The kids were in the living room, watching *Toy Story* for the umpteenth time. Debbie dropped two knives into the dishwater and began to wipe the counter.

"Don't forget that Penny's singing tomorrow night, at Mass," she said.

"I won't," I promised.

"You'd better not. She'll never forgive you."

"I won't," I said, a second time.

She nodded. "Did I see you at Miriam O'Kane's today?" she asked, not looking up from her work, as though this were part of the normal conversation.

"Who? Miriam . . . Oh, Mrs Pow — Miriam Powell. Yes, I was going to call in to see her husband. He asked me on Sunday to look into an intruder in his father's room. Remember — after Mass?"

"Oh. Is that what you were talking about? I thought maybe Miriam had asked you."

"No. I haven't seen her since . . . I don't know when."

"This morning, apparently. So your Sergeant said. Caroline, isn't it? Miriam was there when I phoned you, she said."

"Yes, that's right. Just called in to see what progress had been made."

"I'm sure she did. You didn't mention it on the phone."

"No, I didn't think much of it, I suppose."

"Mmm," she said. "Did you make any?"

"Any what?"

"Progress," she said, then went in and sat with the children, while I finished the dishes in silence.

■ ■ ■ ■

TERRY BOYLE

■ ■ ■ ■

CHAPTER FIVE

Tuesday, 24th December

I answered the phone on the second ring at 3.30 a.m. that morning, having had difficulty sleeping. Debbie lay beside me, hunched away from me so that, even in sleep, her resentment over the reemergence of Miriam Powell in our lives was clear. She stirred with the ringing of the phone, but I answered it before it woke the children. It was Costello. A body had been found in a burned-out car on Gallows Lane by a local farmer, Petey Cuthins.

Gallows Lane was so called because, several hundred years ago, before the courthouse was built, this was where local criminals were executed, left hanging from the branches of three massive chestnut trees on the approach into the town, a warning to all visitors. On a good day it provided a panoramic view of Counties Donegal, Derry and Tyrone.

The fire had abated by the time I arrived, a hoar of mist sizzling lightly off the scorched bodywork of the car. Costello had already arrived on the scene with two uniforms whom I recognized but couldn't name, their faces pale, eyes red-rimmed, working silently through their tiredness. Petey Cuthins was standing against his gate, several hundred yards away from the wreckage, trying to keep his pipe smouldering. He nodded a greeting when I got out of the car and muttered "Merry Christmas" through teeth still clenched on the pipe-stem. His face was dark under the hood he wore. I nodded over at Costello, who was telling the uniforms where to place the crime-scene tape. I took a quick glance inside the car, thought better of looking more closely, and went back over to Petey to wait for my stomach to settle.

"Heard the bang — must've been the petrol tank. Nearly sent my cattle haywire." He gestured with a slight nod of his head towards the charred body in the car. "Nothing I could do, Ben. Couldn't carry much in a bucket from the house. By the time I got here there wasn't much sense in getting the fire brigade out: fire was almost dead. Weren't gonna do him no good anyhow."

The registration plate, though damaged,

had not been destroyed, the raised numerals revealing that it was a new car — a Nissan Primera, as far as I could tell. The driver was alone; from the size I guessed it was a man, but the body was so badly burned I couldn't be sure.

Costello sent the two officers about their business then approached us. The female officer smiled sadly as she passed with a roll of blue and white tape which she tied onto the hedge behind us and began to unwind.

"Do you think it crashed?" Cuthins called, reluctant to go any closer to the car. To the right of the driver's side I could see a pool of vomit in the grass — presumably Petey had seen more than enough already.

"I don't think so," Costello said, patting me on the back as a gesture of greeting. I guessed he was right: there was no sign of denting on the bodywork, no signs of impact on the area around where the car had stopped. I peered in at the body of the driver, the smell of burnt flesh thick in my mouth and nostrils. "The handbrake is on," Costello pointed out. "And the ignition is turned off." Which meant the car was parked when whatever happened to it had occurred. Costello shook his head slowly, "An awful business, boys. An awful business."

I stepped away from the car and spat the taste from my mouth as Costello took out his phone and called Burgess who had reached the station, giving him the registration number to trace. "Best get a doctor up here. And a few more pairs of hands. It's going to be a long night."

The SOCO officers had to go over to Strabane first to borrow arc lights and a generator from the PSNI. Occasional needles of sleet darted now through the mist, trapped in a fluorescent glare, just as the first gash of red cracked on the horizon. Burgess called back, having run the registration number through Garda Central Communications. The charred remains still strapped inside the car now had a probable name — Terry Boyle, an accountancy student from Dublin, whose parents lived in Letterkenny. Costello asked me to break the news to the family, sending female officer, Jane Long, with me. Just as we were about to leave, I saw John Mulrooney struggling up Gallows Lane towards us to fulfil the slightly ridiculous task, as medical examiner, of pronouncing dead something which was little more than skeleton and pulp.

"Jesus, Ben, it's Christmas Eve," he said, stopping beside us and stubbing out his cigarette, which he had held clamped in his mouth as he'd slipped plastic galoshes over his shoes. I noticed that he was still wearing his pyjamas under his corduroy trousers, the paisley material creeping out over his shoes. "What have we got?" he asked, gesturing towards the car.

"Spontaneous combustion?" I suggested.

Mulrooney steeled himself and went over to the car, holding his breath against the smell. I watched him take a biro from his pocket and use it to poke at the skull, angling it slightly for a clearer view.

He stepped back and spat, much as I had done earlier. It's on just such occasions that you regret knowing that all smells are particulate.

"Looks like a simple shooting," he said, and it took me a moment to realize he wasn't being flippant.

"What?"

"Look," he said, indicating with his pen. "Entry wound here; exit wound presumably out the other side. Two murders in a week. You know that might make Lifford the killing capital of Ireland."

"Very funny," I said.

"Any ideas about when it might have happened?" Costello asked, shifting closer to the car.

"None. But to cross the 't's and that —
for what it's worth — he's dead."

Terry Boyle's mother, Kathleen, clutched a
used Kleenex in her hand, her face raw, her
eyes red and puffy. Jane Long's eyes were
not much better. She shifted in the seat and
put her arms around the older woman's
shoulders. I crouched in front of Mrs Boyle,
though she seemed to look through me.

"I'm very sorry, Mrs Boyle," I said, realizing not for the first time the inadequacy
of the expression. I took her hand in mine
and sat with her as she cried some more.

"Mr Boyle?" I said.

The woman shook her head. "Lives in
Glasgow."

"Best get someone to check on him," I
said to Long, the implication being that she
should both break the news and ascertain
his whereabouts.

"Shall I make some tea?" Long suggested,
reaching for her radio as she headed out of
the room, grateful, probably, to escape the
stultifying grief for a few minutes.

"Jesus," Kathleen Boyle repeated over and
over, her body shuddering.

And, with that, I found myself both questioning His existence and praying all the
harder that He would transcend time and

space and bring comfort both to this woman and to her son, who surely did not deserve to die in such a manner.

"Any ideas who might have a slight against your son, Mrs Boyle? Someone maybe he had a falling out with?"

She shook her head, her tissue clamped to her face. "He's only just home," she snuffled. "Back from university. Went out to some disco."

"What about a girlfriend, Mrs Boyle?"

She nodded, but did not, or could not, speak.

"Was he with her last night?"

A shake of the head this time. "She lives in Dublin. He said he was just going out for a drink. Not meeting anybody. Are you sure it's him?" The words tumbled out together.

"We're fairly certain, Mrs Boyle."

"Do I need to identify him or something? Can I see him?" she asked, her expression lightening a little, as if by grace of her seeing the body she might somehow will her son back to life again and forget this terrible night as no more substantial than a nightmare.

"No, Mrs Boyle. We'll identify him," I said, not wishing to explain that her son was now beyond even her recognition. Before we left the house I would have to find something from which a DNA sample could be taken for comparison should dental or doctor's records prove inconclusive.

While Kathleen Boyle wept, Long and I sat in that room, drank tea and did not speak. We could not leave her — not as police officers, not as fellow human beings.

Her sister arrived at around eight o'clock and convinced her to try to get some sleep. Long and I finally made our way back to the station after requesting that should Mrs Boyle think of anything useful — anything at all — she should contact us, day or night. I sat in the car and lit a cigarette, and could think of nothing but my tiredness and the cold which seemed to have permeated my very bones.

The murder team met on Tuesday morning at 9.30 to report on progress in the Cashell case, though we had all spent the night on the Gallows Lane incident. On the way in, Costello called me to one side. "How's things?" he asked. "At home, I mean."

"Fine," I said a little taken aback at his sudden avuncular manner. "Why?"

"We got a call from Mark Anderson this morning."

"Oh."

"He says your dog has been worrying his sheep and you don't care."

"The only thing likely to worry his sheep is his pervert son. Does he not think we have enough bothering us without him phoning in about a bloody dog?"

"Well, that's what I said. In not so many words."

"You?"

"Oh, aye. He went straight to the top. Why speak to the monkey when you could be speaking to the organ grinder, eh?" He laughed without humour and went into the office where we were meeting. I followed him, cursing Mark Anderson and his sheep.

Before we discussed the progress on Angela Cashell's murder, Costello gave us the low-down on the death of Terry Boyle. The state pathologist was conducting the post mortem as we spoke, and hoped to have a report with us later in the day. A forensics team were working on the car to see what could be found, but the fact that it had been set alight meant they would have difficulties finding anything of much value.

"Why burn it?" Holmes said. "I mean, you've shot the poor bastard. Why burn the car then. It's like a 'fuck you', isn't it?"

"Maybe there was something in the car?" Williams suggested.

"Maybe there was some*one* in the car," I said. "Would explain what he was doing parked up there in the middle of the night. Maybe the killer was in the car with him and burnt the car to destroy any evidence."

Costello brought us back to Cashell again. "We'll wait to see these reports. Caroline, I'd like you and Jason to follow up the Boyle inquiry. Report back to Inspector Devlin here, daily. Inspector," he said, referring to me by rank rather than name, thereby making it all official, "I'd like you to continue pushing the Cashell case until McKelvey's found. Let's see if we can get one case tied up at least."

Holmes and Williams nodded their agreement. Holmes looked exhausted, due in part to his visiting many of the local bars and clubs to see if anyone recognized Angela Cashell from a photograph he had got from Sadie. He had felt obliged to partake of a number of complimentary Christmas drinks in each pub and had arrived on site in the middle of the night a little the worse for wear. He told us that Sadie had informed him that Johnny had been refused Christmas bail as a flight risk and would be up before Strabane magistrates on Friday 27th.

As well as speaking to local publicans, Holmes had visited the nightclub in Strabane which Angela had reportedly attended on Thursday night with someone fitting the description of Whitey McKelvey. The club owner didn't remember her, but had provided a tape of his security camera footage for that night, which Holmes placed on Costello's desk.

Williams had contacted most of the local jewellers and secondhand shops, both in Strabane and Lifford, but no one remembered having seen or been offered the ring. She told us she was planning on trying Derry shops later that day. She had asked two of the secretaries in the station to go through the stolen items list which Burgess had printed out for her late on the previous afternoon. The list ran to 112 pages for the past six months.

Costello then provided us with the full report from the state pathologist, including toxicological findings. And we discovered just how Angela Cashell had died.

At some time, probably after seven o'clock on Friday night, Angela Cashell had eaten a cheeseburger and chips and drunk Diet Coke. She smoked several joints through the rest of the evening and drank vodka — again, probably, with Diet Coke. At some point she took what she may have believed to be an Ecstasy tablet, no bigger than a one cent coin and speckled yellow and brown. The tablet was of very low purity and had been cut with, amongst other things, talc, rat poison, DDT, nutmeg and strychnine.

Shortly after taking the tablet, and perhaps even as a consequence of it, she began to have sex with someone who wore a condom, as we had been told earlier. Perhaps during the act itself, the compound of chemicals she had taken caused something in her brain to misfire; her synapses sparked with electrical currents which eventually sent her into an epileptic seizure. The strychnine was probably responsible for spasms which tore her leg muscles from their ligaments. In addition, her lungs began to slow and enter paralysis, though whoever was with her may not have realized this, for they knelt on her chest and covered her mouth with a cotton cloth until she stopped breathing. Perhaps they realized that the drug would kill her, but wished to speed the process along. Or perhaps they simply put her out of her misery.

After she had died her body was washed and her pants were put back on, inside out. Then two people — for she would have been prohibitively heavy for a person small enough to kneel on her to be capable also of carrying her — must have put her into a car. They drove her to behind Lifford Cineplex several hours after she died and threw her body down to the spot where we discovered it.

We waited until everyone had finished reading, Williams going over the report more slowly than the rest of us. "So," said Costello finally, "it fairly much confirms what we knew already, with a few more details thrown in. Especially the drug thing."

"Yeah," said Holmes. "Not uncommon to get low-grade drugs, especially E tabs. Though in saying that, I haven't heard of any of these substances being found before."

"I have," said Costello and I saw Williams nod slightly, as though in agreement. "Read this and see if it sounds familiar."

He handed each of us a copy of a letter dated September 1996, the paper still warm from the photocopier. The letter read:

Dear Student
As you are aware, An Garda work closely with your school to develop drugs awareness programmes to educate you about the dangers of drugs and ensure that none of you get caught in the cycle of criminal activity which drugs use can cause.

97

However, we are also aware that some of you may be using drugs or have been tempted to experiment with them. Therefore I write to you in particular to be vigilant over the coming weeks.

It has come to our attention that a batch of highly dangerous Ecstasy tablets has appeared on the Irish drugs scene and, while none has reached Donegal to date, it has been decided that all students in all schools in the area be made aware of this danger. The tablets, which are round, are about one centimetre in diameter. They have a yellow/brown speckled appearance and might taste slightly bitter. The Customs Office in Dublin has informed us that these drugs, which originated in Holland, will not have the effect of an Ecstasy tablet, but in fact contain a number of deadly chemicals and poisons, including rat- and flea-killer. The tablets can cause a range of symptoms, including breathing difficulties, convulsions, brain damage, and could cause death.

If someone offers you one of these tablets — or if you are suspicious of anything you are offered — DO NOT TAKE IT.

You can contact Letterkenny Garda station in confidence on 074 55584, or else contact your local Garda station or tell a member of your school staff. You will not get in any trouble and you might help save lives.

The letter was signed by Costello, with a further reminder to avoid the drugs completely. I vaguely remembered the letters being distributed by schools, though at the time I was working in Sligo on a breaking-and-entering team who were targeting local hotels and hostels.

"Sound like the same things," Holmes said, putting the letter down on the table.

"I'm surprised you don't remember it," Williams said, "working with the drugs squad in Dublin."

"Before my time," Holmes replied, then smiled good humouredly. "I'm still a young buck, me."

"God help us all," Williams said and hid her face behind the A4 sheet she held.

"Well, it's probably the same," I said. "So, we need to find out who gave it to her. Was it the same person that she was sleeping with?"

"And did they intend for her to be killed by the tablet or was it accidental?" Costello added.

"Yep. So, Jason, I want you to start bringing in the local drug dealers. Ask about, check bars and clubs again, Strabane and Letterkenny. See if anyone's selling this stuff. While you're there, flash about the photo of Terry Boyle too, maybe find out where he was last night."

"They're not connected though, are they?" Holmes asked.

"Not as far as I know," I said, "but if we can kill two birds with one stone . . ."

"There's no one else, Jason," Costello explained. "I've requested extra help from Letterkenny, but you seem to know the pubs and that. Might have more success than most."

"I'll phone Hendry, just so there's no jurisdiction nonsense about going over the border," I said. "Caroline, keep following up on that gold ring. I'll see if I can speak to Johnny Cashell, though he's looking unlikely; I can't see him drugging and abusing his own daughter. Besides," I added, "I don't think this was a sexual attack."

"Pathologist's report *suggests* consensual, Inspector; that doesn't necessarily mean it *was* consensual," said Williams.

"True. But all the same. Size, drugs, eye witnesses — everything seems to be pointing to Whitey McKelvey."

"If the wee bugger would show his face,"

Williams added.

"Maybe he has though, eh?" Holmes retorted, tapping on the CCTV videotape lying in front of us.

We set up the video and TV in the conference room at the back of the station and played the tape from the start. The tape began at 6 p.m. on Thursday 19th December, the time and date appearing in white lettering at the bottom of the screen. The images jumped from one view to the next every twenty seconds.

Williams leaned forward and fast-forwarded the tape until customers began to appear around 7.20 p.m. With each new arrival we paused the tape, looking for Angela and the person who had accompanied her — whom we assumed to have been Whitey McKelvey.

By 9.30 p.m. the bar was filling up and they still had not appeared, though we had noticed that a young man with a shaved head and a shoulder bag who had gone into the male toilets at 8.50 p.m. had yet to emerge. Holmes concluded that he was either a drug dealer or a homosexual. "Either way, we'll bust him if we see him this side of the border," he added.

As the tape progressed, the lights in the

bar dimmed. Then the screen cut to the doorway and I caught of glimpse of a girl with blonde hair passing underneath the camera. She was dressed in jeans and a blue top, as Cashell had described Angela's outfit that night. Slightly behind her, again half-disappearing from view under the camera, was a thin figure with short, almost peroxide-blond hair, clad in jeans and a white top. The figure did not look up at the camera and so we could only see the top of the head and the bright hair. Holmes paused the shot and we all leaned a little closer to the screen.

"Is that him?" Williams asked, squinting at the screen.

"I think so," I said.

Holmes tapped the screen with his knuckles; "Ladies and gentlemen, Whitey McKelvey, I believe."

It was not as clear a shot as any of us wanted, but it seemed a reasonable assumption to make. We watched a further hour's worth of tape and saw Angela several times: in the queue for the bar, dancing, chatting to a group of girls by the toilets. That shot had almost passed when I saw a face I recognized and everything seemed to fall into place. The clothes were different, obviously, the pink uniform replaced with a tight satin grey top that accentuated every curve. She wore make-up and looked older, but there was no mistaking her — it was Yvonne Coyle, the girl who had been feeding Tommy Powell in his room the day before. At the same time, it suddenly came to me where I had seen her face before. It was with her cheek pressed against Angela Cashell's in a strip of passport photographs, placed carefully between the leaves of an unfinished romantic novel lying under the dead girl's bed.

I phoned Finnside almost immediately, while Holmes and Williams set about the tasks we had agreed earlier that morning. Mrs McGowan told me, with some annoyance, that Coyle had phoned in sick, having left early the day before.

"Are you sure she's alright to have here?" Mrs MacGowan asked. "You know, I'd rather not have staff involved with Gardai."

"As far as I know, Mrs MacGowan, Yvonne Coyle has done nothing wrong. I want to speak to her about something completely innocuous," I lied. "She witnessed an accident."

"I'll tell her to contact you if she returns tomorrow —"

"Thanks Mrs MacGowan."

"Though if she doesn't, she needn't bother . . ."

I put the receiver down quickly to avoid hearing the rest. Picking it up again, I phoned Strabane PSNI station and asked to be transferred to Inspector Hendry.

As I had expected, Hendry didn't care about our people going across the border to question bar owners, though it was technically not allowed. Some policemen on both sides of the border could be sticky about it, but generally we all knew that we were chasing the same people. The bad old days, when collusion and suspicion had prohibited any contact, were passing, if not yet past. Hendry also agreed to the more unusual request that I interview Cashell in the PSNI holding-cell — so long as I was a silent partner, technically off-duty, and Hendry asked the questions on my behalf. Finally, I asked him if Whitey McKelvey had been spotted yet, though I knew that, if he had, Hendry would have phoned us to boast about the efficiency of the northern police in comparison with their sleepy southern counterparts.

"No sign here," he said, "though I hear rumours from the travelling community that he's over your side. Apparently a branch of his family has set up camp outside of Bally-bofey."

"I've heard nothing about that," I said, a little rankled at having not received this information myself.

"That's because I haven't told you until now. I'm telling you: British Intelligence, best in the world!" he laughed.

"See you in an hour," I said, and hung up. I immediately rang through to Ballybofey Station and was transferred to a Sergeant Moore, who promised to investigate the tip about Whitey McKelvey being in their area after I had given him a description and some background on the boy. I cautioned him to keep it low-key; I didn't want the boy running again.

I had decided not to ask Hendry for Yvonne Coyle's address; the cost of having to listen to more crowing about Intelligence was too high for such basic information. I decided instead to do some rudimentary detective work and checked a northern phonebook someone had "borrowed" from a phone box just over the border a few years earlier. There were no Coyles listed for Glennside. I tried Mrs McGowan again, suitably apologetic for my earlier abruptness. She gave me the address immediately, with commensurate curtness. I decided to visit Yvonne before seeing Johnny Cashell, on the off-chance that Angela might have mentioned her father to her friend at some stage.

I had to ring the doorbell three times before I heard the thud of someone running down stairs and the clunk of the deadbolt. Then Yvonne Coyle answered the door in a pink dressing-gown one would expect to see on a child, with a teddy-bear embroidered on the breast. Her hair was quite short and, being wet, appeared dark. Her skin still sparkled with moisture, smelling unmistakably of shampoo and soap.

"Oh . . . I . . . Can I help you?" she said, gripping the lapels of her gown in one fist, the other hand holding the door ajar.

I introduced myself and added, "I'd like to speak to you, Miss Coyle, if you don't mind," smiling to seem less threatening.

"About Mr Powell?" she said, affecting an appearance of boredom.

"I think you know what about." I said.

"Well, I can't help you. The bitch fired me, so it's not my problem anymore."

"Mrs MacGowan fired you. Why?"

"Thanks to you, I guess. She's only just off the phone. Said I was bringing her establishment into disrepute." As she spoke she mimicked her former employer's voice with a fair degree of accuracy. Certainly enough to make us both laugh.

"Sorry, Miss Coyle; I told her you hadn't done anything wrong. I . . . Look, can I come in for a few minutes? I have some questions about Angela Cashell."

She tried to pretend to be surprised at the mention of Angela's name, but gave it up as a bad job and swung the door open. "Ten minutes. Give me a chance to get changed first. I'm only out of the shower," she said, pointing to her wet hair, which was dripping water onto the floor. "Though I suppose you already worked that out, you being a policeman and all. Go in and sit down; I won't be a minute."

I went into the room towards which she had gestured. It was a small living room, with a brown sofa and two mismatched easy chairs arranged around a TV set and an electric fire. A CD player and a stack of CDs sat by one of the chairs. I glanced down the spines of the discs and noticed a few Divine Comedy albums, which reminded me of the one I had seen in Angela's bedroom. I suspected I knew now where she had got it. An ashtray full of butts rested on the arm of the sofa, so I sat beside it and took out my cigarettes. "Do you mind if I smoke?" I called up the stairs.

"Long as you can give me one; I'm all out," she replied, coming downstairs, "and I'm too lazy to go to the shop." Yvonne came in and sat in one of the easy chairs. She had not changed out of her dressing-gown, but had wrapped a towel around her hair turban-style. The gown had loosened very slightly, so that the flushed skin at the base of her throat and the top of her chest was visible. She leaned forward and took the cigarette which I offered her, and I could see the swell of her breasts as the gown fell slightly open. I looked away, but she had already caught me looking and smiled slightly as she rearranged her gown. I began to regret not asking Caroline Williams to accompany me.

"I'm out of matches too," she said, and leaned forward again. I battled with myself to look her in the eyes as she lit her cigarette off my Zippo, and in so doing, I noticed that her eyes were two different colours: one green and one almost grey. Seeing her now, without make-up, I also realized that she was not as young as she had seemed when I had seen her at Finnside. I guessed she was in her late twenties. Her skin was smooth and well-toned, but had begun to wrinkle around her eyes.

"So, you're off sick," I said. "Hope it's nothing serious."

"Nothing more than a hangover. Still, I'm not sick anymore: I'm unemployed."

"Sorry about that. I —"

"Don't worry about it. It was a shit job anyway — feeding old gits like Tommy Powell his stewed apples, while his prick of a son tried to look up my skirt. Good riddance."

"Thomas Powell? The son was trying to . . ." I gestured in the general vicinity of her legs.

"Oh, aye. All the time. Thinks he's flash. A bit too old for my taste."

"He's the same age as me," I said, half-pretending to be offended.

"Oh," she replied, and smiled at me. I knew I would be interpreting that all the way back to the station. Time to move on, I thought.

"So, what can you tell me about Angela Cashell, Miss Coyle?" I asked.

"Please, call me Yvonne. What do you want to know about Angela?" she replied. This wasn't going particularly well.

"When did you last see her?" I asked, fairly sure I knew the answer.

"Friday morning. She stayed here on Thursday night. She left the house at the same time as me. I was in work at lunch-time. I gave her a lift over to Lifford. She was meeting her sisters at the cinema."

"What was she wearing?"

She thought for a second. "A red top and a skirt she borrowed from me. She didn't have a change of clothes, so she took some of mine."

"What about the clothes she had been wearing?"

"They're upstairs. I was going to keep them — as a reminder, you know. Guess that sounds kind of stupid. Do you need them back? Only I've washed them — you know, if you're looking for evidence or anything. Sorry," she said, wincing exaggeratedly at her actions.

"I shouldn't think so," I said; they would serve little forensic purpose if Angela hadn't been wearing them at the time of her death. "Did she say where she was going after the cinema?"

She paused slightly. "Home, I think."

"Are you sure?"

"I think so."

I decided to approach it from a different angle. "Why did she stay with you on Thursday?"

"I'm . . . I was her friend. Why wouldn't she have stayed with me?"

"Why Thursday? Why didn't she stay at home?"

"She was at a club in Strabane; handier for her to stay here."

"Did she go to the club with you? Or did you meet her there?"

"I met her."

"Who did she come in with?"

Another pause. "I don't know."

"Are you sure?"

"She had a lot of friends. Angela wasn't shy that way."

"Who was it?"

"I'm not sure," she said. "It might have been one of the travellers, but I don't know. He doesn't come near me. Angela wouldn't tell me if she was with him."

"Why not?"

" 'Cause she knows I don't like him."

"Why not?"

" 'Cause he was using her."

"In what way?"

Nothing.

"In what way, Yvonne?"

"She . . . I don't want to say. It's not fair on her."

"Yvonne. Angela was murdered by some-one. I need to know everything about her — good and bad — if I'm going to find out who did it."

She thought about it, taking two drags on the cigarette in quick succession, before leaning over and grinding it out in the ashtray. She sat back in the chair and pulled her bare legs up under her, wrapping one arm around her knees.

"She let him do things. To her. Sex and stuff."

"Why?"

"For money. So she could buy things."

"What kind of things?"

"Drugs, usually. She got into drugs kind of recently, after she met McKelvey. He met her in a club in Strabane. Gave her something for free, got her drugs for a while when she had money; when she didn't, she paid for them in different ways." She blushed slightly. "She never mentioned him in front of me."

"What kind of drugs?"

"Es mostly. McKelvey got her them, or gave her money to buy them off someone else."

"Was she with McKelvey on Friday night?"

"I don't know. Might have been. She said she had a date. Wanted something nice to wear; she took my red jacket. I'd only worn it once myself. Still, it looked better on her."

"Could she have been meeting someone

other than McKelvey on Friday?"

"She might have been. McKelvey wasn't her only one. She had a lot of friends, like I said."

"Did you see McKelvey on Thursday with her?"

"I thought I saw him, but I can't be sure."

The conversation was flowing fairly easily, so I decided to return to Johnny Cashell. "Did she tell you what she and her father had rowed about on Thursday? The night she stayed with you?"

A pause, while she weighed up her options. In the end she decided to be honest. "The usual. He was spying on her dressing. Used to do it all the time. She said that one time she was in the shower; when she came out he was in the bathroom, cleaning his teeth or something. Acting as if there was nothing wrong with it. She said he gave her the creeps. If you ask me, McKelvey is no better, mind you."

"Did Angela's father ever do anything to her? Anything he shouldn't?" I asked, struggling to make the question direct without being crass. "Did he touch her or anything?"

"I don't think so. I think he just liked to watch her."

"Why didn't you tell us this when she

died? Why keep it to yourself? It could help."

"I guess I didn't want to get involved. Plus, John Cashell might be a dirty old man, but I couldn't believe he'd be a murderer. Liam McKelvey is a different matter."

"Did she tell you who gave her the ring?"

"What ring?"

"The ring she was wearing. The gold ring with the stones; her initials on it."

Yvonne looked confused. "Angela didn't wear a gold ring. She wore nothing but silver. Can I have another cigarette?"

She leaned forward again and took the cigarette. I held out my lighter for her and she steadied my hand in both of hers, though it was not shaking. Her hands were hard from work, but warm. The touch of her skin made my guts contract as if someone had winded me. She held my hand a little longer than necessary, then slowly let go, the tips of her fingers running across the backs of mine, catching slightly on my wedding ring.

Johnny Cashell was sitting in Interview Room One in Strabane police station. It was like every other interview room I had ever seen: a single wooden desk against one wall, the surface engraved with initials and scarred with cigarette burns and rings where hot mugs of tea had whitened the wood. The walls were painted institutional green and covered in scrawls and obscenities, and beside the desk someone had left burn marks from a lighter flame. The room smelt of sweat and smoke, both emanating in copious quantities from Johnny, who shifted continually in the straight-backed wooden chair he had been given, oblivious to the fact that such rooms are designed to ensure maximum discomfort. In fact, it was rumoured that the old RUC used to cut an inch off the front legs of these chairs so that those sitting on them kept slipping forward and could not get settled.

Cashell prodded at his stomach and the bulging around his abdomen under his T-shirt showed that he was still wearing a dressing for the knife wound he'd received. He looked unkempt, his stubble a dirty grey in contrast with the redness of his hair. His T-shirt seemed to be annoying him, and he tugged at it, pulling it off his chest throughout the interview.

I had given Hendry a list of the questions I wanted asked and had filled him in on events while we had waited for Cashell to be brought up to the interview room. Consequently, I was content enough to sit and listen. We had decided to keep things informal.

"So, Johnny, you told Inspector Devlin here that you last saw your daughter last Thursday, the 19th of December. Is that right?" Hendry said.

"What? Aye. That's right. Thursday."

"Was there a reason why she didn't come home that night?"

"Staying with friends, probably."

"Any reason she was staying with friends?"

"Jesus Christ, do you need a reason to stay with a friend? Maybe she was with a boyfriend and didn't want us to know. What the fuck is this about?"

"Did you have a row with Angela on Thursday, Mr Cashell?"

Johnny looked up and peered at Hendry more cautiously, alerted by the use of his full name, sensing a change in tone — a change in direction. "Might have done; can't remember."

"Did you? Yes or no?"

"Well, if you're asking, you know I did. So just get to the point."

"What did you row about?"

"Family stuff."

Hendry laughed. "Oh it was family stuff alright." Then, so quietly that I wasn't even sure he actually said it, he muttered, "You're a smoker, Johnny. Do you like to roll your own?"

"What?"

"Did your daughter accuse you of spying on her getting dressed?"

Cashell exploded, getting to his feet, "You fucking . . . ! Devlin? What the fuck's going on?"

A constable who had been standing at the door behind Cashell — another feature designed to cause discomfort — moved forward and placed a hand on Cashell's shoulder, forcing him back onto his seat.

"Did she accuse you of watching her getting dressed?" Hendry persisted.

Cashell did not immediately reply; instead he glared at me, his chest heaving, his breathing laboured and nasal. Finally, he exhaled slowly; "I . . . I stumbled in on her, by accident."

"That's not what we hear. Apparently this wasn't the first time, was it, Mr Cashell? You watched her take a shower one day too, we're told. Were you attracted to your daughter, Mr Cashell?"

"You fucker!" he spat, then turned to me as if I represented in some way the last voice of reason. "Devlin? What the fuck's going on here? You don't seriously think I —"

"Did you fancy your daughter Johnny? It's

nothing to be ashamed of. She was a good-looking girl. Wouldn't even really have been incest anyway, would it, Johnny? 'Cause she wasn't yours anyway. Isn't that right?" Hendry seemed to take some pleasure from the last comment and the effect it had on Cashell.

Johnny's mouth opened and closed, struggling to respond like a fish gasping for breath, but his brain wouldn't function. Tears welled in his eyes as he stared, as though in a trance, through me and beyond the walls of the room to wherever he stored his memories of his girl. Again I saw her lying exposed in a field, without dignity. No one spoke as a single tear escaped from the corner of Cashell's eye, then he quickly rubbed at his face with the palms of his hands and lifted a cigarette and lit it. He stretched his mouth like an animal yawning, attempting to swallow back his tears.

"Did you kill her, Johnny?" Hendry said, his voice warm with camaraderie, but Cashell simply shook his head.

"Did you ever have sex with her? Or try to have sex with her?"

Again he shook his head and did not speak, as though afraid of the words he might use and what they might say about him.

"Did you want to?" Hendry asked.

Cashell looked at him again, defiance flaring in his red-ringed eyes. "I didn't kill my daughter."

"Why did you go after Whitey McKelvey, then? Jealousy? He was having sex with your girl."

"No. I . . . he . . . I found drugs in her trouser pockets. E tabs, I think. One of my other girls said Angela was spending a lot of time with him. I . . . I put two and two together. Thought maybe he'd drugged her or something. Raped her. She wouldn't have slept with that piece of shit by choice."

"Why him? It could have been anyone," I said, waving a pardon at Hendry for the interruption.

"Muire told me Angela took her to the cinema on Friday, and then was going to meet her boyfriend. He was the only boy I knew she was seeing. People in the village talk. I heard she'd been with him on Thursday night. I just . . . I just assumed she was with him on Friday night, too."

"Did he give her the ring?" I asked.

"What ring?"

"Angela was wearing a ring with the initials AC on it; some kind of moonstone with diamonds around it. A gold ring. Did McKelvey give it to her?"

119

Johnny Cashell's face blanched and he smacked his lips and tongue several times as though thirsty, again looking at some unspecified point just beyond me. "A ring?" he asked, almost to himself.

"Yes. Does it mean anything to you? Could he have bought it for her?"

"I don't know nothing about no ring." While he said it with finality, he seemed distracted. I could see that he was thinking about something, but I didn't know what else to ask.

A few minutes later Hendry wound the interview to a close. As he was being led to the door of the room Cashell looked at me and said, "Oi, Devlin? Whip-round, my arse. Since when did Gardai have a whip-round for the likes of me?" Then he shuffled out of the room, his shoulders slumped, and I couldn't work out whether what he had said had been an expression of gratitude or contempt. Hendry looked at me quizzically, but said nothing.

I returned to my own station after the interview and phoned Ballybofey, only to be told that Moore was out of the station. I left a message for him to contact me as soon as he came in.

Jason Holmes was in the interview room

with one of our local characters, a thirty-four-year-old named Lorcan Hutton, who had spent several years in detention centres and jail for drugs offences but still continued to sell in the town. He was the antithesis of what you'd expect of a dealer. His parents were very wealthy, both doctors in the North. He had blond curly hair and an athletic physique. Despite his periods in prison and rehabilitation centres, he was a regular in the dark areas of bars and clubs, where teenagers — his acolytes — gathered around him, hoping for the free hit that would never come.

In fact, an IRA punishment beating, which had left him with two smashed ankles and puncture marks over his legs and arms from baseball bats studded with nails, had not stopped him, though it had driven his family out of Strabane and into Lifford in the mistaken belief that the IRA wouldn't come across the border.

Holmes announced for the benefit of the tape recording that I had entered the room and then suggested a break. Hutton shrugged, while his solicitor, a Strabane man called Brown, earnestly asked him whether he had been treated badly and what questions he had been asked.

Holmes and I stepped out of the room.

"How's it going?" I asked.

Holmes shook his head. "Nothing. Knows nothing about E tabs. Never even seen one before. Shut tighter than a virg—" He stopped short as Williams approached.

"Did I miss a famous Holmes simile?" she asked, smiling.

"Nearly. You're just in time."

"What's up?" she said, waving a sheet of paper in her left hand.

"Nothing. Lorcan Hutton has joined us for a chat. Brought his lawyer."

"What?"

"Yep. I invited him to the station; he picks up his mobile and phones. The fucking lawyer was here before we were."

"Jesus." She allowed a respectful pause before telling us of her success. "Guess what? We got a hit on the ring. Two hits, actually."

"Great. What?"

"I kept phoning round jewellers and that, and this morning got a woman in Stranorlar who recognized the description of the ring."

"Any names come up?" I asked impatiently. Williams looked a little hurt at my lack of appreciation for her storytelling and continued.

"I couldn't find any of you, so I went on

122

myself. Seems that about a month ago, a young traveller boy tried selling her a number of items, including the ring. She remembered the ring in particular because she has a moonstone ring herself. Said it was very unusual. Offered him twenty euros for it, thinking he wouldn't know the value. Told her to go fuck herself and left the shop. She thought he was playing hard to get, that he'd be back for the money, but she never saw him again."

"Is she sure it was a traveller?"

"Oh yes. Made a big deal out of showing me the can of air freshener she said she'd *had* to spray after he went. A blond boy, she said. Hair almost white. Big ears."

"Whitey McKelvey. Jesus! Good work, Caroline," Holmes said.

"Thank you." She smiled warmly. "Anyway — here's the interesting bit. She said she told the other Garda who had asked."

"What other Garda?" I asked.

"She said that a Guard had called into the shop one day, just out of the blue, and asked her about the ring. Had a sketch of it. She said she told him then; gave a full description of the boy. A young Guard."

"Who was it?"

"I don't know. I've contacted Letterkenny and they're to get back to me about it," Williams said. "But I figured that it meant the ring must have been stolen, not bought. Guess what?"

"What?" I said.

"It was. Stolen, I mean. In Letterkenny, a few weeks earlier."

"Makes sense," Holmes said.

"What does?" I asked.

"McKelvey steals it from Letterkenny, tries to shift it, doesn't get the money he expected and so gives it to his girlfriend in return for . . ." He looked at Williams. "For you know what."

"I suppose," I agreed a little reluctantly. "Who reported it stolen?"

"Someone called Anthony Donaghey. Said it was a family heirloom, belonged to his mother."

"Anthony Donaghey. *The* Anthony Donaghey?" I asked in amusement.

"I don't know. *An* Anthony Donaghey, certainly," Williams said, annoyed at my tone. "Why? Who's Anthony Donaghey?"

"Ratsy Donaghey," I said, looking to Holmes for agreement.

"Right, right. The drug dealer. Right."

"More than a drug dealer. Fulltime asshole. If that ring belonged to his mother, I'll . . . I don't know what I'll do. But it's not his mother's. She spent her days cleaning the local primary school; she didn't buy gold-and-diamond rings."

"Maybe she ran a sideline, same as her son," Holmes said, laughing.

"Maybe we should have a talk with Mr Donaghey," Williams suggested, pointedly ignoring the previous remark.

"You'll have a hard time doing that," a voice behind us said. We all turned to see the oily face of Mr Gerard Brown, lawyer to Lorcan Hutton, about whom we had completely forgotten.

"Why?" asked Holmes.

"He was found dead in Bundoran last month."

"Client of yours, too, was he?" Williams asked, smirking.

"Occasionally," Brown replied, without a hint of irony. "I take it my present client is free to go now."

I nodded at Holmes. "Try him one last time. Make it clear," I said, as much for Brown as for Holmes, "that we will ignore any admission of knowledge about drugs in the area, if Mr Hutton reveals such while giving us information which pertains to this murder inquiry."

"I'm sure my client will do his best to help the Garda," Brown said. Then he and Holmes went back into the interview room.

"So, what do you think, guvnor?" Williams said, stressing the last word.

"I think Holmes is right." Her face fell slightly. "That was bloody good work, Caroline."

She blushed. "What about Donaghey?" she said.

"Check where he died. Contact the station involved and see what they say about his death."

"Do you think there's a connection?" she asked.

"I don't see how there could be, but best check, eh? Meantime, we wait to see if McKelvey turns up in Ballybofey."

"Why Ballybofey?" she asked, and I filled her in on all that I had learned that morning. Then Williams went to her desk, while I began to work through some of the many message sheets that had gathered on my desk since Angela Cashell had died.

The top pile related to Terry Boyle. Apparently he had been seen in three different pubs on the evening he died, though no one remembered him leaving with anyone. Someone had run a standard record check on him the previous night and had reported that he was charged with possession of marijuana in Dublin when a first-year student. He got off with a fine and community service. An appeal for information had just started to filter out through the media — by tomorrow, I expected my messages pile to have grown considerably. I read and was able to scrap immediately the note from Williams, saying that she had got a possible hit with the ring in a second-hand jewellers' in Stranorlar, and couldn't wait for me to return. She added that Holmes had gone out to pick up Lorcan Hutton.

Burgess had left two notes that morning to say that Thomas Powell had phoned enquiring about the state of inquiries regarding his father's intruder. Burgess had spelt both words correctly, though had used them the wrong way around.

On Saturday night, five cars along Coneyburrow Road had had their wing mirrors smashed off by a drunken man seen staggering along the road. The following day, all five owners had phoned to say that the culprit, a local schoolteacher celebrating the Christmas holidays, had called on each that morning and apologized before offering to pay for all damages.

That same night, four bottles of gin were stolen from an off-sales office at the back of the local pub. The thief had tried to escape out of the toilet window, dropping and smashing three of the bottles in the process.

On Sunday morning, a Derry man phoned to report seeing a wild cat along the main Lifford road the previous night as he returned home in a taxi following a wedding. He was unable to describe colour or size — only that it was dark and bigger than a normal cat.

Finally, while I was sitting there, the pathologist's report was left on my desk by Burgess. Terry Boyle's identification had been confirmed using hospital notes which mentioned two breakages in his femur from childhood accidents. Cause of death was attributed to a single gunshot wound to the head, delivered at point-blank range from a handgun. He had certainly been dead before his car was set alight. Stomach contents revealed he had drunk in excess of the legal drink-driving limit, which made me wonder whether he had stopped in the lay-by where he was killed to sleep off the drink. There was no sign of the drug which had been found in Angela Cashell's stomach, which further convinced me that the two killings were linked by nothing more than geography.

An hour and three coffees later, I became aware of a figure standing before me and looked up to see Garda officer John Harvey, a young uniform with light brown hair and glasses, holding his cap in his hand.

"You wanted to see me, sir?" he said.

"Did I?" I asked.

"Yes. Sergeant Williams said I was to see you about the stolen ring. I was the one called to the jewellers about it."

I invited Harvey to sit, and he did, carefully, as though attending an interview. Harvey was a part-timer, but clearly loved the work and compensated for a limited intellect by being fastidious and deferential to all the full-timers in the station, especially detectives.

"I brought my notes, sir. And a copy of the report I wrote." He smiled as he offered me the two typed A4 sheets and his notebook, in which he had recorded the interview in longhand. The notes confirmed exactly what Williams had told us, with a vague description of the boy, as provided by the jeweller in Stranorlar.

"Could it be this Whitey McKelvey, sir?" Harvey said, eagerly.

"Could be. Why did you go to the jewellers in the first place?"

"Sergeant Fallon asks some of us part-timers if we'd go around local second-hand shops every so often with stolen-goods lists. I wasn't doing anything that day, so I volunteered. I don't know if he followed it up, though."

I figured Fallon probably hadn't. Stolen rings were low priority; simply by sending someone like Harvey out to check, Fallon had covered himself should anyone make a fuss that their loss wasn't being treated seriously. In reality, we all accepted that stolen goods generally stayed lost. I could also understand why Fallon picked people like Harvey to do the job: he had clearly approached it with the same seriousness as he would a murder inquiry. In fact, I decided to follow Fallon's lead.

"John, perhaps you could help me with something else. Tommy Powell in Finnside Nursing Home claims he had an intruder in his room last week. I promised we'd send someone out to check. Would you take a run out, if you get a chance?"

He nodded eagerly. "I'd love to," he said.

"Thanks," I replied, looking back to my paperwork in the hope he'd take the hint and leave. He didn't.

"My pleasure, sir. If there's anything I can do to help with the Cashell case. You know, I could . . ." He didn't get any further, as Burgess shouted that Costello wanted to see me.

When I went into his office, he was speaking to someone on the phone and had a copy of the *Belfast Telegraph* on the desk in front of him. He spun the paper round to face me while he agreed with whatever was being said to him on the other end of the line. Then he pointed at an article on the front page, apparently a story concerning the latest UN debate over the efficacy of Hans Blix's Inspection Team, and the inevitability of a war in Iraq. I failed to see the relevance of the story and shrugged my bewilderment. Costello frowned and stabbed a finger at the bottom of the page, without interrupting his conversation. I sat down when I saw the short piece to which he had pointed, under the heading, "Puma on Prowl in Donegal?"

The story told, in sensational detail, how sheep in the area of Lifford were being terrorised nightly by an unidentified creature. It also quoted an eyewitness, the Derry man who had spotted the creature on the way home from a wedding, giving a much fuller description than the one he had provided for our desk sergeant when he had phoned that weekend. He had, he said, contacted the local Garda, but felt that his complaint was not taken seriously. Now poor animals were suffering due to Garda reluctance or inefficiency. As a side-bar to the story, the paper had included a table of facts about pumas and what to do if you encountered one, including the suggestion that, when face-to-face with a puma, it is best not to panic, but rather pretend that it is not there.

By the time I had stopped reading and put the paper down, Costello was holding the phone in his hand, the mouthpiece covered. "Do you know anything about this?" he said, lifting the paper, as though to check whether the story was still there, then throwing it across his desk. It skimmed across the polished surface and slid onto the floor. I picked it up.

"A bit. The Derry man left a message. I only got it today. I thought we had more important issues."

"Well, this might explain Anderson's complaints about his sheep."

"Possibly," I agreed.

"Except we look like spare pricks at a funeral not doing anything about it. RTE have been on the phone. Again."

"Twice in one week. We've hit the big time."

"Three times," Costello corrected me. "You got the pathologist's report, I take it?" I nodded. "What do you think?"

I recounted my thoughts on reading it, including my view that perhaps Terry Boyle

132

had parked at Gallows Lane to sleep off the effects of overdrinking. Costello let me speak, then passed me a booklet of typed sheets.

"Forensics' report," he said. "Bloody detailed. I've one of those forensics boyos on the phone, except he's put me on hold. Car was parked and the engine was off when he was killed, they say." With that, we both heard a tinny voice over the phone line. Costello listened for a few seconds before announcing that he was putting the phone onto speakers, which took rather longer than it might have. Eventually, I was introduced to Sergeant Michael Doherty, who had written the report.

"We discovered a fair bit from the car, Inspector," Doherty began. "The victim was likely shot by someone standing outside the car. On the driver's side. We recovered the bullet from the bodywork behind the passenger seat. Ballistics tests are being carried out at the moment. I'll say this — it must have been a scare for whoever was sitting next to him."

"Was there a passenger?"

"Almost definitely. You see, blood spattering is a definite science, Inspector. When your victim was shot, his blood should have spattered all over the inside of the car. But around the passenger seat, there's significantly less blood than there should be. My guess is that someone was sitting beside him — someone who was covered in blood when they got out of the car. Now, their seats were pushed right back and, though your victim's clothes were badly burned, we can tell his trousers were unbuttoned and unzipped when he was killed, so I'd say he was up for some hanky-panky." Doherty laughed in a vaguely embarrassed way and continued, "The important thing is that your victim's window was wound down. Obviously the glass was blown out in the fire, but the mechanism was down near the bottom of the door."

"His window was open?" Costello interrupted. "So what?"

"The weather wasn't great that night. I don't know about you, but if I'm about to strip off for a bit of action in the back of the car, the last thing I'd do in the middle of winter is wind down my window. A bit chilly round the nether regions, eh?" His laugh rattled from the speaker again. "No, my guess would be —"

"That he opened the window to his killer," I said.

"Just so," Doherty agreed.

"Why not just shoot him through the

window?" I asked, as much thinking aloud as seeking a response.

"Maybe whoever did it wanted to be sure that they had the right person. Or wanted to see his face. Or wanted to make sure they didn't hit whoever was sitting beside him in the car."

"Maybe," I agreed.

Doherty made a few final observations, then hung up. Costello had listened grimly to the whole conversation without speaking. He sat opposite me, his hands clasped. "So," he said finally. "What do you think?"

"Seems like forensics have done the thinking for us: he picks someone up — or is picked up by someone — parks in the lay-by for a bit of sex; there's a tap on the door, opens the window and bang."

"What about the person in the car with him? An accomplice?"

"Hard to see it otherwise. How did his killer know where to find him, unless he followed him? Why not kill the passenger too? And why burn the car, unless they were scared that the passenger had left some evidence. Either that, or it was some poor innocent out for a night's fun who's wandering around Lifford in shock, covered in blood."

"Jesus, Ben, we need to clear up some of

this quick. Two killings in a week. We'll start to look incompetent."

When I came out of the office, Harvey was still sitting opposite my desk. He stood when I approached, his cap held in his hand.

"Everything alright, sir?" he asked.

I nodded. "Can I help you with something else?" I asked, lifting some of the paperwork from my desk.

"Sergeant Burgess asked me to tell you that Officer Moore from Ballybofey was on the phone, sir," he said. "He said it was important."

Ten minutes later we were on our way to pick up Whitey McKelvey.

CHAPTER SIX

Tuesday, 24th December

It was late afternoon and the sky was the colour and texture of slate. The moon was beginning to shine from behind a thick bank of cloud that threatened snow, and the air was cold and dry.

Three cars left Lifford station on the way to Castlefinn where, Moore had reliably informed me, McKelvey was staying with some cousins who were camped in a picnic area. I knew the place he mentioned. Learning from the problems encountered in Strabane, Donegal County Council had placed height-restriction bars across the entrance to all public areas — lay-bys, car parks and so on — to stop the travellers from using them. The group that had taken over the area outside of Castlefinn had arrived in the middle of the night in early August and had spent several hours dismantling the restriction bars. They then moved into the area *en masse,* before re-erecting the bars, thus apparently materializing in the picnic spot like a ship in a bottle.

The area was not ideal for picking up McKelvey. While there were only two entrance/exit points, it backed onto an area of woodland and fields. If McKelvey made a run for it we would have difficulty catching him. We had decided that Holmes, Williams, Harvey and I would approach the caravans from behind, waiting in the trees in case McKelvey came that way. Costello himself, who knew the family, would knock on the caravan door and ask to see McKelvey in the hope that he might come peaceably. Several uniforms would accompany him, while two cars blocked the exits.

We stopped about a quarter of a mile short of the campsite and my team got out of the cars and began to pick through the bramble hedges that lined the road into the field beyond. By following the perimeter, we would eventually come up behind the site. The field was sodden from the autumn rains and it had now frozen into thick brown ridges like waves, over which we tripped and stumbled. We had misjudged how long it would take to reach the camp and Costello radioed several times, impatient to get moving. Just as we reached the treeline directly behind the caravan, the snow began. Great fat flakes at first, drifting lightly around us, like eiderdown. Then the snow grew thicker and fell with greater speed, gathering on the branches of the trees and settling on our backs and shoulders. Holmes began to stamp his feet and blow into his hands for heat. Williams shuddered involuntarily and Harvey offered her his jacket. Momentarily, she looked offended, then smiled and took it. I couldn't tell whether Harvey was blushing at her smile or from the cold, but I was left to wonder how consistently Williams practised her feminist beliefs.

A buzz of static on the radio, and Costello announced that he was moving in. I drew my baton and saw the others follow suit. Holmes flicked open the catch on the slip for his pepper spray, and I wondered what he expected from a seventeen-year-old traveller boy. The snow fell increasingly heavily, the pattern of the falling flakes became almost hypnotic, and I realized that I was not paying attention to what was happening. I heard a thud as Costello knocked on the door. Then voices. Almost immediately, the curtains across the back window of the caravan, which was in darkness, were pushed back and the window opened. A small figure began to climb out, one thin leg first squeezed through, then another. Finally, the figure dropped silently to the ground and approached the trees between Holmes and Harvey. As the figure moved into the trees, Harvey flicked on his torch, momentarily lighting the startled face and the shock of black hair. Then the figure ran, with Harvey and Holmes crashing after him. I heard Williams shout and assumed that she, too, was after the boy.

I was about to shout to them to tell them it wasn't the right person, when I saw a second figure climb through the window and make for the trees. This time there could be no mistake. Even in the darkness, the luminescence given off by the snow forming at our feet was enough to reveal the almost white blond hair and pale marble skin. Whitey crept along the undergrowth on his belly, seemingly impervious to the brambles and the snow. When he felt he was safe, he stood and began to pick up speed.

He was about fifteen feet from me, moving quietly towards the fields. I can only assume that he did not hear me approach behind him over the din of the shouting and crashing of Williams and Harvey and the growing chorus of raised voices from the picnic area, where I guessed Costello was being lectured on police discrimination.

Eventually, I pushed out of the trees completely and, sticking to the perimeter of the field, was able to catch up with Whitey just as he emerged into the moonlight. I placed my hand solidly on his shoulder, my baton in the other hand, and began to speak.

I recall exactly what happened next, viewing it as if in slow motion. Whitey turned his head and I saw in his eyes a mixture of fear and aggression at being cornered. Then he grabbed my hand and clamped his teeth on it. I felt his teeth cut through my flesh, until eventually they connected, jarringly, with the bone of my hand. I could taste blood in my mouth. He shook his head as a terrier might with a toy, before releasing my hand. I screamed. Then something inside me snapped, audibly almost, and I felt a surge of adrenaline rush through my system. Without thinking, I turned and swung my right fist into McKelvey's face. I felt the cartilage of his nose shatter beneath my fist, felt the hard crunch as my knuckles connected with his cheekbone and his teeth, and saw his head snap back as blood and spittle spurted from his mouth.

He fell to the ground, legs splayed, and I lifted my foot and stamped down with my heel on his crotch. McKelvey doubled up, his face contorted with hatred and embarrassment, and I noticed a stain widen on his trousers as his bladder emptied. He looked at the mess he had made on himself, touched the wetness with his fingertips as though he could not believe his own eyes, and then held the moist fingers towards me. "I'll fuckin' kill ya," he spat, scrambling to his feet as he cupped his genitals in his hands.

I almost chased after him again, until I felt a hand close on my arm and I spun to face Williams, my fist raised. I saw a momentary flash of fear, or something deeper, flit across her face, and I lowered my fist in shame, stammering my apologies. I watched as my colleagues crashed through the undergrowth in pursuit of the boy.

Then the pain in my hand sharpened as the adrenaline dissipated; I doubled over with shock and pain and vomited into the snow, bile mixing with my blood, which appeared as black as oil under the moonlight. I felt momentary relief before a searing pain gripped my insides and I vomited again, retching over and over until I felt Williams's hand on my shoulder. I spat the sour taste out of my mouth, wiping away the thick strands of saliva with clean snow. Williams was busy wrapping her scarf around my hand and calling for help. Then, in the distance, I saw Whitey McKelvey being shoved towards me, Jason Holmes towering behind him with one hand clamped tightly on McKelvey's neck and the other holding his handcuffed wrists behind his back. When McKelvey stumbled and slid in the slush and snow, Holmes simply pulled on the cuffs, snapping the boy's arms back sharply, so he had to fight to regain his footing quickly or risk dislocating a shoulder.

When he got abreast of me, he pushed McKelvey onto the ground then placed his boot on the back of the boy's neck, pushing his face into the snow and mud. "Are you all right, sir?" he asked. Red spots flickered and flitted before my eyes and everything went dark.

I came to a moment later and, for a second, could not remember where I was or why these people were staring at me through a snowstorm. Gradually my mind began to work again and I tried to stand. Williams helped me to my feet, while Holmes lifted McKelvey and again began pushing him towards the cars. I saw Harvey to my left, leading the black-haired boy, who was also in cuffs. I noticed a cut on his cheek and the beginning of a bruise, livid and purple, flowering below his eye.

"What happened to him?" I asked, nodding over at Harvey and the boy.

"He ran into a baton," Williams said. "Lucky I stayed here with you. Where would you men be without women, eh?" She put her arm around me and pressed her head against mine, and in that brief moment of warmth I could only ask myself the same question.

"I'm sorry I . . . you know . . . raised my hand to you," I managed to say as she helped me towards the flickering blue lights cutting through the branches of the trees around us. She patted my shoulder lightly in what I took to be a sign of forgiveness. "I shouldn't have hit him, either," I added.

"No one needs to know, sir," she said. "These things happen, eh?"

I nodded, grateful for the opportunity to forget that my shame at hitting the boy had been equalled by the satisfaction I had felt in doing so.

Three uniforms kept the irate group of travellers at bay as the two boys were placed in separate cars and taken back to Lifford. I wanted to go with McKelvey, but Costello wouldn't allow it, telling me I was to get to the doctor's surgery before anything else. Holmes and Williams took McKelvey, but promised not to begin the interview without me.

The snow was falling so fast that the windscreen wipers of the car would not clear it. It had lain dry on the car bonnet like powdered sugar and now blew back onto the windscreen as we drove.

The doctor gave me a tetanus shot and stitched and bandaged up my hand, showing me first where the skin and ligaments could be pulled back to reveal the yellow-white bone beneath. Again, the bile rose in my throat and I had to swallow it back to stop myself being sick. As he gave me a bottle of painkillers, he broached a subject I had not wanted to consider.

"I've taken a blood sample for testing, you know," he said, looking me in the eye. I nodded and did not speak. "HIV, hepatitis, that kind of thing; I'll get the results for you quick as I can. There's a three month incubation period with HIV, though; might have to get that done again in the spring. It's unlikely, Inspector, but all the same — better be safe than sorry, eh?"

"Safe . . ." I said, unable to articulate the thoughts which darkened my mind.

Now I sat in the patrol car as we carefully wound our way down the snow-covered streets of Lifford and slid to a halt outside the station, nausea continuing to gnaw at my stomach while I tried to reassure myself that McKelvey was too young to have diseases such as those the doctor had mentioned, yet acutely aware that his age, perhaps, made it all the more likely.

When I got into the station, several people whose faces I hardly recognized enquired after my health and some patted my back or shook my uninjured hand. The doctor had elevated my arm in a sling — for comfort, he said, but it had the effect of drawing attention to the injury.

I was shuffling up to the interview room when Costello appeared, two steaming cups of coffee in his hands. He offered me one.

"How's the hand?" he said, motioning towards my arm with his own cup.

"Fine. I'm on a painkiller trip. I'll tell you, I can understand the attraction of drugs."

Costello laughed, thinking I was joking. "Feeling up to talking to our latest visitor? We held back, just for you."

McKelvey was in our holding cell, sitting on the edge of the lightweight metal bench which was suspended from the ceiling with thick wires. He was wearing black jeans, which were moulded to his legs and groin,

and a pair of Nike trainers. On top he had
been wearing only a white T-shirt when we
picked him up, but someone in the station
had given him a blanket which he had
wrapped around himself. His hair looked
bleached blond, almost white at the tips,
like an albino, and despite its length, his
ears stuck out almost at right angles to the
side of his head. One of the earlobes had a
nick taken out of it; the other was pierced
with three gold studs. His face was thin and
narrow, his eyes wide and blue, his cheek-
bones high, all of which, combined with his
skin-tight trousers, gave him a feminine appearance. One of his eyes was badly bruised,
the lid almost shut, and the knocks he had
received had affected his nose, for he spoke
with a harsh, nasal twang.

Harvey cuffed McKelvey and led him up
to the interview room where we had set a
table and enough chairs for McKelvey and
the murder team. When McKelvey was
brought in and sat down he slouched auto-
matically and reached over to lift one of the
cigarettes from the pack I had left in front
of me. I put the packet in my pocket after
taking one myself. If necessary, we could
offer him one later in barter for information.

Costello introduced all present for the

benefit of the twin tape recorders which were running beside us. Costello then asked McKelvey, for the second time, to confirm that he had waived his right to a solicitor. McKelvey laughed and said something unintelligible which we took to be agreement.

"Liam. Do you understand why you are here today?" Costello asked as a gentle opener.

"Aye. CSA. Can't take knickers off a bare arse, know what I mean."

We looked at each other, trying to make some sense of what he had said. Eventually Williams said, "What? Could you . . . could you explain that for us, Liam?"

"CSA. But you should be thanking me. Them sluts were sluts till I got them up the duff. They don't realize that, but they're slags and nobody respects them, see? Then I get them up the duff. They get respect then, wit' their sprogs. All claiming benefits anyhow. I get them slags respect. An' a good seeing to," he said, winking at Williams, "know what I mean, like."

"Jesus," Williams said disgustedly, "it would take more than drugs, son." Costello shot her a warning glance.

"Liam, did you know Angela Cashell?" Costello asked.

"Fuck's sake, course I do. Haven't I jus' tol' you. She was a slapper — no one'd go near her. I got her respect."

"You got her respect," Holmes interrupted incredulously. "How exactly did you do that?"

"I'm not talking to you," McKelvey snapped, literally spitting. Costello announced that the interview was suspended for a break and called us outside, leaving Harvey in the interview room with the boy.

"What in God's name is going on in there?" he asked as we came out.

"He thinks he's been lifted for not paying child support," Williams explained. "The CSA in the North."

"He also seems to believe that by leaving girls pregnant, he's doing them a favour by removing the stigma of being a 'slag' and replacing it with the honour of being a single mother to a litter of little Whitey McKelveys," I said.

"And he seems to think that Angela Cashell was pregnant, too."

"Was she?" Holmes asked with concern. "You know, that would be a double murder."

"No. If she was pregnant, the autopsy would have shown it. The question is why did he think she was pregnant?" I said.

149

"Unless she told him she was," continued Costello. "But why would you want that piece of shit to think he was father to your baby. Especially if there was no baby?"

"Perhaps she wanted to keep him," suggested Williams. "Maybe she thought he was going to dump her, so she said she was pregnant in the hope that he'd stick around. Or maybe she thought she was. At that age, it's difficult to rely on the time of the month. If you're a week or two late, you convince yourself you've been caught."

"Do you?" I asked, smiling.

"Oh yes," Williams said. "And it doesn't stop when you're past being a teenager."

"Maybe she wanted money. Tells him she's pregnant and needs money for the baby," I suggested.

"Or for an abortion," Williams agreed.

"Maybe McKelvey thought she was pregnant and killed her to avoid having to pay anything," Holmes suggested.

"No," Williams said. "You heard him in there. He doesn't give a shit how many babies he has, he has no intention of paying for them anyway. Why would one more be any different?"

"Shit," I said, as a growing realisation dawned. "That scuppers one theory."

"What?" Holmes asked.

"Well, we know that McKelvey did a runner when he saw Johnny Cashell looking for him after Angela died. We'd assumed that that was a sign of guilt for her death. But what if it wasn't?"

"You mean, what if he thought Johnny was after him for getting his daughter pregnant?" Holmes said.

"Exactly," I said.

Costello nodded towards Holmes and Williams. "Look, I'd like you two to sit out of this one," he said. "We'll try him first," he said to me, "with you leading. If we don't get anywhere, we'll swap. Okay?"

I could tell that both were annoyed about being left out of the interview. As the two of them headed into the room beside us, where they could watch and listen unseen, I asked Costello why in particular he had excluded Williams, who had been getting on fine.

"Don't want to have a lady have to listen to that kind of chat. No place for a girl like Caroline," he said, his tone serious, his face set. I wondered whether to point out that comments like that would have him before an industrial tribunal for sexist behaviour. In the end I said nothing, but followed him into the room, taking time to nod in the direction of the two-way mirror, through which I knew Williams and Holmes would be watching.

We sat down and I took out a cigarette and lit it. I could see Whitey's gaze following the smoke and he licked at his lips and fidgeted in his seat.

"So, you knew Angela Cashell?" I asked and he confirmed that he did. "What about her father?"

"Bloody lunatic," he said.

"Why?"

"Psycho bastard tried to burn me fuckin' home down. Should be liftin' him, not the likes of me."

"Why did he come after you Liam? Why'd you think he tried to —"

" 'Cause she were up the duff," he stated, folding his thin arms across his chest.

"What? Because you got her pregnant?"

"Aye, why else?"

"Not because he thought you'd killed her?" I asked, as casually as possible.

"Aye, right." He laughed. "Me kill her. What would I kill her for? Wasn't she givin' me me hole?"

"You're a born romantic, Liam," I said, earning a glance from Costello.

"What about drugs, Liam?" Costello asked.

"What about them?" he said, grinning inanely. "Yes, please," he laughed, looking from Costello to me and back to see if we shared his estimation of his sense of humour. Neither of us spoke. "Oh, sorry, sir, I forgot. I'd never do that." He spluttered a laugh again, spittle bubbling on his lips.

"No drugs, then Liam. Not for you?"

"I don't do drugs. I'm telling you; I don't need them."

"Not even something to get you in the mood, you and Angela maybe. Before . . . you know?"

He giggled strangely. "I don't need nothing, me. You might at your age, but not me."

"What about Angela? Was she taking drugs?"

"I don't know. Ask her. Give us a fag, mister."

Costello thumped the table with such force it made me jump, whatever the effect on McKelvey. "We can't ask her — she's dead. So watch your mouth, son."

For a moment McKelvey looked slightly stupefied, but quickly regained his bonhomie. He behaved as though this whole thing was a big joke — three friends having a laugh. "Aye, good one. What? Have you got me in for murder, like? Aye, right."

"Actually, we do Liam. So I'd start answering some questions if I were you, son, starting with where you were on Friday night." Costello leaned forwards on the table as he spoke, his size formidable in such a small room.

McKelvey was silent a moment, his face aghast. Then he shouted, "Piss off! You're not pinning nothing on me. I want me lawyer." He leaned to look around us at the mirror behind us. "Oi, you in there. Get me a lawyer. I want me lawyer."

"Listen, Liam. It's very simple, son," I said. "We have a number of questions which we would like you to answer. If you help us, and answer them fully and honestly, we'll have you home this evening. If not, you're in here over Christmas until the court opens on the twenty-seventh. Help us and we'll see you right."

McKelvey said nothing. He folded his arms sullenly and slouched further in his seat, staring at some indistinct point on the scarred surface of the table. I hoped we had deflected his attention away from his request for a lawyer — it would only complicate things. "Where were you on Friday night last?" I asked, taking his silence as a sign of reluctant acceptance.

"Don't remember," he said, without looking up.

"Try!" Costello said.

"I was in Letterkenny. With me cousins."

"Where?"

"About."

"Where about?" I asked.

"Everywhere! I don't know, do I? I had a few drinks in me," he spat.

"When did you last see Angela Cashell?"

"Last Tuesday, I think."

"Are you sure?"

"Aye, of course I'm sure."

"So you remember what you did last Tuesday, but not Friday?" Costello queried.

"I got off, didn't I? 'Course I remember it."

"You didn't see her, say, on Thursday night?"

"Are you deaf?" He leaned towards the tape recorders and raised his voice for comic effect. "I haven't seen her since Tuesday. Do you understand?" This final phrase he said as a deaf person might. Then he laughed forcibly, any real bravado having long since abandoned him.

"So, if I told you we have video footage of you and Angela Cashell on Thursday night together in Strabane, you'd say I was lying would you?"

"Aye. I didn't see her on Thursday, alright?"

"Okay, okay, Liam, whatever you say." I looked to Costello, signalling that I was done for now.

"Tell me, Liam, I have to ask. Angela Cashell was a good-looking girl. Whatever attracted her to you?"

"Animal fucking magnetism, isn't it?" he said, not missing a beat, his teeth exposed in a grin.

"But seriously," Costello said, not breaking his stride either, "what attracted her? Drugs? Money? What?"

"I gave her things nobody else could," McKelvey said, almost offended that his charms were not immediately apparent.

"What? Scabies?" I asked and thought I heard a snort from behind the mirror, where Williams and Holmes were still watching. I immediately regretted the comment, but Whitely spoke before I could apologize.

"Aye, babies," he said, though I was unsure whether he actually misheard me or just chose to ignore what I had said.

"There must have been something else," Costello said. "Were you paying her?"

"No!" McKelvey replied, beginning to redden. "She needed money sometimes. That's the way she is. I gave her it if she was stuck. Said her da was a bleeding tight-wad."

"Did she ask you for money when she said she was pregnant, Liam?" Costello asked

156

with conspiratorial warmth.

"Aye. Said she needed two hundred quid to take care of it, know what I mean? Couldn't ask her da."

"What did you tell her?"

"Told her it wasn't my problem."

There was a pause while Costello seemed to consider something, biting at the inside of his cheek. Finally he asked, "Would you have taken care of her and the baby?" The relevance of this question was lost on me.

"Not my problem. She got a shag. What more does she want?" He folded his arms on his chest and nodded once, with arrogance, as if to emphasize his position. "Know what I mean?"

Costello shook his head sadly, and I realized the question had been personal: a vain attempt to see if there was even a shred of decency in Whitey McKelvey.

"Liam," I said, redirecting the interview, "I want to go over some stuff, because I think you've not been totally honest with me. So I'm going to ask you once more. Were you giving Angela Cashell drugs?"

"I said no already."

"Were you buying her drugs or giving her money for drugs?"

"I gave her money for stuff. I don't know what she spent it on."

"What about the ring, Liam? Did you give her the ring?"

"What ring?"

"Gold ring, greeny-blue stone in the middle with diamonds around it. You know the one. You lifted it in Letterkenny a month ago. Tried to sell it in Stranorlar. Refreshing your memory now, Liam?"

"That. I sold it," he said, refusing to look at me, staring instead at the mirror behind me. "Some bitch bought it off me in a disco."

"Who?"

"Don't know."

"Where?"

"Don't know," he said, smiling.

Costello stood up, suddenly. "This interview is concluded at 7.55 p.m. on Wednesday 24th December." Then he turned off the tapes and called into the intercom beside the machines. "Would someone come in and take this piece of shit to the cells?" He added softly and a little sadly, "Then hose this place out . . ." Finally, he turned to McKelvey and said, "You disgust me, you . . . fucking animal," as if he could think of nothing worse to say. His shoulders slumped, as though he realized that Whitey McKelvey, of all people, had somehow inveigled him into revealing a side to his

158

character that he would rather not have acknowledged, and he left the room.

"You shot yourself in the foot with this one, buddy." McKelvey said nothing, but gave me the finger. Then, when Harvey came over to take him down to the cells, I too left the room and joined Costello and Williams and Holmes next door.

"Well?" I said.

"Not much, is there?" Williams said. Then she smiled, "I liked the scabies line though."

"It was a cheap shot," I said.

"It's him," Holmes said. "He's a liar through and through. We know he was with her on Thursday night; sure we have it on tape. If he's lying about that, he's lying about the whole lot." He snorted with derision. "I say we charge him now."

"No," Costello said. "We've seventy-two hours. Hold him over Christmas. We'll start again on Boxing Day. If we need to, we can charge him then. Let the wee shite stew for a few days without his turkey and ham. Agreed?" We all shrugged assent. "The only problem now is who'll do tonight?"

It's difficult on any night, never mind Christmas Eve, to get volunteers to man a station in a village the size of ours. Generally, one of us takes a mobile and the station is locked up for the night. McKelvey had screwed that up. Someone needed to be in the station while he was being held.

"I'll do a session before midnight," I said. "Debbie will divorce me if I do the whole night. Anyway, Penny is singing solo at midnight Mass tonight and I can't miss it or *she'll* divorce me, too."

"I'm out," Williams said. "I have to play Santa all alone."

"I'll do the nightshift," Holmes piped up. "I have no one waiting for me; I don't mind. Everyone else has someone to go home to."

"Aren't you going home for Christmas?" Williams said, and I realized that I didn't even know where "home" was for him.

"No. My mother died years ago. My father is in care but he's so far gone I could stand right beside him and he wouldn't even know I was there. So that's me. Little orphan Jason."

Williams looked taken aback by his sincerity. "Come to mine for dinner tomorrow. It'll just be me and Peter . . . and the cat." She seemed to have blurted the offer out without thinking, and instantly blushed.

"Thanks, Caroline," he said. "I might."

The two of them looked at each other momentarily, before turning back to me and Costello to dispel the awkwardness which we all felt.

"Fine, Jason. If you're happy enough to do it, that's great," Costello said. "We'll get Harvey to hold the fort until . . . eight?"

I nodded my agreement — if I did 8.00 to 11.30 p.m., I'd still be in time for Mass.

"Benedict, you take the mobile just in case." He began to walk away, then called over his shoulder, "And a happy Christmas to you all!"

As he turned to walk away, I saw Williams mouth *"Benedict?"* to Holmes, who shrugged.

"Only to Elvis," I said, with a wink, realizing that they hadn't known my full Christian name.

"I heard that," Costello shouted, from his office.

By the time I got home it was almost seven o'clock. Debbie was getting Penny changed into her Christmas clothes, which she had been given early as a special treat for singing at midnight Mass. I watched as the two of them fixed one another's hair and giggled about girlie things. Shane and I did the manly thing by sitting in front of the TV and not speaking. But then, he was only ten months old.

Around five to eight, I got ready to go to the station. I left the house with Debbie's warning ringing in my ears: "If you miss Penny's solo, the door will be locked when you get home. Sleep with Frank."

I made it to the station in five minutes or so, the traffic was so light. Harvey opened the front door, yawning.

"What's up?" I asked.

"Nothing, sir," he said. "Quiet as a mouse in there. I took him tea and a sandwich about an hour ago."

"Fair enough, John. Best get home, eh?"

"Going to see my sister, sir. Christmas presents and that."

"Have a good evening. Happy Christmas, John. Thanks for your help today."

"My pleasure, sir," he said, shrugging on his Garda overcoat. "Merry Christmas."

I checked on McKelvey a few minutes later: he was sleeping on his side, his breath wheezing slightly, presumably a result of the blows he had received during his arrest. I lifted the empty cup and plate which he'd left at the side of his bed. He muttered quietly in his sleep and shifted onto his back.

I sat in the station until 11.30 p.m. reading three-day-old newspapers. When Holmes arrived, I packed up and headed to

Mass, not bothering to check on McKelvey, who was getting a better night's sleep than the rest of us.

I sat in the church and listened to my daughter sing "O Holy Night", her voice cracking a little on the top notes. I looked at Debbie to see tears well in her eyes as she watched our little girl stand at the lectern and hold the attention of all the people in the church. I was aware of a sensation deep in my mind, an awareness of what the doctor had said about hepatitis or HIV. I would have to ensure that I did nothing which might endanger my family. Debbie would sometimes use my razor to shave her legs. What if I nicked myself and she used it? What if Penny or Shane picked up something from my cutlery — or if I kissed them goodnight? Something in my breast felt raw and exposed as my daughter's voice rose above the choir's in the final chorus, and I wished to be a child again myself, to be held in my mother's arms and told that everything would be alright.

As if instinctively sensing my need, Debbie took my hand without looking and squeezed it tenderly. Her thumb ran across the back of my hand, caressing the knuckles, and I felt her tense when she rubbed the gauze dressing where McKelvey had bitten me. Instinctively, afraid that some blood may have soaked through with which she might come into contact, I pulled my hand away. She looked down at my hand and then at my face. Smiling a little bewilderedly, she took my hand again in both of hers. Her openness and generosity made me grateful all over again that she had ever married me. This thought would come back to haunt me later that evening, as I almost threw away such a precious gift.

CHAPTER SEVEN

Wednesday, 25th December

It was raining as we drove home, a thin steady drizzle which created dirty haloes around the neon of the street lamps and smeared the windscreen with each sweep of the wipers. The journey passed in silence as Penny lay dozing, stretched across the back seat.

As I swung the car into our driveway, the headlamps raked across a silver BMW which had been abandoned in front of our doorway, and I felt something in my stomach collapse in on itself.

"I wonder who this could be," Debbie said, then got out of the car.

My parents had watched Shane for us while we were at Mass and my mother opened the door. "You've got company. In a bit of a state, too," she said, rolling her eyes.

Miriam Powell was sitting on the old leather armchair facing the door as we entered the living room, attempting to affect an air of sophistication, despite the smell of gin that hung around her. Her eyes were bloodshot and she was clearly having difficulty focusing. My parents excused themselves and left as Debbie carried Penny up to bed. Miriam watched with a fixed, insincere smile as I kissed my daughter on the forehead and told her I loved her. "I always knew you'd make a good father, Benedict," Miriam said. "I've always said that."

"There's little to it, Miriam. When you have kids as good as those two of mine, you can't help but be good."

"I have no children," she stated matter-of-factly.

"I know." I felt I should add some note of commiseration, but I had always suspected that their childlessness was by choice.

"Could you offer a lady a drink?" she said, in a slurred attempt at humour.

"Gin. Right?"

"You could be a barman, do you know that, Benedict?" she replied, and laughed — a shrill, empty laugh that rang out too long.

In the kitchen, I fixed her a gin and tonic, omitting the gin because she was driving. When I returned, she was standing at the hearth, admiring our family photographs.

"Thank you, Benedict. I have always relied on the kindness of . . . well, not strangers certainly, but —"

"That's a role you were never any good at, Miriam," Debbie said, standing in the doorway. "Even at college, you were never weak enough for Blanche."

"Deborah! Happy Christmas, dear," Miriam said, turning suddenly and moving to kiss Debbie. In her haste, the cuff of her woollen jacket caught on a picture of Penny on her first day at school and the picture fell to the ground, shattering the glass.

"Oh fuck! Was that me?"

"Don't worry, Miriam," I said, reaching down to pick up the pieces as she did the same. Hunkered down, wavering unsteadily, she fell against me, gripping my arm for balance and spilling some of her drink over my shirtsleeve and the picture lying on the floor. Then she started to giggle, as I helped her to her seat. She held out her glass, presumably in a request for a refill, and I noticed Debbie surreptitiously shake her head.

"So, Miriam, what can we do for you?" she said, still standing in the doorway.

"I'm here to see your husband. And you, of course, Deborah." She smiled and extended the glass again, which I took from her and set on the coffee table.

"Tommy Senior tells me you called with him, Benedict. We appreciate it," she said, slurring her words only slightly. Despite her state, or perhaps because of it, she held herself perfectly erect, her head haughtily tilted back, but her eyes were glazed and a hint of red was blooming on her cheeks. She was an attractive woman, more so now than ever. Her skin was still dark and supple, her figure trim and well proportioned. Debbie had once commented that anyone could have that body if they hadn't had two children, but it was clear that Miriam worked to keep her shape. As though sensing my admiring glance, she straightened herself further, so that her breasts pushed against her jacket and strained at the buttons.

Debbie coughed. "Ben always does what he says, Miriam. He told me about your husband's father. I was sorry to hear it."

"Have we anything to worry about?" Miriam asked me, as if Debbie had not spoken.

I assured her that her father-in-law was safe, as best we could tell, and that I had assigned an officer to follow up the complaint. I felt ridiculous, speaking in my policeman voice in my own living room after midnight on Christmas Day, especially as it was clear the Powells could have phoned for such information.

"And where is your husband?" Debbie said, sitting on the sofa as it became apparent Miriam would only leave in her own time.

"Oh, drifting about. Doing his Santa routine — delivering his very own little present. Emptying his sack!"

An awkward silence followed, none of us sure how to take her final comment.

"I feel I have disturbed your evening," Miriam said, trying to stand up with dignity and almost succeeding. "I shall impose on you no longer. Good evening and happy Christmas. Deborah . . . Benedict . . ." and she stumbled against the coffee table. Again, I reached out to steady her and she gripped my bandaged hand and squeezed it while she righted herself, causing me to wince.

"I'm alright," she stated emphatically, fishing in her purse for her car keys.

"Miriam, you can't drive home like this," I said, and Debbie rolled her eyes. "We'll phone you a taxi."

I tried four different numbers, in Lifford and Strabane, but none was answered. Eventually it became clear that one of us would have to take her home, and Debbie

169

made it even clearer that she wouldn't do it.

The conversation on the journey was strained until we reached Miriam's driveway.

"Did I see you sitting outside my house the other day?" she asked, smiling coquettishly. "Afraid to come in?"

"I . . . I got a call on the mobile and had to stop."

She wagged her finger back and forth in front of me and tutted. In the confines of the car, I could smell alcohol and cigarettes off the heat of her breath. "You weren't sure whether to come in, Benedict. A woman knows these things."

I didn't know what to say and so said nothing.

She continued, "It was nice. Kind of like a first date again. The nervous boyfriend waiting in the car?" She raised her eyebrows inquisitively.

"Goodnight, Miriam," I said, trying to sound as firm as possible. "I have to get the kids' presents ready for the morning. Merry Christmas to you and Thomas."

"Debbie's a lucky woman," she said. "I was once, too." She smiled and waggled her finger at me. "Ah, I remember. You couldn't control yourself with me once." Again she smiled coyly, but the impression in the darkness was anything but coy.

"A lot of water under the bridge since then," I said. "Goodnight then."

"Goodnight, Benedict," she said. "Merry Christmas."

She leaned over to kiss me on the cheek, and so I leaned towards her. However, at the last moment, she moved her head slightly and the corners of our mouths connected with a tingle, like static. Her lips were moist from her lipstick and I felt them tug slightly on mine. The gentle teasing of her lips, the warm haze of alcohol which filled my mouth and nose, the under-scent of coconut which seemed to radiate from her skin — all took me back fifteen years. I shifted slightly in my seat, pressing my lips on hers, hearing her moan deeply, feeling the cool wetness of her mouth. Our teeth knocked together slightly, like a teenager's kiss. Feeling her tongue in my mouth, I touched the tip of it with mine. I placed my hand to the side of her face, her skin warm and soft; my other hand, thick with bandages, touched her neck fleetingly, then lower, slipping inside her jacket as she groaned and shifted her body against mine, her own hands moving down my chest. She pressed my face against her neck and whispered something hoarse and urgent which I could not decipher. I could feel the fabric of her underwear, the sheen cool and smooth to my touch. Unbidden images of my wife came to my mind and, with those, the sharp recollection of the threat of infection I carried. The haze lifted and I pulled away from her quickly.

She opened her eyes and smiled at me, attempting demure but managing only satisfied. Then, without another word, she got out of the car and staggered to her front door, waving over her shoulder without looking back. As I watched her, I became aware of a movement at the window and I looked up to see Thomas Powell watching me from their living room. Despite the fact that I sat in shadow, he held eye contact for a few seconds. Then he closed the blinds, leaving me sitting in the darkness, which seemed to grow around me and thicken as I wiped his wife's lipstick off my mouth.

When I got home, Debbie was laying out the last of the presents on the armchairs. She did not speak when I came in, nor as I began to build the buggy we had bought for Shane. When she was done she said simply, "You missed a bit," pointing at the corner of her mouth. Instinctively, I rubbed at my mouth, and Debbie looked at me as if I were someone whom, after ten years of marriage, she suddenly did not recognize.

"You . . . you . . . bastard," she hissed, unable to find a more succinct way of expressing her feelings for me. Then she went up the stairs to our bedroom and I sat on the living-room floor, a screwdriver hanging useless in my hand, as I listened to her soft sobbing, muffled by our pillows.

I lay on the sofa with Shane's blanket over me and felt sorry for myself. The wound on my hand throbbed under the bandages to the same rhythm as the guilt and regret hammering behind my eyes.

At 2.45 a.m. I was sitting on the back doorstep, smoking my fifth cigarette. I tried to see the Star of Bethlehem, as if that might offer some hope, but rain was falling now in sheets, cold and sharp as needles, bouncing off the ground and hammering applause on the corrugated iron roof of Frank's kennel.

At 3.15 a.m. I began to feel drowsy, my eyes heavy. More than once I jerked awake as the heat of my cigarette burnt my fingers. I became aware of a sensation in my groin and for a few seconds struggled to make sense of it, then realized it was my mobile phone, which I had set on silent vibrate so it would not ring during Mass. It was 3.45

a.m. when I learnt that Whitey McKelvey
had died in custody.

CHAPTER EIGHT

Wednesday, 25th December

Outside the station, in the pounding rain, a number of cars were already parked, some abandoned more haphazardly than others.

John Mulrooney had again been called as medical examiner and was checking McKelvey's arm muscles for signs of rigor. McKelvey lay twisted on the floor, partly under the bed. He was not wearing shoes and one of his grimy white socks hung off his foot. His eyes were open, his face contorted in pain, from which even death seemed to have offered no release. His chin was still wet with saliva and flecks of spit could be seen on his cheek, the whiteness standing out against the fresh purple bruise. One of his eyes was ringed with black, and blood was crusted around his nostrils. Beside him on the floor lay several tablets, which fitted the description of the one found in Angela Cashell's stomach.

Someone was taking photographs. Jason Holmes sat outside the cell, being comforted by another officer as though he were a relative. Someone else brought him a cup of tea, though probably with something stronger added.

Costello appeared from his office. "Devlin!" he called, then went back inside. I followed him in, taking a seat in front of his desk.

"What the fuck happened?" he began.

"I don't know, sir. I've only just arrived."

"I'll tell you what happened. Somehow, someone didn't search the fucker properly when he came in. Looks like he took a dose of his own medicine." He calmed a little. "Jesus Christ, he's twisted so bad they might have to break his legs to fit him in the box." He blessed himself, kissed his thumb and motioned heavenward.

Mulrooney knocked on the door, then came on in. "Ben," he said, nodding. "Happy Christmas."

"You get all the good ones, eh Doc?" Costello said, and Mulrooney grimaced in acknowledgement.

"Goes with the territory. Fairly simple, folks. Looks like he took some of those tablets beside him, if what you said about the Cashell girl is true." He had obviously

176

been informed of the cocktail she had taken. "Dead less than an hour, I'd say."

"Is that it? Clean-cut and simple?" Costello asked, with more than a little hope in his voice.

Mulrooney grimaced again. "I'm not entirely sure. There's bruising on his face from his arrest, I'm told. One of his fingers is also badly bruised, possibly broken. Could have been when he was lifted. Looks like someone hit him a fair smack in the face," he said, glancing slightly towards me. "Badly bruised. I hope he deserved it, but it might complicate things."

Costello's face blanched. "You're sure?" he managed.

"Fairly much. If you need me for anything else, leave it until Boxing Day." He smiled ruefully as he waved goodbye and left.

Costello moved to behind his desk and dropped heavily into his chair, grunting as he did so. "What happened, Benedict?" he said in a tone both friendly and weary. But I said nothing.

He looked at me for a moment, waiting. I wanted to come clean and tell him all that had happened, but I could not speak.

"What happened, Inspector?" he asked again, the change in mood evident.

"I'm not sure, sir. Everything was fine

when I left. He was lying sleeping, I think."

"You *think!*" he said. "What about this bruising to his face?"

"Picked up during his arrest, sir?" I offered.

"A punch in the face?" he snapped, loud enough, I imagined, for those outside his office door to stop and pretend they weren't listening to our conversation.

"Go home, Inspector," he hissed. "And get your story straight. Because in the morning I'll have to announce an internal enquiry to the press, the McKelvey family and every shit-head who's looking to run down this force. Someone's going to take a fall, Inspector — and it won't be me."

I left his office in silence, absorbing, but not fully comprehending, all that he had said. Those outside were no longer even pretending not to have heard. I saw Williams with her son, who was wrapped in a blanket, lying asleep across three chairs in the waiting area. Williams was standing with her hand on Holmes' shoulder, and he sat, head bowed, staring at the floor. She must have spoken to me for he looked up at me, then he shrugged off her hand and came over.

"What happened, Jason?" I asked.

"I don't know sir. He . . . he kept goading

me. Acting like he was off his head. I might have smacked him about a bit. Nothing serious, though. Nothing to do . . . this," he said, gesturing slightly towards the floodlit cell with his head.

"Nothing serious! He's fucking *dead*, Jason," I hissed, trying desperately to keep the conversation between us.

"Well, I'm not the only one who smacked him about a bit, sir, am I?" With that he looked towards Williams, who held my gaze awkwardly for a second and then looked away.

"Don't worry," he said. "We'll say nothing. Your secret is safe with us." He placed his hand on my shoulder, as Williams had done to him, and kneaded the muscle slightly. I looked at him, my mind buzzing with thoughts, my jaw muscles seemingly beyond my control.

I stood outside, under the wash of the streetlamps, as the first light of a Christmas dawn turned pink the edges of the mountains behind the town and the rain began to ease. It felt fresh on my face after the heat of the station and my inclination was to walk down along the river, down to where Angela's body had been discarded one week earlier, but I realized that it was dawn and the children would soon be up for their presents.

As I drove into the driveway, I noticed our living-room light on, and realised that I had missed my son's first Christmas morning and Penny's face when she opened her presents.

I ran into the house, hardly bothering to shut the door behind me. Debbie was standing in the living room, Penny peering down from the top of the stairs.

"What's happening?" I asked.

"I told the kids I had to check first if Santa had been. Now he's been, we can bring them down." Her face revealed her disappointment. I tried to say thank you but only managed to mumble incoherently. "We'll get the kids settled with their toys, then we'll talk," she said. "This is their day — don't spoil it for them."

And so, for an hour, my self-absorption left me and I played with my children and my wife, and recalled again all the Christmases of my own childhood and longed for that magic again.

Then, over breakfast, while the kids played, I told Debbie everything: the arrest and the bite and my attack on McKelvey, nearly punching Williams, the incident with Miriam in the car, McKelvey's death, and

Costello sending me home. As I spoke I felt the familiar catharsis of confession and began to feel a little better — though aware that reconciliation requires penance and reparation as well as simple admission of guilt.

Debbie listened without talking. She drew back from the table while I spoke of my encounter with Miriam Powell, but not when I told her of my attack on McKelvey, even when I revealed the visceral thrill I had felt. When I finished she stared at her hands for a few seconds, then got up and went over to switch on the kettle.

"I'll make more tea," she said, as I swivelled in my seat to watch her moving around the kitchen.

"What do you think?" I asked, needing some response, but at the same time afraid that she would answer.

"You're a stupid bastard, that's for sure. I can't believe you kissed Miriam Powell. Anyone but that . . . slut!" She lifted the teapot, then put it down and turned to face me, leaning against the cooker. "Did you not see it coming? Are you blind? Is this a man thing? I mean, for Christ's sake, Ben, could the signals have been any clearer?"

"I'm sorry, Debs," I said, resisting the urge to excuse myself by pointing out that Mir-

181

iam had started it.

"I know you are, Ben. But that doesn't necessarily make it alright."

"I know."

"God, I'm so angry with you. Miriam bloody Powell. I'm warning you, Ben — keep that woman away from me or you'll be investigating another murder, I swear."

I said no more, and eventually she sat beside me again and refilled our cups with hot tea.

"You'll have to speak to Costello. Tell him the truth." It took me a second to realize that we were not still talking about Miriam Powell. Debbie continued, "Maybe you shouldn't have kicked him, but you're only human — I'd be surprised if you hadn't done something. But you need to tell Costello, in case he thinks you're involved more seriously. Holmes will tell him. You know that."

"Maybe not," I argued, weakly.

"Oh, come on. A uniform, starting out? Taking the heat for an Inspector? He'll rat you out first chance he gets to save his own skin."

"That doesn't mean I should rat him out," I said.

"I didn't say that. I said you have to tell Costello what you did. Let Holmes deal with his story. Costello has always dealt fairly with you. Square it with him."

"What if they fire me?"

"Then they fire you! We'll deal with it. Not telling Costello the truth is just going to make it worse. Drink your tea, have a smoke and then go and see him before this gets further out of hand."

Costello lived on the road to St Johnston in a house which had once perfectly suited himself and his wife and four children, but which had become increasingly empty as, one by one, his children had left for college or to get married. The youngest, Kate, had gone to university in September. Now, Costello and his wife Emily shared the five-bedroom house and a silence broken only by the occasional echoing creak. The house had recently been whitewashed and the garden was carefully tended, the roses pruned for winter, the hedges carefully shaped.

Costello did not look surprised to see me. He turned and walked back into the house, leaving the door ajar. I followed him in, slowly, closing the door behind me. Emily was standing at the door to the kitchen, a dishcloth in her hands. Behind her, sitting at the table in her nightdress, with a spoonful of cereal in her hand, was Costello's youngest daughter, Kate, presumably home for Christmas.

"Hey, Ben," she called out, raising her spoon in a half-salute.

"Hiya, Kate," I said, as Emily came forward and took my hand in hers.

"Merry Christmas, Benedict. How are Debbie and the children?" she asked gently.

"Fine, Emily. Merry Christmas to you, too," I replied, watching as Costello lumbered into the room which he called his office.

"Tell them I send my love," Emily said, then ushered me towards the room with a kind smile I was unsure I deserved.

I knocked on the oak-panelled door and went in. Costello was sitting at the roll-top desk which he had bought at an auction in Omagh and which I had helped him move into this room. He had on half-moon glasses and was reading an electricity bill.

"What do you want, Benedict?" he said wearily, peering at me over the rim of his glasses before returning his full attention to the bill.

"I need to tell you what happened; my involvement. I should have told you last night. I'm sorry." And for the second time that morning I recounted the events which had unfolded the previous night. Several times Costello stopped me for clarification.

"So you hit him when he bit you?" he asked when I had finished.

"Yes."

"And he was alive and healthy when Harvey left?"

I nodded.

"And you didn't check in on him before you left?"

I shook my head. It made little difference — he had died in any case on Holmes' watch.

"Did you see Holmes search McKelvey when he lifted him?"

Again, I shook my head. "I was out of it with the bite and that. I just assumed he had when they brought him in."

"Do you know if Holmes did anything to the boy when he was in custody?"

Neither of us spoke for a moment.

"I thought so. Have you any cigarettes?" he asked.

"I didn't know you smoked." In the five years I had known him I had never seen him do so.

"Cigars sometimes, at night. But it's too early for a cigar. Use that for an ashtray," he said, emptying paper clips out of a ceramic finger-bowl sitting on the desk. He smoked, looking out the window, puffing the cigarette as though it were a cigar, while I smoked nervously beside him.

"McKelvey was an animal, Benedict. In my opinion, he deserved everything he got. The death in custody thing is bad because we look stupid. He should have been searched thoroughly when he was brought in. Holmes should have kept an eye on him and his hands off him. There should have been more than one officer in the station overnight, for God's sake, Christmas Eve or not. Your bust-up with him *should* have been reported . . . Jesus, every part of this thing is ballsed up." He ground the cigarette out, folding the filter down onto the tip to ensure it was extinguished.

"But," he continued, "he killed that poor girl with those drugs. I hope the wee shite suffered before he went, because that's as much justice as Angela Cashell will get. It would've been better for all of us if Johnny had succeeded in burning the bastard alive last week. So, the question is, where do we go from here?"

"Internal Affairs?"

"Probably. I'll let Dublin decide that. In the meantime, whether it's right or not, we pin everything on McKelvey. I want that as the official line." As he spoke, he counted off each point on his fingers: "He was seen with the girl; we know he lied about seeing her on the Thursday night; we know from Coyle that he was providing her with drugs; we know they were sexually active; we found the drugs which killed Angela Cashell on his body when he died; physical description fits the size of the killer. Everything fits, so long as the post mortem shows an overdose of those rat-poison tablets as cause of death."

"What about the bruising?"

"My inclination would be resisting arrest. Holmes brought him in, didn't he? He's going to have to take some of the heat for this, whether he likes it or not. Probably best if he takes it for an overenthusiastic arrest rather than criminal negligence."

"Makes good PR," I said.

"Well, that's how it is. We'll put Holmes on suspension for a week. With pay. He can work behind the scenes on the Boyle killing — long as he's not seen around the station. And McKelvey as a dead murderer rather than a dead victim will help. So, this is what you do, Benedict," he said, leaning towards me and tapping me on the knee. "Go into the station and collect your files. Then get this concluded. Put everything we have on McKelvey and leave no loose ends. If we can tie this up, we can focus on the Boyle boy. Today."

The station was buzzing when I arrived, and I was able to get into the murder room and collect the blue lever-arch folder containing the notes on McKelvey without too many people noticing me.

McKelvey's body had been moved and the cell lay empty, the floor marked with white chalk outlines where tablets and body had been found. I left through the back fire exit to avoid having to talk to anyone and drove home.

Debbie was preparing dinner and the kids were playing in the living room, so I sat in the kitchen and reported all that had transpired with Costello. Debbie listened as she peeled potatoes and checked on the turkey in the oven, piercing the tender flesh to check if the juices ran clear. Then I set to work, drawing all the strands together and trying to fit McKelvey at the centre. The difficulty was that we did not have hard evidence: no smoking gun, no signed confession. But then, most detective work is circumstantial — fingerprints and DNA are useful only when a suspect has been arrested. But I did my best with what we had and tried to ignore the moral implication of the task I was performing. I knew that McKelvey probably had killed or contributed to the death of Angela Cashell, yet, as things were, I would never know for certain, and so I would always harbour doubts. I was bothered by the fact that I could not find any logical motive. As McKelvey had said himself, she was providing him with sex — why would he kill her?

With breaks for dinner and family, I had the report finished for 8.30 p.m. and, after we put the kids to bed, I asked Debbie to read it through to see if everything made sense. She read it twice, both times looking bewildered, flicking between pages to double-check some piece of information.

From her expression, I knew there was something that did not read right. "What is it, Debs?" I asked. As she replied, I realized what had been niggling me since Costello had run through the facts that morning.

"Why was he wearing a condom?" Debbie asked. "McKelvey. Why would he wear a condom? According to this, he didn't care that his girlfriends got pregnant. In fact he seems kind of proud of it. Especially if he thought she was pregnant. Wearing a condom when you're already pregnant doesn't seem to make sense."

Something cold shivered down my spine

and settled deep inside me, causing me to shake involuntarily.

"Unless maybe it was an AIDS thing. You know, an STD issue or something," Debbie suggested, but I knew now that was not the case.

"No," I said. "It's been bothering me too. If he believed Cashell was pregnant, they'd obviously already had unprotected sex. Why would he suddenly worry about STDs that night?"

"Maybe he didn't want to leave evidence, DNA, you know."

I considered it, then shook my head resignedly. "Maybe. But that would mean he intended to kill her; that he had planned ahead and knew he would need to wear a condom to prevent being caught. It just doesn't fit. We had assumed it was an accident, a drug-trip that went wrong. At the end of the day, McKelvey didn't have cause to kill her. That's what that report *doesn't* say. He had no motive."

"He thought she was pregnant. Maybe he was afraid she'd tell someone," Debbie suggested.

"The same boy would've *wanted* her to tell someone. Another notch in his bedpost." I felt my back prickle with sweat and my face blazed. "McKelvey doesn't fit. We were following the wrong line all along. I've missed something." What I could not vocalize was the fact that, because of it, an innocent eighteen-year-old boy had died on a Christmas morning, while the rain washed the streets outside.

I phoned Costello first and told him what I had concluded. He listened, cursed, then told me to leave it with him until morning so he could sleep on it. We arranged to meet at the station at 8 a.m. I asked about Holmes and was told that, as we had discussed, he had been suspended with pay pending an enquiry. Costello did not mention the beating to him, nor had Holmes told him about it.

Next, I phoned Williams and started to tell her. In the background I could hear music playing, some kind of dinner jazz. She sounded a little tipsy and I could hear the rubbing of her hand on the receiver, as though she was covering it, to speak to someone.

"Sorry, Caroline," I said. "Have you company?"

"Kind of," she said, giggling in a way I had not heard her do before.

"Someone I know?"

"Maybe, Detective."

"Is Holmes with you?" I asked, unable to suppress the surprise in my voice.

"Uh huh," she said with a laugh.

"How did he take the suspension?"

"He's a little pissed off. He has to carry on doing the work, but nobody's allowed to know. Bit of a pisser. He'll get over it, though."

"Listen, Caroline, this is important. I don't want you to tell Holmes what I'm about to say — if it turns out McKelvey was innocent, it'll hit him hard. His head could be on the block for this."

Despite her earlier playful manner, she seemed to sober quickly and listened without interrupting. I asked her to meet me the following morning in the station.

At bedtime, I went out to give Frank a dog biscuit and fresh water for the night. But when I opened the door of the shed where we kept him when the weather was bad, he wasn't there. I went back into the garden and called him several times, but to no avail. I called to Debbie for a torch and we set about searching the hedgerows and ditches near the house. I shone the torch briefly into the field where Anderson's sheep were grazing and was relieved not to find him there at least.

Returning to the garden, I heard a familiar

snuffling from the shed. Frank was lying inside, his head down, his tail wagging halfheartedly, waiting to ascertain my reaction to his absence. His coat was wet with rainwater from the long grass of the fields bordering our property and cuckoo spit hung off his ear. I tried to find how he had got out of the shed, shining the torch into the corners and behind the junk we had piled against one wall, but I couldn't see anything obvious. I ruffled the hair on the dome of his skull and locked up the shed behind me.

Later, in our bedroom, I had to explain to Debbie why I had lifted my toothbrush away from the others in the bathroom, and why I was setting up the spare mattress. I cried as I told her my fears about AIDS and whatever else McKelvey might have been carrying. She knelt down on the floor beside me and held my face in her hands. Kissing me softly, she promised me that everything would be alright — and I almost believed her.

At 2.30 a.m. we were woken by Penny's screaming. Crossing the gallery to go to the bathroom, she had happened to glance downstairs towards the front door of our house, she said. Someone had been looking back in at her. She saw the door handle twitching, she said. He looked evil, she said.

We told her that she had had a nightmare, that she must have still been half asleep. Then I went out to the front of the house to check, while Debbie took Penny into our bed. I had to refill the kettle with water three times to completely wash away the muddy footprints from our doorstep in case Penny should see them the following morning.

CHAPTER NINE

Thursday, 26th December

Boxing Day broke with spectacular blue skies and an explosion of a sunrise on the mountains behind the house. I had not slept again, keeping watch all night, until the sky turned to grey and the remaining puddles from the previous evening's rain froze and sparkled under the first rays of the morning sun. There was no wind, only a sharp chill that would keep the grass stiff until afternoon, so that it crunched beneath your feet as you walked. I told myself that it was a new day and tried to dismiss from mind our late-night visitor.

At 7.15 a.m. I threw warm water on the windows of the car to defrost them, then left the engine idling while I gathered my notes for the meeting with Williams and Costello. By the time I came back out to the car, the water on the windscreen had frozen again. Inside, my breath condensed and froze to ice on the interior of the glass. I sat in the car, letting the engine warm up, and smoked a cigarette. The details of the case had bubbled inside my head all night. Having gathered all the evidence the day before to prove that Whitey McKelvey had killed Angela Cashell, I now had to start proving that he hadn't.

I reached the station twenty minutes early, but Costello was already there and Williams arrived soon after me. Just before 8.00 a.m., a blue van pulled up outside. Several minutes later, a smaller white van with a radio antenna on the roof wound its way around the bend in the street and slid to a halt against the concrete posts outside the front doors.

A young woman, wrapped tightly in a sheepskin jacket and wearing gloves and a scarf, picked her way carefully along the pavement and into the reception area of the station. We heard her introduce herself as a radio news reporter for 108 FM, a local independent station. I had heard her once or twice before on the news, though she was much younger than her voice suggested. She was wondering if we would like to comment on either the death in custody of William McKelvey or the attack on livestock the previous night by the "Wild Cat of Lifford."

I wandered up to the reception desk and listened in. Mark Anderson had contacted the radio station that morning to say that one of his sheep had been mauled the night before and its innards removed from its body. He had told the receptionist at 108 FM that he had asked twice for assistance from Gardai, and both times nothing had been done.

I was hoping to hear more details, but Costello cut the discussion short, telling the young lady that he would be making a statement later and there would be no comment until then.

Our meeting was brief. First, Costello informed us that ballistics had found a match on the gun used to murder Terry Boyle. Apparently it had been used in a filling-station robbery in Bundoran a year or so previously.

Costello then turned his attention to Angela Cashell and the fallout from McKelvey's death. He had decided to run with McKelvey as our killer for now, while we checked background details again. If another party entered the frame, in his words, we would deal with the McKelvey fiasco as necessary. If our investigation yielded nothing, we were to fold it quietly away and McKelvey would, to all intents and purposes, remain Angela Cashell's murderer.

I asked him about the ring which Mc-Kelvey claimed to have sold.

"Forget about bloody rings, Benedict. I want a quick result. Don't ignore the obvious just because it is obvious!"

Williams and I returned to the murder room with the files. We worked through the morning, examining the anomalies and loose ends which hung over the initial investigation. I became increasingly convinced that the ring which Angela Cashell had been wearing was somehow central to the whole thing.

"Why?"

"She was stripped naked; her clothes were kept or destroyed; someone washed her body; used a condom. Everything seems to have been done to reduce the possibilities of forensic evidence. Everything was removed, except her pants and this ring. Why leave her pants?"

"Well, the panties suggest some form of respect. Some residual affection or liking for the girl. Someone wanted her to have some dignity."

"Her father?"

"Maybe. Worth looking at again, certainly. Or a woman," she suggested.

"Why?"

"I dunno. It just seems like something a woman would do. It was a conscious decision to put her underwear back on her. I don't think a man would do that. In fact, you'd think if sex was involved somewhere, he'd want to *keep* something as intimate as that — a trophy, you know?"

It made sense. "What about the ring? It has some significance. None of her family or friends knew about it."

"Whitey McKelvey did. Maybe he did give it to her."

"More likely than him selling it to someone who then came back and killed her," I said.

"So, he steals it from Ratsy Donaghey, gives it to Angela Cashell, and she gets killed wearing it."

"Do you think it's worth killing over?"

"I dunno. Maybe we should get it valued."

"But if it was worth anything, surely whoever killed Angela would have taken it," I pointed out.

"True. So, it's a message."

"To whom?"

"I don't know. But you're right. We'll follow it up."

I asked Williams whether she had had any luck contacting the Garda in Bundoran who had dealt with Donaghey's murder.

"Not yet. He's off until tomorrow, I'm told. I need to speak to him about the gun used to kill Terry Boyle, too. What do you think is the Donaghey connection with Cashell? Drugs?"

"Maybe," I said, "but he was a different generation. More of an age with Johnny Cashell than Angela. Follow it up anyway. Get that video of the bar again as well. McKelvey denied being with Angela that night. Let's recheck it and see if he was lying or not. In the meantime, I'm going to a wake."

"Whose?"

"Angela Cashell's. Her body was brought back on Christmas Eve. She's to be buried tomorrow. I want to see Sadie Cashell before that."

"Is it not a bit early? It's only just gone ten?"

"Morning's the best time for us; less chance of a fight brewing." I lifted my keys. "Do you want to come?"

"Are you kidding?" she said, grabbing her coat.

A wake is a long-held tradition in Ireland. The body is laid out for two nights before the burial. Neighbours and friends congregate — ostensibly to pay their respects, but

200

on occasions the wake becomes a party. Mourners comment on how well the deceased looks, as though he or she were not dead. Plates of cigarettes are passed around like sandwiches. At some stage the whiskey is opened and passed among the mourners; someone produces a tin whistle or a fiddle and a full-scale ceilidh breaks out, with people jigging and reeling around the coffin and resting their empty glasses on the white satin lining.

The following morning, the wake-house smells like a pub that has been left unaired. Tea-stained cups are gathered and washed; sandwiches are made in preparation for the next night, which promises to be even bigger than the previous.

Sadie Cashell was sitting by her daughter's coffin when we entered the house and, despite the early hour, three neighbours sat with her. I gave her the Mass card I had had signed by Father Brennan on the way in, offered my condolences, and stood beside her at the coffin and prayed three Hail Marys for the redemption of the soul of Angela Cashell. Sadie leaned over the coffin, pushed a wisp of Angela's blonde hair back from her face and arranged the ruffle at the throat of the shroud she was wearing. I finished my prayers and laid my hand gently on Angela's, which were joined in front of her, intertwined with a rosary. Her skin was cold and hard, almost like wax. Her expression was one of serenity: angelic. It was an appearance certainly preferable to my last sight of her, lying on a bed of leaves and damp moss, the empty winter sky reflected in her unblinking eyes.

I sat beside Sadie on one of the hard wooden chairs which a neighbour must have lent her and passed her a half-bottle of Bushmills that I had bought in McElroy's Bar out of hours.

She held my hand in both of hers, which were shaking slightly, and rubbed the back of my hand with her thumb. She told me that Johnny had not been released for the wake, but hoped to be back for the funeral. She told me how the other girls had taken it. Muire had run away the day before, but was found by a neighbour walking to Strabane. Then she asked if we knew who had taken her daughter from her, and I told her that I thought we did and that, if she believed in God, he would be facing justice. She smiled and gripped my hand tighter.

"Sadie," I said. "I want to ask you a favour. About the ring Angela was wearing. Do you have it?"

"Why?"

"Listen, Sadie, I know it wasn't hers, but I don't care. Keep it if you want. But I'd like to borrow it for a day or two. I think it might have something to do with what happened to her."

She seemed initially unwilling, but eventually agreed and, with some reluctance, turned away from her daughter's coffin and left the room. I heard her going up the stairs and moving about above us. Half a minute later she returned with the ring, still sealed in the plastic evidence bag in which the pathologist had placed it. She handed it to me without a word and sat again beside her daughter.

"Have you touched this, Sadie?" I asked. "Since you got it back. I need to know — for fingerprints."

She looked at me and shook her head, once.

"I'm sorry, Sadie," I said. "I had to ask." I told her that we had to leave and she stood to walk us out to the door.

"Johnny was angry at me, you know. For taking that money," she said. "He told me we don't need a copper's charity."

"We all need a little help sometimes. Johnny's just raw over Angela. It's understandable."

"She was his favourite, you know. In a

strange way, she was his favourite. He treated her as if she were his own daughter."

I took her hand in mine and looked her in the eyes. "She was his daughter, Sadie, and I'll not let anyone say any different."

She pulled me close to her quickly, gripping my arms in her hands, and muttered something into the nape of my neck. I felt the wetness of her tears against my skin.

By the time we arrived back at the station a fairly large group of reporters had gathered across the road in front of the visitors centre. Someone was holding court before them. He was too slim to be Costello. For some reason I was not wholly surprised when I realized that the figure in the dark suit decrying Garda incompetence was Thomas Powell, attempting to assume the mantle his father had passed to him. It was perhaps no accident that he had chosen the road in front of the old courthouse, from whose roof eighteenth-century recidivists were hung in front of crowds of thousands, to give his lecture on crime and justice in Lifford.

"In the past weeks, three young people have died, one while in Garda custody, and yet nothing seems to have been done. Livestock is being slaughtered by a wild animal of some sort, but again nothing has been done." He scanned the group as he spoke, making eye-contact with as many of them as possible, perhaps trying to remember faces for future press conferences. Then, his eye caught mine and I swear he smiled. "Instead, we have officers following personal agendas while we suffer the effects of their incompetence." He pointed in my direction. "Perhaps Inspector Devlin here would elucidate further on what Gardai are doing to clean up this mess?" He turned to the cameras, dictaphones and microphones, clearly assuming that I would stick to Costello's "no comment" dictate. "My father campaigned tirelessly against Gardai incompetence and I regret that I seem to have to do the same and represent the people of Donegal with an impartial voice."

"Let's take the fight to him, shall we?" I said to Williams, and walked over to stand beside him in front of the reporters. I felt Williams tug at my jacket, saw the panic register on her face; then she stepped back, away from the glare of the lights.

Powell was alerted to my presence by the radio reporter I had met earlier. "Inspector, any comment on these claims?"

I raised my hand and waited until the gaggle quietened a little. I spoke slowly and clearly, without looking at Powell, who stood beside me, his arms folded. "I've just returned from visiting one of three houses on both sides of the border, where a family has spent Christmas in mourning for the loss of a child. I think perhaps we should respect that, rather than using their coffins as soap boxes from which to electioneer, don't you?" I smiled sweetly, then turned and walked into the station. Costello glared at me from his office door, having watched the performance from between the slats of his drawn blinds.

I asked Williams to take the ring to Patsy McLaughlin, one of our oldest forensics experts, a man known for his care in lifting evidence.

While he checked the ring for fingerprints, I phoned my father, the man Powell Sr had described as the "furniture man." My father has worked with antiques all his life and, consequently, knows most of the older and more knowledgeable antique dealers in the area. I didn't know if the ring was an antique, but it looked old enough to at least be worth checking. I also wanted some indication of its value, for it seemed no more plausible that such an object should belong to a drug dealer like Ratsy Donaghey than to Angela Cashell.

My father said he would phone me back in five minutes. Half-an-hour later, he got back to me to say that he had found a man in Derry, Ciaran O'Donnell, who would look at the ring. I arranged to meet them at O'Donnell's shop on Spencer Road at 5.00 p.m., by which time I hoped Pat McLaughlin would be finished with it. As it transpired, he was done with it much sooner, for an hour later he and Williams arrived at the murder room with the news that they had found nothing, which didn't explain why the two of them seemed so happy. McLaughlin explained.

"I laughed when she brought it. Do you know how many sets of prints you get off something like a ring? But there was nothing. Do you realize what that means?"

"Obviously not, or I'd be smiling like you two. Astound me," I said.

"Think about it, Detective. Your prints aren't there, are they?"

"Of course they're not. I didn't touch it . . ." I said impatiently

"What about the pathologist? Her prints aren't on it either."

"Because she wears gloves when she's working," I said, my excitement rising fast as I reached the clear conclusion.

"Exactly. And so did whoever put the ring on the girl's finger, because *she* clearly didn't do it herself. Someone was very careful about putting this ring on her."

At five o'clock we met Ciaran O'Donnell and my father outside his shop, an old unit built on a slope off Spencer Road in Derry. The slope runs down to the River Foyle, which splits the city in half. Having been closed for Christmas, the shop was bitterly cold, making my fingers so stiff and blue that I pulled my coat sleeves down over my hands and balled them into fists. The air was musty and damp underneath the sweet smell of furniture polish that pervaded every surface.

O'Donnell was an old man, bent slightly from the mid-section of his spine. His hair grew symmetrically on both sides of his bald dome in wisps of grey and white. He wore thick-lensed glasses, which he removed to examine the ring, putting a jeweller's loupe in his right eye. He sat at an old oak desk and flicked on a tiny desk-lamp and examined the ring in minute detail for a few minutes, turning it in various directions, brushing it lightly with a tool that resembled a tiny toothbrush. Then he set it down and lifted a green book from the bookcase in the corner of the room. He carried the book to the desk, put the glass in his eye again, and examined the ring with his left eye shut, then perused the book with his right eye shut. Finally satisfied, he put everything on the desk in front of him and called us over.

"An interesting piece," he began. "The ring is eighteen-carat gold with a moonstone insert, surrounded by twelve rose-cut diamonds. What's interesting about this is — well, two things, really — one of the diamonds has been replaced. It's a very neat piece of work, but it's sourced differently from the others: there's a slightly pinkish tint to it under this light. The second thing, which isn't really interesting, is that this is not an antique. I'd say it's thirty years old at most."

"Any idea about where it came from?" Williams asked.

"Well, there's good news on that front," he said. "It was made in Donegal. By Hendershot & Sons to be precise. They were very exclusive jewellers during the '70s and '80s, though they've disappeared into the woodwork recently, so to speak"

"How can you tell that?" I asked, while my father smiled and nodded his head.

"Very simple, really. They stamped the

ring with their own mark beside the gold mark."

"What about the engraving, the 'AC'?" I asked.

"No idea. Except I think it was engraved when the ring was made; the inside surface of the engraving is as dulled as the rest of the ring. More recent work would leave a slightly shinier surface."

"What would you recommend we do now?" I said, glancing at Williams.

"Well, you're the policemen — police *officers* — so I wouldn't want to say. But I'd contact Hendershot & Sons and see what they can tell you."

"I thought you said they'd vanished into the woodwork," Williams said.

"Yes," he said. "In terms of market share and so on, they have. But they're still open. It was a side street off from the Atlantic last time I was there, but that was some years ago and they may have moved. Check the phonebook."

We thanked Mr O'Donnell for his help and I promised my father we would visit him and my mother soon. "Do," he said. "And give the kids a hug from me." I promised I would. Then Williams and I drove home.

"Well, do you fancy a trip to Donegal?"

she asked as we drove past Prehen Park and up the Strabane Road.

"Why not? Especially if I get mileage allowance for it."

"We could kill two birds with one stone and head on to Bundoran — check out the officer in charge of the Ratsy Donaghey killing while we're at it," Williams said, smiling.

Before I signed out of the office for the evening, I received a call from the doctor who had attended me on Christmas Eve, whose name, I learnt, was Ian Fleming.

"My father was a Bond fan, if that's any use to you," he explained, though I had not passed comment. I nodded into the receiver. Then I realized that he couldn't see this gesture and managed a grunt, despite the dryness in my throat.

"Good news, Inspector," he said. "All clear so far — a late Christmas present."

I almost wept as I thanked him.

"Don't forget. Check again in a few months' time. Without giving too much away, I spoke to the boy's GP this afternoon at the dogs. Explained about the bite. He checked for me. Figures the boy was clean, too. So hopefully . . ."

Debbie let slip a tear or two when I told

her, then made tea, as it seemed the only thing to do. I invited her to join Williams and me the next day, in case she wanted to go shopping in Donegal, but she had promised her mother she would take her to Derry. We ate dinner in companionable silence, though I suspected that my kiss with Miriam Powell still played on her mind.

At around 8.45 p.m., we heard Penny calling from upstairs. She had gone to bed twenty minutes earlier and normally took after her mother in that she fell asleep as soon as her head touched the pillow.

Her bedroom is at the front of the house and we found her kneeling on her bed, her head and half her body hidden underneath the curtains while she watched something out of her window. She lifted the curtains above her head slightly when she heard us and invited us into her makeshift tepee. Then we saw what had got her attention.

On the road outside, a number of the local farmers were gathering with shotguns and torches. In the middle of the group, Mark Anderson was standing like some tinpot general, issuing orders and pointing first at a scrap of paper in his hand and then to various points in the fields around our house. Someone was taking pictures, and in the light of one of the flashes, Anderson evidently saw our three faces peering down at him from the bedroom for he pointed us out to the photographer and said something that caused him to laugh. Unable to hear anything, we watched him silently throw back his head with his toothless mouth wide open, then splutter and cough, before spitting onto the ground.

I went downstairs, pulled on a jacket and went out to see what was happening. The photographer was writing names in his reporter's notebook and seemed to be packing up. I called him over.

"What's going on?"

"They're searching for the wild cat that's been killing Mr Anderson's livestock." He was barely out of his teens and still had the fresh red scars of acne across his cheeks and around his mouth.

"The last time he was called Mr Anderson was in court, sonny," I said, "so I wouldn't waste it on him now. Where are they going with the guns?"

"Haven't you heard, *mister*," he said, bristling at the "sonny" comment. "Thomas Powell has offered a reward of a thousand euros for whoever can capture the cat, dead or alive. Says the Garda aren't doing anything so he has to instead. Care to comment, Inspector?" the boy said, smiling at his guile.

"Yeah, you're standing in my driveway. Piss off."

I went back into the house and put on a jumper and waterproof coat and my rubber boots. Then I padlocked Frank in the shed, just as a precaution.

I found Anderson about a quarter of a mile up the road, standing at the gate of his field, which ran all the way down to our home and up another mile or so to his own house. The moon was high and the sky clear, and in the lilac light the veins which had burst on Anderson's cheeks and nose through years of drinking stood out. As he talked, his toothless gums seemed purple and angry.

"I warned you I'd deal with things," he said, as I approached. "You're a bit late now."

"A wild cat's a little different from my dog. Are you sure whatever's worrying your sheep is an animal? How *is* Malachy, by the way?"

"Are you here for a reason?" he sneered, choosing to ignore the implication in my question.

"Just thought I'd keep an eye on things. Don't want someone shooting you by accident, now, do we, Mark?"

I chose a slight rise in the field to lie against and joined two other men there. One I recognized as a clay-pigeon shooter from Raphoe, though I did not know his name. The ground beneath us had frozen to iron and the cold seeped up through my body so that I had to shift continually to keep warm. And there, in the frost, we lay and waited, straining against the dark to see shapes shifting around the sheep, whose wool seemed all the more brilliant in the moonlight. The holly hedge around the field was thick and lush now with big blood-red berries. Small animals skittered through it. Directly above us was a weeping birch whose branches were so heavy they trailed along the ground.

At around 10.30 p.m. someone shouted, and at one corner of the field the loud clear cracks of shotguns rang out a second after the bright gunfire flashes. A number of the men lying about clambered to their feet and ran to the spot where something had been seen, while two men argued about who had shot first.

"Looks like someone's made a grand," the Raphoe man said, getting to his feet. I followed suit, only to have my legs buckle under me with stiffness from lying in one place so long in the middle of winter. I hobbled behind the men to the spot where a group had gathered, but even before I got there it became apparent, from the disgusted shakes of collective heads, that the quarry was not the wild cat they had hoped. Instead, in the middle of the circle of men, lay the body of a fox, its side shredded by the shotgun blasts, oozing blood as black as tar onto the sugar-frosted grass. Its tongue lolled in and out of its mouth, its breathing was laboured and harsh. With each breath, a fresh spurt of blood pumped out of its side. My companion from Raphoe loaded a shot in his gun, placed it above the fox's head and fired so close that blood and tissue spattered on his shoes and the barrel of the gun. The air carried the smell of cordite and burnt fur.

"Do we go home then?" someone asked disappointedly.

"Weren't no fox attacked my sheep," Anderson said, spitting on the carcass. "Leave this here — might attract whatever that thing is." He half-heartedly kicked the body, which flopped over on the grass, then wiped his boot on the back of his trouser leg. "Back to your positions," he said, then fixed his cap on his head and trod back to where he had been hiding.

I returned to the mound again and lay in a different position this time and lit a cigarette.

"Best not do that," the other man, whose name was Tony something, said. "Them cats could smell smoke miles away. That'll scare them off."

"If this cat can smell the smoke of one cigarette, but can't smell the stink of thirty Donegal men lying in a field of sheep shit, it deserves to get blown away," I said, then inhaled deeply for effect, though the air was so cold it burned my lungs. The Raphoe man laughed and took out a tobacco tin to roll a cigarette, so I gave him one from my packet.

"Aren't you hunting?" he asked, noting the fact that I was the only unarmed man in the field.

"Nope. Just making sure nobody shoots anybody else," I said, adding, "or my dog."

"What?"

"Anderson thought it was my dog that was attacking his sheep. I suppose I should be grateful that this cat has appeared."

"I suppose so, officer," he said, joining with my laugh.

I smiled. "I know your face. I can't place you, though."

"You gave me a speeding ticket a few years back. You were in uniform then."

"Shit," I said. "Sorry."

"Don't be. I was doing a hundred and two along the Letterkenny Road. I was lucky I wasn't killed. I got off light, all things considered."

I recalled the event now and remembered the face, although the man had had a moustache then. He seemed to assume that I remembered his name, so I didn't want to ask. "A red Celica was it?"

"Close enough. A red Capri."

"Have you still got it?" I asked. "It was a lovely car, even as a blur."

"No. Wife had a kid; I got rid of the car. Driving a family car now."

"This is lovely," the man called Tony said, "and I hate to interrupt, but could you two shut up?"

We sat in silence for another hour or so, smoking periodically. The evening was so still the smoke hung in a silver cloud above our heads. At around 12.30 a.m. I stood up to stretch the stiffness out of my legs, and it was while doing so that I saw a black shape snaking its way down from the top of the field just above us. It crept slowly towards a group of sheep that seemed to be sleeping, its belly pressed so close to the ground its coat must have been dusted with frost. I couldn't tell what it was as it slinked down along the furrows tractors had made in the field.

"Stand up," I hissed to the two beside me, and they did so, rubbing their legs while they straightened up. The Raphoe man spotted the shape then and loaded a shell, as did Tony.

They both shouldered their shotguns together, steadying the barrels. The Raphoe man shifted his stance a little, widening his legs so he was standing in a solid position. I noticed the mist of his breath stop as he took aim, and I found myself instinctively holding my own breath as I watched the shape slow and stop, as if it too were suddenly aware of the events which were about to unfold. Afterwards, I would recall that he shifted his aim just slightly in the final milliseconds before he shot, though I cannot be sure.

Slowly then, he pulled the trigger, a fluid movement, and his gun jerked as the blast echoed across the field and left my ears ringing. Tony fired a second later, another sharp crack, like a stick being snapped. Then the three of us set off at a run, stumbling through the furrows and sliding across the sheep dung, scattering the slumbering sheep who watched us with wide, terrified eyes. As we ran, we saw the black shape dash back the way it had come, its running erratic. We reached the spot where it had been when shot, and saw the black blood of its wound spattered on the white grass. We followed its path, the grass greener where the frost had been disturbed by the creature, and saw more blood on the ground. Then the path disappeared into a thicket hedge and we could follow it no further.

"Hard luck," I said to the man from Raphoe, who smiled slightly.

"Time to go home I think, partner," he said, shouldering his shotgun and picking his way carefully back down the field, while others ran to see what had happened.

I walked back down the road to the house about half an hour later and went around the back of the house to check that the shed was locked. I rattled the padlock on the bolt and was turning to go into the house when I heard a soft whimpering from inside the shed. I unlocked the door and went in.

Frank lay in the corner, curled up, blood congealing on the floor of the shed beneath him. He raised his head an inch and looked at me, but his usually bloodshot eyes were pale and dull. He licked ineffectually at the area on his flank where the shot had skinned him, and I noticed that his right ear, which before had hung almost to the ground, was tattered and torn, the surface bloody and dark. His snow-white chest was pink and red with blood, though I could not tell if he was bleeding there or if this had come from the wound to his ear.

He yelped weakly when I lifted him and carried him out to the car. I set him on the back seat with a picnic blanket under him, working quickly lest some of the farmers wandering down the field, disappointed with the night's hunt, should see him and realize what had happened. I quickly ran up the stairs to Debbie, who was sitting up in bed reading a magazine. She had heard the shots earlier and was interested to hear what had happened. I told her to call the emergency vet in Strabane, as I was afraid if we took him to a Donegal vet, word would eventually filter back to Anderson.

I had to wait outside the surgery for twenty minutes until the vet arrived and she helped me carry Frank onto the steel table in the surgery. There, she gave him a shot that knocked him out in seconds, before washing his wounds. I told her half of the story, saying that I had been shooting at a fox and that the dog had run into the line of fire.

"Oh, right," she said, "I thought maybe it had to do with the cat hunt over there." She brushed one of her bangs back from her face with a bloody, gloved hand and smiled before returning to cleaning the wounds.

The shot had skinned Frank's leg but there were no deeper injuries. His ear was badly torn and was about half its original length, which meant that part of his ear, a scrap of bloodstained velvet, was lying in Anderson's field. She bandaged his ear, tying it up behind his head, and put a dressing over the thick white ointment on his leg. Then she went into the storeroom and brought out a bottle of pills, antibiotics to reduce infection.

Finally she checked his eyes and teeth and helped me carry him back out to the car.

"I hope you weren't shot by accident, too," she said, nodding at the dressing on my hand, while I manoeuvred Frank onto the back seat.

"No, I was bitten."

"By him?" she said, looking concerned.

"Oh, no," I said. "By a person." I closed the back door of the car while she looked at me, now more concerned about my mental wellbeing than my physical health.

"Figures," she shrugged finally, taking the money I offered her.

CHAPTER TEN

Friday, 27th December

I left the house at 7.30 the following morning and drove to Williams's house, a two bedroom bungalow in Ballindrait. As I approached, a blue Sierra drove past, the windows misted and icy, but I was almost certain that the man hunched over the steering wheel, looking like he had been hurried out of bed, was Jason Holmes.

I did not ask Williams about it until we passed through Ballybofey twenty minutes later. "Did I see Holmes leaving your house this morning?" I asked in as innocuous a manner as I could.

"Yes, Father, you did," she said, looking out the side window. "He slept on the sofa," she added, turning to look at me.

"Hey, I didn't ask. Nothing to do with me," I said, holding one hand up off the steering wheel in mock placation.

"I know," she said. "And I'd keep it that

way, unless you want to end up like your dog."

"Fair enough. I was only going to ask how he's doing. With the McKelvey affair."

"Fine, I think," she said. "He doesn't say much. By the way, he thinks he may have a hit on the Terry Boyle thing. A barman remembered seeing him leave some night-club in Raphoe with a girl on the night he died. Small girl — brown hair. He's going there today to get a description, maybe do up an e-fit." She rolled down the window and dropped out the gum she had been chewing.

"That's littering," I protested.

"As I was saying," she continued, ignoring my comment, "I think he's alright with it. So long as he thinks McKelvey is guilty."

"Did you tell him where we were going?"

"Yeah, though I said we were following a lead on McKelvey, tying up loose ends, checking out the ring. He wanted to know what he was missing. You know?"

"Understandable," I said.

We arrived on the outskirts of Donegal around an hour later. We called first at Hendershot & Sons Jewellers which was, indeed, still beside the Atlantic restaurant. From outside, it looked quite rundown: the woodwork around the door and the sign above the window were sun-faded and blistered. The windows were dusty and the shop appeared so dim inside that at first we thought it was closed. Inside, the style was old-fashioned with a lot of mahogany cases brimming with gold and diamonds which glittered under the spotlights embedded in the ceiling. The shop smelt of air-freshener, perhaps used in an attempt to disguise the deeper smell of tobacco.

The manager was a young man with wavy brown hair and an expensive smile that glittered like the stone in his tie-pin. We explained our visit and showed him the ring. He examined it and suggested that we leave it with him for an hour while he contacted his father, who had made most of the jewellery they had sold during the '60s and '70s.

So we drove on to Bundoran, forty minutes towards the coast. For years Bundoran would have passed for a 1950s coastal village: bleached cottages, rundown shops with curling yellowed sunscreens on the windows, the Atlantic buffeting the coastline even on calm days. Recently, however, it has transformed itself, with amusement arcades and surfing shops, flickering neon signs, restaurants with Wild West facades, and bars crammed with old Irish paraphernalia. In the early mornings, the streets are littered with broken beer bottles and vomit. By lunchtime, however, the town again presents its family-friendly face.

We parked outside the Garda station and went in to meet Sergeant Bill Daly. The window in reception was so low that you had to bend slightly to address the man behind it. It was almost like a taxi office. Williams introduced us both and asked for Daly.

Soon we were buzzed through and welcomed by a middle-aged man, whose black hair was greying at the temples. His skin was tanned like leather, with wrinkles deeply etched around his eyes, and he squinted slightly in the glare of the fluorescent lights overhead. He took us to an interview room.

Daly excused himself and returned after a few moments carrying a small cardboard box on which he balanced three cups of coffee and a thin green folder. He set down the box and sat opposite us, blowing on the surface of his coffee and squinting at Williams.

"So, you're here about Ratsy. Take a look; ask anything you like," he said, gesturing towards the green folder.

Williams opened it and placed it between us on the desk. The notes were brief and concise.

Ratsy Donaghey had been found in his flat overlooking the local playgrounds and swimming pool on 5th November, tied to a chair, his mouth gagged. His arms were covered with cigarette burns. Ultimately, his killer had slit Donaghey's wrists and left him to watch while his blood poured down his hands and dripped off his fingers onto the ground. Vital reaction indicators around the wounds suggested that he lived for perhaps another twenty-five to thirty minutes as he watched the life drip out of him, struggling against his restraints with such violence that he cracked three ribs.

"Any leads?" Williams asked when we finished reading.

"None," Daly said, draining his coffee and beginning to fold down the lip of the paper cup.

"Nothing?" I asked.

"Nope. Not a thing. Ratsy Donaghey was murdered by someone, but we don't know who and, to tell you the truth, we don't really give a shit."

I was not wholly surprised: Donaghey was a career criminal who had made his money selling drugs for years. No policeman was going to waste effort on the likes of Donaghey when the crime rate was rising and police recruitment numbers dropping.

"Let me tell you a story about Ratsy Donaghey. He bought his little pimp-pad here fifteen years ago, as well as one in Letterkenny and two others in Sligo and Cork. He gave free samples of drugs to youngsters of twelve, then got them to steal cars for him; he took out the radio, they got a free joyride. When they dumped it, Ratsy stuck syringes used by some HIV hypo up through the driver's seat. Some poor bastard in a uniform finds this stolen car, gets in to check it out or drive it back to the station, gets a dirty needle in the ass and AIDS for nothing. That's Ratsy Donaghey."

AIDS again. Why did everybody talk about AIDS all the time? I'd never noticed it before. I reminded myself that I'd been given the all clear. Then an inner voice reminded me that I had three months to wait to know for sure.

"It's still a crime," Williams said, though without conviction. It took me a moment to process the conversation and work out what she was talking about.

"The only crime involved in this would be wasting tax payers' money investigating the fact that someone did us a favour. And while you're defending him, you might be interested to know about the ballistics match you asked about — we never got anyone for that, but Ratsy Donaghey was our number one suspect. Held up a sixty-year-old man locking up a filling station; fired a warning shot above his head when he refused to hand over his cash; guy had a heart attack. He survived, though, or we'd have had a murder case on our hands. Ratsy Donaghey was a piece of shit and good riddance to him."

"There'll be other Ratsy Donagheys," I said.

"There already are. But while they keep taking each other out, they save us the hassle."

"Do you think that's what happened here?" I asked.

"Probably," he replied. "Could be an unhappy customer, new competition, a Provo punishment. Honestly, I don't give a shit. So long as Ratsy suffered a lot before he went."

"Did you find cigarette butts or any physical evidence?" I asked.

"Oh, no. Everything was washed and cleaned and left tidy. No prints, no fibres, nothing. Whoever did it was a pro."

"Fair enough."

"Now, what's the connection with your case?" he asked, leaning back in the chair and stretching.

"None, maybe. A piece of jewellery turned up on a list of items stolen from Donaghey's flat in Letterkenny. It's connected with a case we have ongoing."

"That's it? Hell, it must be quiet in Lifford."

"It is," said Williams smiling. "His gun was used in a murder a few days ago. Though, presumably, Ratsy didn't use it himself."

"Maybe he sold it. Maybe it was stolen along with this ring you're talking about."

"Maybe," I conceded. "Any chance we could see Donaghey's flat?"

"Not a hope. Day after he died the council came in and fumigated the place. They moved a Romanian family in last Monday. Didn't tell them the history. Just hoped they don't see the bloody big stains all over the floor. Everything he owns that wasn't auctioned by the state is in that box."

While Williams continued, I opened the box and flicked through some of the contents: a packet of cigarettes, a set of keys, a bundle of letters, and photographs. Absent-mindedly flicking through the bundle of pictures, I found one I recognized. It took me a moment to place it or, rather, when I had last seen it. A woman sat on a flight of steps on a beach. It was the same photograph I had seen tucked behind a vine of ivy on the tree where Angela Cashell had died.

"Who's this?" I asked Daly, holding the photograph up.

"His mother?" Daly guessed. "If he had one."

"I'll hold on to this, if you don't mind," I said, impatient to get back to Lifford to Angela Cashell's murder site to confirm that the pictures matched.

"Nothing you can think of as odd? Nothing that marked this out from a normal drugs kill?" Williams asked, suspecting, perhaps, that the journey had been a waste of time.

"Nothing. Apart from the cigarette-burns torture thing. I only hope whoever did Ratsy videotaped it. Now *that* I'd pay to see."

We stopped for lunch at a chippy while I explained to Williams about the photograph. She offered to phone Holmes and ask him to pick up the picture for us, just so we'd know it was secure. Then we headed back to Donegal town to the jewellers, stopping on the way so I could buy a chocolate cake for Debbie. I hoped that the ring would yield some answers. Instead, it raised more questions.

■ ■ ■ ■

We arrived back at the jewellers around 3.30 p.m. to be introduced to Charles Hendershot, an old man with white hair and a thick handlebar moustache. He was small and stooped, his movements considered and careful. His fingers were tapered and feminine, his skin as fragile as aged paper. He sat behind the main sales desk on an antique chair cushioned with red velvet, his feet crossed at the ankles. The ring and a tattered red leather-bound ledger sat in front of him. His head shook ever so slightly as he spoke.

"I remember this ring," he said softly, after we had sat down with him at the back of the shop. "I remember every piece I make. Each is different. Each is a piece of art." He raised a slender finger towards us, speaking mostly to Williams, who sat turned towards him, her hand resting lightly on the arm of his chair. "You know, I was asked to make a piece for the Pope in 1979, when he came to Drogheda. I was asked to make a cross by the President himself."

"Really?" Williams said and he smiled at her in a way that was almost boyish.

"1978 I made this piece. June 1978. I

found it here in the ledger. I changed my styles each year. That year I did rose-cuts. They're an antique cut, but I did them then, and again in '85 and then in 1991, but never again with moonstones."

"How did you remember it was June?" Williams asked, and I believe she fluttered her eyelids at him.

"Easy, my pet," he said, patting her hand lightly with his own. "The moonstone. It's the birthstone for June: that and pearl. So June 1978. I remembered it and I was right," he said as he leaned forward slowly and tapped the ledger. "It's right there."

"What about the 'AC', Mr Hendershot?" I asked. "Did you engrave that?"

"Yes. It should have read 'From AC'. Too much on a piece like this. So they settled for 'AC'."

" 'From AC', not 'For AC'?" Williams asked.

"Yes. Odd that. Really, it's the lady's initials that should go on a piece. You remember that, young man, when you buy this lovely girl a ring," he said, pointing at me in a way that reminded me of my grandmother. Williams smiled at me expansively, probably because he had called her a girl, as well as lovely. "But it was 'From AC'. I checked."

He opened the ledger and, licking the tips of his fingers, flipped the pages slowly, while I tried to curb my impatience, tapping my open palm against my thigh. He looked deliberately at my hand and stared directly at me before returning his attention to the book, turning the pages even more slowly until he found what he wanted.

"A Mr A. Costello from Letterkenny. I can't remember the face. Faces escape me."

"A. Costello," Williams said jokingly; "surely not the Superintendent."

"No," I said. "He's Olly — Oliver."

Hendershot was still reading through the ledger. "Yes, Mr Alphonsus Costello," he said. In that terrible moment, while my vision spun and my thoughts struggled to make sense, Williams's joke suddenly wasn't funny anymore.

"Who was the girl? His wife?" Williams asked.

"I don't think she was his wife," the old man said, pursing his lips and shaking his head slightly. "But, you see, you're in luck here. One of the diamonds has been replaced."

"Yes, we were told."

He turned and looked at me sharply, like a chiding schoolmaster, then spoke exclusively to Williams for the rest of the conversation, even when replying to questions which I asked. "Anyway, pet, I noticed one of these diamonds is different from the rest. A pink diamond. You see, the lady who was given the ring returned it to us in November of that year, saying one of the diamonds had fallen out and had been misplaced. That never convinces me. Some people would actually take out the stones and sell them, then come back and say the stone was lost. However, this piece cost quite a bit and so I replaced it with another rose cut. I had to send the piece back to her."

"Do you have an address?" I asked.

He looked at his book, then back at Williams. "Her name was Mary Knox. She lived in Canal View in Strabane."

Williams looked at me and smiled in a shy, concealed way. We had driven to Donegal to discover that a ring, which had been deliberately placed on the finger of a murdered girl, had been bought twenty-six years earlier by our own Superintendent for a woman who was not his wife. And we were both keenly aware that he must have recognized the ring when he saw it and yet said nothing. And we had to wonder how the same ring ended up in the possession of a drug-trafficking miscreant like Ratsy Donaghey, only to be stolen in the month prior to his own death. I suspected that Mary Knox, whoever she was, was the only person who could answer any of these questions.

As Knox had given an address in Strabane, and as Costello was clearly involved with her in some way, we decided it would be best to ask Hendry in the North for information. We could have asked Burgess, but he was unlikely to complete the task without Costello getting wind of what he was doing.

I called Hendry on his mobile and when he answered he was slightly out of breath, his voice fractured.

"I hope I didn't interrupt something, Inspector," I said.

"Only my day off, Devlin. What is it now?" he said, in a tone which I hoped was mock exasperation. "I tell you, I should have taken this case myself, 'cause I've ended up doing most of the work anyway."

"I need some info on a lead we've run up on the Cashell murder. Mary Knox."

"As in Half-Hung McNaughten," he laughed.

"Same name, two hundred years on. Lived in Canal View in Strabane twenty-six years ago, if that's any help."

There was silence on the other end of the line and Williams and I looked at each other. Williams shrugged and was about to speak when Hendry's voice crackled over the speaker again. "Give me ten minutes and I'll call you back," he said, all trace of humour gone. Then the line clicked and went dead.

It was almost half an hour later when he phoned, by which stage we were approaching Lifford.

"I needed to check something, but I was right," he said cryptically. "You'll not have much luck with Mary Knox. She disappeared in 1978, presumed dead."

"What happened to her?" I asked.

"Exactly what I said. She disappeared one day. Vanished off the face of the Earth. New Year's Eve 1978 to be precise."

"Inspector Hendry, Sergeant Caroline Williams here, sir. You said 'presumed dead'. Why?"

"Pleased to meet you, Sergeant, so to speak. Call me Jim. We presume she's dead because no one ever heard of her again; no bank accounts or savings touched, nothing. Plus she lived a . . . salacious enough lifestyle, shall we say."

"Nicely put, Jim," I said.

"I said the lady could call me Jim, not you, Devlin," he replied, laughing.

He promised to gather up whatever he

could when he went back to work (another reminder that we were eating into his day off) and hung up.

When we got back, I dropped Williams off at her home and asked her to get Holmes to leave the photograph from Angela Cashell's murder site in the station for me. Then I went back home myself to leave the cake for Debbie. When I went in she was baking fairy cakes with Penny, and Shane was sitting in his highchair, biting on a plastic block. He smiled at me when I came in, holding aloft his arms to be lifted.

"A kiss for my favourite girls," I said, kissing them both on the foreheads, before going over and lifting Shane, who clung to my shirt, giggling and kicking his legs against my belly.

"How was Donegal?" Debbie asked.

"Eventful," I replied and told her what we had discovered. "How was home?"

"Fine. Pity we didn't have this cake two hours ago, though, when we had a visitor, isn't that right, Penny?" Debbie said. But Penny had taken one of the freshly baked buns over to Frank, whose bed had been set up in the kitchen. He looked up and whimpered a little, though he snuffled down the bun in one mouthful and wagged his tail limply, while Penny scratched the pink area beneath his jaw. "Miriam Powell called," Debbie continued.

"Here?" I asked.

She nodded grimly. "We had a very interesting chat about all kinds of things: how lucky I am, mostly; how shit her marriage is; how distant Thomas is; and so on and so on."

"Did she mention the other thing? The other night?"

"No. She apologised for being drunk, though she smelt as bad this afternoon. She wants you to call her about her father-in-law. I trust this time it won't involve any physical contact."

That night we all sat on the sofa and ate chocolate cake and watched films I had rented from the video store. Penny fell asleep, curled up beside Debbie with her legs stretched across my lap, and we wrapped her in a blanket and carried her to bed. I stood at her window and watched as a group of gunmen — a smaller band than the night before — trudged up past our house to Anderson's field in search of the elusive sheepkiller, which I suspected was actually lying downstairs in my kitchen.

Then Debbie stretched across the sofa, her head on my lap, while I played with her hair and stroked her neck and shoulder muscles. Debs fell asleep in minutes, so I sat in the quiet and watched rubbish and enjoyed my home and forgot about Angela Cashell, Terry Boyle, Ratsy Donaghey and Whitey McKelvey for a while.

At around 2.30 in the morning, I woke suddenly, having heard in my sleep the sound of breaking glass. I lay in the semi-darkness for a moment, watching shadows and orange light flicker and dance on the bedroom ceiling. Then I heard more sounds of cracking, and the whine of metal, screeching like an injured beast, and I realized what was causing the flickering orange light on the ceiling.

Downstairs, I saw that someone had smeared dog excrement on the door and windows of the house before throwing a lit petrol-bomb into my car. We managed to get the children safely into the back garden, away from the blaze, when the petrol tank exploded, blowing in all the windows at the front of the house and leaving pools of flaming petrol on the lawn and dripping from the branches of the trees surrounding our home.

■ ■ ■ ■

MARY KNOX

■ ■ ■ ■

CHAPTER ELEVEN

Saturday, 28th December

It took twenty minutes for the fire brigade
to arrive. By then the car was no more than
a smouldering wreck and Debbie's parents
had arrived to take her and the kids to stay
with them for the night. Several lads from
the station arrived with odd bits of wood
and plastic to cover the windows until
morning. Finally, Costello himself arrived
and made coffee with a nip of whiskey. He
sat in the kitchen with me and tried to figure
out who had attacked my family.

"It's a . . . it's a bloody disgrace is what it
is," he said. "We'll hang the blackguards
when we get them."

"*If* we get them," I said, knowing that if
my car had been bombed because of something to do with the Cashell case, then Costello himself was a suspect. Not that I
thought he would be standing in the middle
of the countryside at two in the morning,

petrol-bombing cars. But that didn't mean he couldn't get someone else to do it.

"So, who do you reckon?" Costello asked.

"I'm not sure, sir. Someone connected with the case, perhaps. Someone pissed off at me for some reason. Mark Anderson, getting back at me for his sheep being killed. Maybe the person Penny saw the other night. God only knows."

"Firebombing smacks of Johnny Cashell," Costello suggested.

"Except he's safely in jail in Strabane."

"Aye. Maybe some of McKelvey's crowd," he replied. "Taking their anger out on someone."

"Maybe."

Next morning, the glaziers arrived to begin fixing the windows at the front of the house. I helped the salvage crew clear the last twisted scraps of metal off my driveway and hitched a lift with them to the station, where I picked up an unmarked car to use until my insurance paid for a new one. Then I drove to Strabane.

I passed under the tin sculptures of musicians and dancers which dominate the local skyline, standing some twenty feet tall. The winter sun was a lemon mist above the hills to the east, twinkling weakly off the burnished metal of the statues.

I went first to the library. In addition to the books and CDs, internet access was available, though even at this early hour it was booked solid. I asked for the microfiche machine and copies of the *Strabane Chronicle* from 1977 to 1979 and, fifteen minutes later, started winding my way through the ribbons, one at a time, looking for mention of Mary Knox. I went immediately for the first edition in 1979, which was 4th January. The headline read, rather unimaginatively, "Woman Missing", though at least it made my search easy.

Police are appealing for information regarding the whereabouts of Strabane resident, Mary Knox, who has been missing since New Year's Eve. Knox, in her early thirties, is described as being of average height and build. She has dark brown hair and brown eyes and was last seen wearing a floral print dress and black boots. Anyone with information regarding Miss Knox's whereabouts is asked to contact Strabane Police Station on 36756.

The following edition, dated 11th January, provided more information, under the heading "Fears for Missing Woman." More importantly, it included a photograph showing a woman sitting on some steps leading to a beach. It was the same photograph I had removed from Ratsy Donaghey's box of possessions:

Police are still appealing for information about missing woman Mary Knox, who disappeared on New Year's Eve. Miss Knox moved to the area three years ago, having lived in Manchester, and has a pronounced English accent. She is described as being of average build, with brown hair and eyes. Miss Knox was a well-known figure in local circles and was last seen wearing a floral print dress and black high-heeled shoes.

The change of tense in the last sentence was conspicuous, perhaps an unintentional slip by a copy-editor, perhaps a pragmatic acknowledgement that, after eleven days, Mary Knox would not return. Over the following weeks the articles grew shorter and shorter until, eventually, a week passed with no article at all and Mary Knox was forgotten.

I had to go back almost eight months before I found mention of her name again.

Hendry's comments about her lifestyle had made me suspicious, so I had looked at the Court Report page in each edition, and sure enough, in April of 1978, her name appeared: Mary Knox, of no fixed abode, had appeared before Strabane District Court charged with soliciting and prostitution. She had pleaded guilty after the court heard evidence from Sgt Gerry Willard, who stated that he had seen the defendant provide sexual services in exchange for money in a lay-by on the Leckpatrick Road. RM Edward Benning warned Miss Knox that she would face a custodial sentence if she persevered in such behaviour. He stated that he had spared her on this occasion because of her dependants.

As the editions slid past me on the screen, Mary Knox's name appeared four more times: twice for soliciting, twice for being drunk and disorderly. In one of the soliciting cases, the officer giving evidence was identified as Constable James Hendry. Knox's dependants were not mentioned again.

I phoned Hendry and asked him to meet me for lunch, which, by the time he arrived, consisted of sandwiches wrapped in wax paper, eaten on a park bench outside the library. The sun was low in the sky and our shadows stretched along the pavement.

"Anything on Knox?" I asked, trying to eat and talk at the same time and doing neither with any great success.

"Fairly much what I told you yesterday."

"You didn't tell me you arrested her."

"Did I? I don't remember, but I'm sure I did arrest her. She was one of those characters everyone in the town knew. Rumour was that she was piecing off a bit of action to anyone in uniform who would give her a free pass." He added quickly, "Not that I ever availed of the offer myself."

"Was she working this side of the border or on the other?" I asked, wiping mayonnaise from my mouth.

"Both, I guess," replied Hendry. "She had quite a range of clients, all things considered. If she'd been inclined to mediate, she'd have been a one-woman peace process."

"No thoughts on what happened to her?" I asked.

"She's dead," Hendry said, in a matter-of-fact way, rolling his wax paper into a ball and pitching it at the bin beside our seat. The paper hit the rim and skittered onto the road. A woman walking past with her two children looked at it, then at us, and scowled. "I'd say she's buried under a housing estate, or in the woods, or under a beach or car-park somewhere," Hendry added.

"Who did it?"

"Hard to say, really. At the time, the IRA had 'disappeared' quite a few people: informers, non-informers, people who spoke out against them in the local shops. Disappeared and never seen again. Provos wouldn't admit it then, but it's coming out now. Tortured them to find out what they'd said, then dumped the bodies on building sites. So that was high up on our list. The other possibility was some customer, unhappy with the services she provided. Maybe a john she was blackmailing, threatening to tell his wife. Whoever did it probably never killed again. She just vanished."

"The newspapers talked about her 'dependants'. Who were they?" I asked, lighting a cigarette and offering Hendry one.

"Two kids. A boy and a girl. Damned if I know what age they were, though," Hendry said, drawing on the cigarette, then looking at the tip to ensure it had lit fully. He blew the smoke out with an audible sigh, wiping crumbs from his moustache as he pulled at it.

"What happened to them?"

"I've no idea. I'd nothing to do with the

disappearance. I encountered her occasionally. Knew her by reputation, really." He looked at his watch. "I better go. Take it easy, you hear," he said, waving as he walked off back to his station. Then he stopped and came back. "Thought you might want to know. Johnny Cashell was up yesterday. Fined five grand. Got off light all things considered, even if in some ways he did the community a service!" he laughed.

After picking up Hendry's discarded litter, I returned to the car. So Johnny Cashell had been back in Lifford yesterday — shunting him right back to the top of the list of suspects for burning my car. And also putting him nearer the top of the list of people I had to speak to. First, I drove along the Derry Road to the new council offices, where I asked for the registrar. The woman who came out to help me was a heavyset, reticent lady, who seemed to whisper when she spoke. I explained to her that I was looking for birth certificates for the two Knox children, and gave her a general idea of the period in question. She took all the details, then told me she would call me when she had copies.

Next, I returned to Lifford, stopping off at the station to confirm what I already knew to be the case: the photograph from the site where Angela's body was found was the same as that taken from Ratsy's flat. Mary Knox. Williams had left a note saying that she and Holmes had gone with a police artist to get a sketch of the girl spotted with Terry Boyle the night he died. I headed straight for Clipton Place to confront Johnny Cashell over the arson attack on my house. It seemed, however, that he had been out the night before celebrating his release and, slightly the worse for wear, was now in the pub, searching for the hair of the dog.

As it turned out, I missed him in McElroy's bar. However, I did find out that Johnny had been there all of the day before — after his daughter's funeral — and had had to be carried into a taxi at three in the morning — which meant he was still lying comatose in the bar when someone torched my car — which meant he slid right back down my list of suspects.

Finally, when I had nothing left to do to avoid it, I drove back over to Lifford and to Powell's house. This time I pulled into the drive where Miriam's BMW sat alone. I knocked on the door twice and was about to turn and leave when I heard the slamming of one of the internal doors. Seconds later, Miriam pulled the front door open, her face flushed and her breathing heavy. Her breath smelt of cigarettes and drink. She stood in the doorway, leaning slightly against the doorframe, and smiled. "Come in," she said, and turned and led me into the living room.

"Debs said you wanted to see me, Miriam," I said, standing by the sofa.

"Sit, Ben, please," she said, doing so herself. As she sat, she ran her hands along the backs of her legs, as though to smooth out a skirt, but it was clearly force of habit, for she was wearing jeans and a white, man's shirt with the top buttons open wide enough to reveal the flush at the base of her throat and the swell of her tanned chest. She seemed to be aware of my gaze for, as she spoke, she fingered the collar of the shirt and rubbed her index finger along the length of her collarbone.

"I wished to apologize for my behaviour in your home the other night," she said, smiling at me girlishly.

"I need to apologize, too, Miriam, for what happened in the car."

She waved her hand, as though wafting my words from the air.

"No need, Ben. Just think of it as two old friends renewing their acquaintance."

"You wanted to speak about your father-in-law?" I prompted, already growing uneasy with the direction the conversation was taking.

"He saw someone again the night before last," she said.

"In his room?" I asked.

"Not quite. Outside. He said he saw shadows at his window, trying to peer in through the crack in the curtains."

I was reminded of our own experience several nights before. Could the two incidents be linked? "He didn't see their face?" I asked.

"No," Miriam replied. "I just thought it might be important."

"You could have phoned me with this, Miriam," I said, standing up.

"I know you're mad at me," she said quickly. "I know you hate me for what I did to you. With Thomas."

"I don't hate you, Miriam," I said.

"You do. You're right. It was horrid of me. But, I've paid the price for it. My wonderful husband. He's standing in the next election. It'll be the first time he's stood near me in years. His waitresses and nurses, they do it for him. He thinks I'm withered up. Used goods, he says." The words tumbled out without pause, as if Miriam were somehow aware that if she stopped now, she would never have a chance to unburden herself again. Or perhaps she just liked an audience. "Am I used goods, Ben?"

"I need to go, Miriam," I said, moving towards the door.

"You used to be a better man than this, Ben. I remember. I remember touching you. You were so excited you couldn't hold yourself back. I remember. You do, as well. I know you find me attractive. Oh, Debbie's a great mother, I'm sure. But would she do what I'd do? Remember you and me down by the water station? We have unfinished business, Ben. Let's finish it," she said, playfully. She moved towards me, swaying gently from side to side, her head lowered slightly so that she looked up at me through her fringe. "No one need ever know," she said. "Just a bit of harmless fun."

She was close to me now and I could feel the heat radiating from her body. Her skin seemed to emanate something more than warmth. I could smell again the exotic coconut of her skin and taste again her mouth, cold and sharp. I wanted to feel the soft tug of her lips. She put one hand on my chest, the tip of a finger finding its way between the buttons and rubbing the hairs of my chest. She ran her fingernail along the skin and something deep inside me began to well up. She smiled at me with her mouth, but her eyes remained slightly out of focus, as though she were not really there, and in their emptiness I saw my children and my wife. I felt again Deb's neck and the softness of her hair. I took Miriam's hand and lifted it from my chest, then moved away from her. Her smile wavered, as if she could not understand what had happened. Then it faltered completely as I moved backwards towards the door.

"Goodbye, Miriam," I said. "I want to go home to my family. I'm sorry if I gave you the impression that there was something else there."

She set her face defiantly against the shafts of winter sunlight streaming down the hallway. "Get out, you useless shit!" she spat. "See if your wife will be a whore for you on the back seat of a car."

As I turned to open the door, I came face-to-face with Thomas Powell, who flashed his most political smile. He looked freshly showered, his hair still damp and slightly spiked. He had recently shaved and smelt strongly of aftershave, despite it being late afternoon. "Have I missed something?" he said.

I did not tell Debbie of my visit to Miriam

Powell, and all evening I debated with myself over the real reason for it. Miriam had sensed the unfinished nature of our relationship; but it was also vanity on my part. Miriam Powell would still sleep with me out of pity, or charity, or some obsessive need to debase herself even further. Perhaps she wanted revenge against her adulterous husband. Perhaps she just wanted to enjoy herself.

If I had not seen the emptiness in her eyes, would I have gone ahead and given myself to her and given away all that was important to me? I told myself that I would not. And, as I kissed my children goodnight and curled up to sleep behind Debbie, I believed that to be the truth.

I dreamt that night of Miriam Powell. She and I were together in the back of a car, parked behind the cinema. We were kissing and her breath was hot and urgent against my ear as she pressed her cheek to mine. Over her naked shoulder, through the windshield, I could see the body of Angela Cashell lying on the grass. Debbie was standing over her, shaking her head. Miriam tugged at my shirt, flicking open the buttons, and I heard shouting. Rubbing the condensation from the the window, I looked across to another car, parked beside us. The light was on inside and I could see Costello with a faceless woman. She had brown hair and brown eyes and her body was scarred and abused. She looked at me and screamed. Then the car I was in began to move. Behind me, flames forked out of the boot and I believed I could hear the petrol bubbling in the tank, ready to explode. My stomach lurched, and when I looked again, Terry Boyle was sitting beside me, the fetid smell of his breath and his scorched flesh thick in my mouth and nose, the charred remains of his hand clasped on my knee. Then Whitey McKelvey was driving, his face contorted and frozen, his hands lying useless on the melting wheel, which spun wildly out of all control.

Chapter Twelve

Sunday, 29th December

I awoke at four in the morning with an irresistible need for food. I settled for coffee and a cigarette, which I smoked at the back door as Frank lay in his basket, watching me with critical eyes. I went out into the garden, which was frozen under a clear night sky. The stars were bright and numerous. The moon was almost new and as thin and curved as a curl of lemon rind. I inspected the outside of Frank's shed while I walked to keep myself warm. At the back, hidden under the branches of the fir hedge, I finally found where the boards had rotted and broken and Frank had been squeezing in and out. Inside the shed, the hole was hidden behind bags of cloths that we had used to cover furniture when we had painted the house. I saw, too, the stain of blood on the floor from the night of the hunt and knew, though I had tried not to think on it, that if Frank were killing livestock, sooner or later he would have to be put down.

I lay on the sofa that night, unable to dispel the thought that whoever had attacked my home would do so again. I sat awake till dawn. Then, having turned on early morning TV, I must have fallen asleep. I woke cramped and uncomfortable, my face hot and stubbly. My eyes were dry and sore and my skin smelt of salt and sweat. Penny stood looking at me, her head bent to one side.

"Did you and Mommy fight?" she asked, with a matter-of-factness that I found disconcerting in my five-year-old daughter.

"No, pet. I couldn't sleep, so I came down here," I said, trying to smile, while I stretched the crick out of my neck.

"Why?" she asked.

"Because I couldn't sleep and didn't want to wake anyone else."

"Okay," she said. "Can you move, please? I want to watch television." Then she sat down at the end of the sofa, having given me just enough time to lift my head out of the way.

As I showered, I ran over the dream of the night before and resolved to face the thing I dreaded: confronting Costello over Mary Knox.

■ ■ ■ ■

For the second time in a week, I found myself walking up Costello's tarmac driveway, my innards constricted. The morning sky was a brilliant blue, the white shreds of cloud contrasting all the more strongly. The sun shone low in the sky, struggling to clear the mountains in the east. However, the temperature had dropped again overnight and a skin of ice was forming on the water in the concrete birdbath in the centre of the Costellos' front lawn.

Emily answered the door and smiled in a confused way. "Is something wrong, Benedict? You look terrible."

I could not look her in the eyes, holding in my pocket the diamond ring that her husband had given to a prostitute twenty-six years earlier. The eldest Costello child was thirty-five.

The Super appeared behind her, tucking his striped shirt into his voluminous brown corduroy trousers. "Benedict," he said, smiling. "Come in." He had not yet shaved and his hair stood slightly on end.

"I'd like a word, sir. If you don't mind," I said, refusing to cross the threshold into their home out of respect for Emily.

He looked a little startled, but nodded and lifted a heavy quilted coat off the hooks beside the door and followed me out to the car. "What's up, Benedict? Is this about McKelvey again?"

I took the ring out of my pocket and held it up between my thumb and forefinger.

"Cashell's ring," he said. "So what?" Then he saw the photograph which I took from my pocket and he said simply, "Ah."

"Who was Mary Knox?" I asked, making it sound more personal than I had intended.

"Let's go for a drive," he said.

In 1976, Ollie Costello was a sergeant with Lifford Garda. He had been married for ten years. On a June night, when the sky was royal blue and the moon was white and low above the hills, he was passing the Coachman Inn nearly an hour after closing time and noticed lights shining from the gap under the closed doors.

He hammered on the double doors and was finally admitted. As the noise of the revellers died around him, he saw a group of men crowded around the edge of a platform which doubled as a stage for the local auctions. None of the group had noticed Costello yet, for their attention was fixed on a woman who stood on the stage above them in the process of peeling her petticoat and underwear from her sweating body. The men cheered as inch after inch of white flesh was exposed, while the woman writhed and wriggled to some silent music that pounded in her head. It was a spectacle both ridiculous and strangely sensual.

"Right, madam, that's enough," Costello said finally, banging on the wooden platform with his truncheon as the gathered spectators hastily dispersed.

"Ain't never been called a madam before," she said, winking down at him while she continued to gyrate, almost naked. He climbed onto the stage, struggling to shift his weight sufficiently to pull himself up, then removed his jacket and put it around her, suddenly conscious of the half-moon of sweat which had darkened the underarms of his shirt.

She wrapped his jacket around her, holding it closed with her hands, and swayed slightly, dizzy as a result of both her dancing and the drink she had taken. Costello put his arms around her to steady her, and took her to the Ladies, where he stood guard while she got dressed. Then he led her out to his car before returning to the bar and cautioning the owner, Harry Toland, for his breach of license.

When he got back to his car, the woman who had said her name was Mary, was sprawled in the back seat, pulling the foot of her tights down slightly to shift the hole in them from her big toe to one of the smaller ones. The car smelt of cigarette smoke and drink and sweat and feet and worn stockings. Costello wound down the window and took out his notebook. He flicked on the light in the car and asked the woman for details. He cautioned her that she could be charged with lewd behaviour and asked if she had someone she wanted to contact. As he did so, he watched her in the rearview mirror, suddenly aware that the beads of perspiration clinging to her face and chest were making him vaguely excited.

She said she'd heard there were men in Lifford who liked to dance with single women. She told him she was alone. Then she took out her cigarettes and lit one. He told her she was not allowed to smoke in a Garda car and she smiled at him with her eyes. She asked him if he smoked and he said, "Sometimes." She took the cigarette from her lips, her lipstick thick around the brown filter, and extended it towards him. He resisted as it touched his mouth, then dragged from it, smiling at her as he exhaled.

She lit another cigarette for herself and told him of her children, a boy named Sean and a girl called Aoibhinn. She spoke of how worried they would be when she did not come home that night. Finally she suggested to Costello that if he let her go home, instead of arresting her, she would perform an act on him which he'd enjoy.

He sat in the front of the car, suddenly cold and warm, excited and scared and unable to reach a decision that would calm the rush of adrenaline he felt. And for a few moments, all thoughts of his wife and children left him and he convinced himself that he deserved some fun in life. He told himself that Emily would never know and so would not be hurt.

He started the engine and drove to the area of waste ground where the old asylum used to stand. He sat in the darkness while she climbed between the two seats and sat beside him. He turned his face away from the streetlamps and closed his eyes and thought only of his breaths that quickened and shallowed until he swore he would hyperventilate. When she was finished, he opened his eyes again and started the ignition, while she put on her seatbelt and fixed her make-up in the vanity mirror. Then he drove her the quarter mile to the border and let her out of the car. She thanked him, and he almost reciprocated. Then she closed the door, waved in at him sadly through the side window, and turned and walked into the shadow of the Camel's Hump, the massive British Army checkpoint which had dominated the area for most of the Troubles.

Costello returned to the station where he went to the toilet and washed himself several times and strained until he forced himself to urinate. He looked at himself in the mirror, water dripping off the fringes of his hair and off his nose and for a moment he thought he would vomit. But the wave of nausea passed, or he swallowed it down; he smoothed his hair back on his scalp, replaced his cap and walked home, allowing the breeze which was rising off the river to cool the redness in his cheeks.

Costello woke the following morning early and sat at his kitchen table in silence while the air around him lightened. He took a walk into Lifford town just after 8.00 a.m. and bought fresh bread and orange juice and a bunch of cut flowers from a bucket outside the local supermarket. He made Emily breakfast in bed and laughed a little too loudly at her jokes. He studied her face carefully and reminded himself of all the things about her which he loved, all the reasons he had married her.

Two weeks later, when he could stand no more, he sat in his car at the customs point and flicked through his notebook until he found Mary Knox's name and address. He wore plain clothes so he could cross the border. He sat outside her house on Canal View, watching the windows for what seemed an eternity. Finally, he went over and knocked on the door. Butterflies fluttered around his insides. A knot thick as a fist caught in the centre of his gut. The door was opened and she was looking at him, standing on her doorstep, his hair brushed, a bunch of flowers bought from the same bucket as his wife's clasped so tightly in his sweating hand that the green paper was staining his skin.

Later, as he left the house, he placed a twenty pound note on the phone table in the hall, while she dressed quietly in the living room.

Over the following months he visited Mary Knox with increasing frequency. Their routine did not change. He sat and waited in his car until she was ready for him. He stood at her door like a child approaching an adult, fear and excitement tightening inside him. He always brought her flowers, even when those from the night before were still fresh.

At Christmas he bought Mary Knox a gold chain which cost more than the gift he bought for his wife. He bought the Knox children a train set and a doll, but was not allowed to present them personally. She bought him nothing and he thought she might give him a free turn, but as he crept out the front door that night she called him back and asked him had he forgotten something. He was so angry he swore he would never go back to her, but he returned four nights later.

One night he saw a figure — another customer — emerge from her door, glancing furtively up and down the street, the orange lamplight glistening off his wedding ring. Costello could do nothing and Knox made no apology.

On his way home he picked up a drunk who was staggering over the bridge towards Lifford and beat him so severely with his nightstick that when the man left the drunk-tank the following morning, his ribs and back were ribboned with purple and red welts, though he could not recall how he had received them.

More and more often, Costello found himself waiting until a man left Mary Knox's house before he could enter. Finally, on one such night in May, as the evening freshened and the last blue faded from the sky, he hit on the idea of a trip to Donegal. He would take her away for the weekend, spend two whole days with her, with no distractions — no other men, no Emily, no twenty-pound payment. He could say he had to attend a conference. He could book under the name Smith, as he had seen it done in the movies. For the first time in months, he felt again the nauseating wave of nerves and excitement return.

It took three weeks to convince Mary Knox. He promised to pay for everything if she would come. He promised to arrange it so no one would know. Finally he promised to buy her something to compensate for the loss of earnings she would suffer over one weekend. She smiled and allowed him to kiss her and agreed. She said she would leave her children with a neighbour; they had an understanding.

It was on that trip that Costello bought Mary Knox the ring which I now held. And, he believed, it was that trip which had signalled the start of the end of their relationship: perhaps because Mary Knox realized how possessive he had become.

As autumn darkened the nights around him, he saw her less frequently. Several nights her house stood in darkness all night. When he did see her, she seemed distant. Her clothes looked more expensive and, though she still wore his ring, it was supplemented now with other items of jewellery. One night when he called, he watched her going out of her house and getting into a black southern-registered car, driven by a Lifford man named Anthony Donaghey. He was tall and thin in an ungainly way, his hair shorn close to his scalp. He wore drainpipe jeans rolled up on his shins and high-laced Doctor Marten boots. Yet, he held the door open for Mary Knox as if he were her chauffeur, and she sat in the back while he drove.

Without any regard for his dignity, Costello followed them back across the border and out to the Three Rivers Hotel that squatted on the Letterkenny Road. He sat in the shadows of the car park for three hours, running his car battery low by listening to the radio, waiting for Mary Knox to reappear. Shortly after one in the morning, she swayed drunkenly out through the front door. Donaghey got out of a waiting car, helped her in and drove her home.

When Costello asked her about the incident several days later she told him he was pathetic, sitting in the darkness watching her. She told him she didn't need a jealous lover. She told him she had someone more important than a policeman to take care of her. He shouted at her so loudly her daughter upstairs began to cry. Mary Knox slapped him on the face and called him a lunatic. His face stung and burned where the print of her hand had already started to turn red. Blindly, he grabbed at the earthenware jug of flowers and threatened her with it. For the tiniest second something like fear flickered in her eyes, then she laughed at him, laughed so hard that tears began to leak down her face. Her laughter followed him out onto the street and all the way home.

He did not see Mary Knox again. Several weeks later, on New Year's Eve, she and her children vanished.

We were sitting now in the lay-by halfway across the bridge between Lifford and Strabane. Traffic drifted past us. Below, where the Foyle began its final journey to Lough Foyle and on to the Atlantic, a lone heron waded in the shallows, dipping its beak curiously into the murk, but was having no success finding food.

"So, that's the whole story, Benedict. Why did I not tell you this before? Hardly my finest moment, was it?"

I said nothing, but ground the cigarette I was smoking into the car ashtray. I wound down the window to let the smoke escape and watched as the heron gave up its search, stretched its wings and lifted itself from the water. "What has this got to do with Angela Cashell?" I asked finally.

"I don't know, Benedict. Honestly. If I thought there was a connection, I'd have told you before now."

"There must be a connection," I said with irritation. "Ratsy Donaghey reports stolen the ring of a woman who disappeared twenty-odd years ago; Whitey McKelvey gets hold of it, tries to flog it, claims he sold it to a woman in a disco, and it ends up on the finger of an almost naked dead girl, the daughter of a local hood. Coincidence is one thing, sir, but this is just a little much."

"I could call the NCIB in. Get some fresh minds on the case. Of course that means that everything will be in the open. Everything."

Regardless of the implicit threat that my attack on Whitey McKelvey would surface once more, I was reluctant anyway to hand things over to the National Criminal Investigation Bureau. My handling of the case had hardly been exemplary, but I felt I was at last on the right track.

"The first question is, how did Ratsy Donaghey end up with the ring?" I said, trying to ignore his comment.

"Well, either Mary gave it to him or he took it from her," Costello said. "And she may not have cared for me, but she cared for that ring. It cost a fortune."

I started the engine and indicated to turn back towards Lifford. "Where are we going?" Costello said.

I looked at him but could not answer.

CHAPTER THIRTEEN

Monday, 30th December

At 9.30 on Monday morning, I met Williams in our storeroom office. She and Holmes had secured an artist's impression of the girl with whom Terry Boyle had been spotted on the night he died. Unfortunately, for all that effort, the picture could have been of any teenaged girl: small, fair hair, attractive; no eye-colour, no distinctive tattoos or piercing. The e-fit would be released to the press, but even Williams admitted that she didn't hold out much hope. Holmes was continuing his suspension at home, watching daytime TV and phoning suspects whose names had been bandied about in connection with Boyle. It was a thankless task, but he was using a Garda cellphone, so it wasn't costing him anything.

"She looks like somebody I know," I said, turning my head to one side, as though looking from a different angle might help me see more clearly.

"She looks like *any*body I know," Williams said. "That's the problem. How's the Cashell case moving?"

I told her all that Costello had told me. When I finished she shook her head in disbelief, then said, "I guess you were right when you said the ring was a message. Do you think it was meant for Costello?"

"Maybe. It's something we'll have to consider. First we figure out what Ratsy Donaghey had to do with all this. I have a feeling that, if he's involved, Mary Knox didn't voluntarily give that ring away."

"Well, I have two bits of news," Williams said. "First off, I checked that video again. Bad news is there was no sign of Whitey McKelvey."

"But we saw her going in with him."

"No," she replied, raising a finger in the air in a way that reminded me of one of my old school teachers. "We saw someone going in with Cashell, whom we assumed to be Whitey. Remember, the guy with the short blond hair and jeans. White shirt?"

"I remember," I said. "What about him?"

"He appears again later. Going to the toilet. I had to go and check in the bar myself last night. He went into the girls' toilet. He was a she."

"Are you sure?" I asked, though I knew it was a stupid question.

"As best I can be. It's hard to tell. The white shirt is kind of baggy. A small-breasted woman, short hair? Yeah, could be a woman. Maybe Whitey McKelvey was telling the truth. He doesn't appear anywhere on the video."

"If he was telling the truth about that, maybe he did sell the ring," I said.

"Let's say he did. How did it end up on Cashell's finger? Unless someone bought the ring specifically for that purpose. Which would have meant tracking down Whitey. Which meant they knew the ring had been stolen. Or maybe Ratsy told them it had been stolen. Maybe that's why he had cigarette burns all over his arms. Maybe they tortured him until he told them about it. They trace it back to McKelvey and buy it from him," Williams added. "Then plant it on his girlfriend's body to make it look like he did it. But why?"

"What if McKelvey wasn't the link. What if the message wasn't for McKelvey or Costello? What if it was meant for Johnny Cashell?"

"It's possible. Should we go see him?" Williams suggested.

"I guess we'd better," I said.

We didn't get any further, though, for my own cellphone rang. It was Kathleen Boyle, Terry's mother, and she had received something unusual in the mail.

"I don't usually open my husband's mail," she explained, sitting on the same sofa as she had the night her son had been murdered. "Only at Christmas. Well, some people don't realize we're separated, you see. They still send cards to both of us, but in his name. You know, Mr and Mrs Seamus Boyle. I open them and send his on to him."

"No need to explain, Mrs Boyle," Williams said, impatient to find out what exactly had been sent.

"Well, I knew this was a Christmas card when it arrived today. I just thought it was late. But the card was blank you see — no message, nothing. Just this inside . . ." She held out a photograph, its subject unclear as the light shimmered with the shaking of her hand across the glossy finish.

When I took the picture from her, I was both surprised and strangely comforted to see the familiar image of Mary Knox, sitting on the steps, frozen in a moment that must have held significance for whoever had taken the photograph — or whoever was attaching it to murders twenty-odd years after her disappearance.

Mrs Boyle caught the glance between myself and Williams. "Do you know who she is?" she asked.

"The question is, do you?" I replied.

"No idea. I've never seen her before. I just thought . . . Well, you said if I thought of anything unusual to get in touch."

"You're sure you don't know her?" I asked again, desperate now to find the link, the relevance of this picture.

"No, I've never set eyes on her, I swear."

"The card was sent to your husband, Mrs Boyle. Would he know her?"

"I . . . I don't know," she said, suddenly taken aback by the thought. "She might be one of his . . . women. But the picture looks so old."

"Can we contact your husband, Mrs Boyle?" I asked. "To see if —"

She nodded vigorously. "Oh, he'll be here later. For the funeral tomorrow." She looked from Williams to me and back, as if somewhere in the space between us she might find an explanation for the death of her son.

After assuring Mrs Boyle that she had done the right thing in calling us, we sat in the car and discussed our progress. There was no discernable link between Ratsy Donaghey, Angela Cashell and Terry Boyle, yet someone had murdered the three of them, and Mary Knox's picture had turned up in connection with all three crimes. Ratsy Donaghey was the same generation as Johnny Cashell and, though I didn't know Seamus Boyle, Mary Knox's photograph had been sent to him, not his wife. I decided the only thing left to do was to confront Johnny Cashell and Seamus Boyle. Before we did, I called Hendry to see if he had found out anything more about Knox's disappearance. He had spent the morning going over case notes for me.

"I told you yesterday. The main line of inquiry at the time was IRA involvement. Of course, that meant that it never went any further."

"Does the name Ratsy Donaghey mean anything? Druggie from Letterkenny."

"Tony?"

"That's him."

"Tony's name appeared once or twice. One of the neighbours said she had seen him a couple of times around the house before the girl vanished. Not just him, mind," he added.

"No word on the kids yet?"

"Nothing. My guess is if she's alive they're

with her. Otherwise, one of her neighbours wasn't spotted for a few days after the disappearance. Went to Dublin to a sister, she said. She and Knox were very close; she looked after the kids, apparently, when Knox was working. Joanne Duffy her name was. Lives in Derry now, somewhere. Why do you ask about Tony Donaghey?"

"His name's come up on this side."

"What did you call him? Ratsy?" Hendry asked, and I explained.

When Donaghey was a teenager he used to hunt and catch rats in the farms around Lifford. On summer days, when the weather was stiflingly hot, he went into Letterkenny and hung around by traffic lights, a live rat in the pocket of his coat. If a single female driver stopped at the lights, with her window down because of the heat, Donaghey would throw the live rat onto her lap. Generally, the driver's first reaction was to leap out of the idling car. Donaghey could then jump in and drive off. He did it six times before he was caught. Rumour also has it that the officer who caught him, who is now a superintendent, broke the bones of Donaghey's two hands with a truncheon as a salutary lesson in the summary justice of Donegal.

"Fair enough," Hendry said. "He was a

bad bastard by all accounts. Reading between the lines here, he was fairly in the frame for the Knox disappearance, and a few others. We had him down as a Provo, for a while anyway, until even they kicked him out. No evidence, though, so it was left in the wind. Sorry."

I thanked him and hung up. Twice now he had mentioned the Provo connection. I couldn't see it. Still, I thought, it would do no harm to check. I picked up my car keys. Williams looked at me.

"I think I need to go to confession," I said.

Our local priest is an elderly man called Terry Brennan. He moved to Lifford four years ago after serving in one of the roughest areas of Derry for fourteen years and, while many assumed him to be a bumbling old relic from the golden age of Catholicism, few knew that he had mediated between the IRA and British government ministers for several years in the late '80s and early '90s. He had no affiliations with either group, yet managed to retain the respect, and, more importantly, the ear of both.

The 10.30 a.m. Mass was not yet over, so we sat in the car park until the small number of woman parishioners exited into the morning sunlight, pulling on coats or fastening scarves around their heads against the cold. Then I went into the chapel.

The sunlight from outside shone through the stained glass at such an angle that the spectrum of colours splashed across the white marble of the altar. Father Brennan was in the confessional; two elderly supplicants knelt at the pew directly outside. The door of the box clicked open and a child came out, holding the door open for a woman who was, presumably, his grandmother. Within less than a minute, she too came out and the man in front of me entered the box. From where I was sitting I could hear his soft murmuring, interspersed with the deeper, more guttural mutterings of Father Brennan. Then the man came out and left the confessional box door swinging in air heavy with the scent of incense.

I went into the box and pulled the door behind me. The atmosphere was warm and close, the smell of polish and wood mixing with the scent of the priest's aftershave. I could make out his silhouette through the grill that separated us. He was looking down at his lap, at a prayer book, his ear close to the grille.

"Bless me, Father, for I have sinned. It has been a few weeks since my last confession," I began.

"Better make it quick, Inspector, my breakfast's being made," Brennan replied in a voice gravelled by years of smoking Woodbines. He laughed softly to himself, a chuckle that resonated like a cough.

"I need a favour. I need to speak to someone who could help me with a case. A prostitute named Mary Knox disappeared from Strabane in 1978. I need to know whether the Provos had anything to do with it. It connects with the Cashell and Boyle deaths, I think."

"They're connected?" Brennan hissed.

"We think so. But no one knows, so . . ." My unspoken request for confidence hung unanswered. Brennan did not speak for almost a minute, the silence interminable in the darkness of the box. He leaned closer towards the grille and, in the half-light, I could see that he had turned his head towards me, a glint of external light catching the frame of his glasses. "I can't promise anything, Inspector. It's a very unorthodox request. Give me a number to contact you. As I say, no promises."

"Thank you, Father," I said.

I heard him moving in the box next to me, preparing to leave. He reached up and pulled the stole from around his neck.

"Father," I said. "I was wondering if you'd hear my confession while I'm here."

He did not speak, but sat again, and I could faintly make out in the gloom that he had placed the purple stole around his neck again and blessed himself. I began to tell him about McKelvey, about Anderson and his sheep and, mostly, about Miriam Powell. He asked me if I had told Debbie what had happened. He asked me if I was sorry. He asked me would I have taken the affair any further and I said, "No."

"God forgives you, Inspector. Your wife, I suspect, will forgive you. Try now to forgive yourself. I absolve you from your sins, in the name of the Father, the Son and the Holy Spirit, amen. Leave your phone on."

Williams and I went to a restaurant on the border called The Traveller's Rest. She ate cereal and toast while I had a full breakfast with bacon, eggs, sausage and tomato. I was wiping my last slice of toast through the remaining egg yolk when my phone rang.

"Devlin here," I said, not recognizing the caller ID on the phone's display.

"The priest said you wanted to ask some questions." The voice was cold, disconnected not just by the anonymity of the mobile phone but by something deeper.

"Yes," I said, though he had not asked a question.

"What do you want?"

"Mary Knox. She was a —"

"The priest told us. What do you want?"

"Did the IRA have anything to do with her disappearance?" I asked and realized that the people at the table beside us were staring open-mouthed at me. I stepped outside, fumbling in my pocket for my cigarettes as I spoke.

"No."

"Are you sure?" No response. "What about Ratsy Donaghey? Was he one of yours?"

"It's a well-known fact, Devlin. The priest told me that —"

"So Ratsy Donaghey didn't have anything to do with Knox's disappearance?"

"I didn't say that. Listen. We did not sanction the . . . disappearance of Mary Knox. Whether one renegade volunteer did is another matter and one for which we accept no responsibility. Such behaviour reflects badly on us."

"I hardly think you're in a position of moral highground," I began.

"The priest told us you were a decent fella," the voice said. "He was wrong. I can understand why they torched your car.

Don't look for this to happen again."

"Wait," I said. "What about Johnny Cashell and Seamus Boyle?"

"Are you fucking stupid? They all worked together." Then the line went dead.

I recorded the phone number that had shown on my display, a northern cellphone number. I phoned through to the Garda Telecomm Support Unit and asked them if they could trace it. Later that day, they contacted me to tell me that the number belonged to a ten-year-old who had reported it lost in her school some days earlier.

"Donaghey did it," I said, having relayed the details of the conversation to Williams. "He was IRA but acted outside of them. When he went into drugs they cut him loose completely. But he must have done it."

"How come the RUC couldn't get him?"

"Extradition proceedings in the '70s were fairly rare. Probably not worth the effort if they couldn't be sure the state would hand him over. Besides, they needed to prove it was him for a case. We don't have to *prove* anything. Suspicion is enough to get us going — give us something to work with. So, let's work on the assumption that Ratsy Donaghey did kill her. Let's say he stole her jewellery. That was the kind of lowlife he was. Twenty-five years later, his house is broken into and the jewellery stolen. So much time has passed he believes he's in the clear. No one will remember a bloody ring, he thinks. And it must be worth something. Maybe he wanted the insurance to cover it. Somehow, someone sees the ring on the stolen items list, though. They make the connection. Ratsy gets tortured and killed. What if it wasn't a rival drugs thing or questions about the ring? What if Ratsy was tortured until he spilled the whole truth on Mary Knox? What if he named names? Let's say he names Cashell and Boyle. A little while later, Cashell's daughter and Boyle's son both end up dead, with photographs of the dead woman, and Cashell wearing her ring."

"How did they get the ring? Check all the jewellers' shops until they get a hit? Follow it back to Whitey McKelvey, get the ring and set him up? None of the jewellers mentioned anyone asking questions except us, and it's our job to do that!"

"Well, who else would have access to the stolen items lists?"

"Don't you read your email? Another new initiative — stolen item lists are being put on the local page of the Garda website. Someone somewhere hopes that the public will do our job for us. Anyone with Internet access could have seen those lists."

"True enough," I agreed reluctantly. "So someone sees the ring on a list; links it to Ratsy. Questions him; makes the connection with Whitey? How?"

"Luck? Grapevine? Sheer coincidence? Maybe Ratsy knew McKelvey had done it. Must be easy enough to work out who's pawning stolen goods in Donegal," Williams said. "The more pertinent question is who would want to kill Mary Knox's killers — assuming she is actually dead?"

"She's dead. Who'd revenge her death? Someone close to her; someone who knew the ring; someone who knew her personally; someone who remembered her after twenty-five years."

"Costello?" Williams said, shrugging slightly as she said it.

"Possibly," I said, pretending it hadn't crossed my mind.

"Why kill Angela Cashell? Or Terry Boyle?" Williams said. "Why not kill the fathers? Why pick on their children?"

"Unless it's Mary Knox's child who is taking revenge. Maybe he'd kill the children of those responsible for his mother's death."

"Or she."

"What?"

"Knox had two children, a boy and a girl. Don't forget, we haven't ruled out a woman's involvement in Cashell's murder. The panties back on? And we know there were two people involved in Boyle's murder: the girl he left the pub with and the person who shot him."

"True," I said.

"So, what do we do now?" Williams asked.

"We'll speak to Cashell and see what he gives us. Have a chat with Boyle tomorrow, after the funeral. Meanwhile, let's see if we can connect Donaghey and Cashell to the Knox murder. And let's see if we can track down what has happened to the two Knox children."

Williams looked at me. "What if we find it's Costello?" she asked, biting hard at her bottom lip.

"Then we arrest him," I said, with more conviction than I felt.

We arrived at Cashell's home just as a TV crew pulled away. Johnny was talking over the hedge to his neighbour, Sadie beside him, smoking a cigarette.

The neighbour nodded in our direction and both the Cashells turned and watched us walking up the pathway to their house. Johnny Cashell stood a little taller and tried to puff out his chest. The effect was diminished somewhat by the fact that he winced — his stomach wound was obviously still hurting him.

"Do I smell bacon?" his neighbour asked, obviously thinking a joke good enough to make once was worth repeating.

"Not over the smell of petrol," Johnny Cashell replied, turning and standing in his doorway, legs slightly apart, arms folded across his chest. "What do you want?" he sneered. "Here to make more accusations about a grieving father? I were just telling the telly people about you. Couldn't solve a fucking jigsaw, so you blame the family."

"I wanted to return this to Sadie," I said, walking towards him holding the ring out. "You'll recognize it, I think, Johnny. Though I dare say the last time you saw it Ratsy Donaghey was pulling it off the finger of a dead woman. Would I be right?"

Sadie stared incredulously, then turned to the neighbour, as if looking for him to share her sense of injustice. Johnny was not quite so blasé. He peered at the ring and a glimmer of recognition registered in his eyes. His tongue flicked nervously on his lips and he laughed just a little too loudly. "More bullshit, Devlin. There are no depths —"

"There's no statute of limitations, either,

Johnny. Doesn't it bother you that Angela died for this? Or that Donaghey set you up, you ignorant bastard?" My voice was rising now and I could feel my muscles begin to hum. Williams curled her hand around my upper arm.

"Best we speak inside, Mr Cashell, don't you think?" she said, guiding the Cashells into their house while I followed. Sadie quizzed her husband in whispers about what I had said.

I placed the picture of Mary Knox on the table and stood facing the Cashells. "We know the ring belonged to Mary Knox, Johnny. We suspect that Tony Donaghey took it from her at the time she disappeared. The ring has resurfaced now, twenty-five years later, and Donaghey has paid the price for it. Someone caught up with him in Bundoran a few weeks ago."

I watched Johnny Cashell attempt to keep his poker face in place. "Someone tied him up Johnny," I continued, "burnt him with lit cigarettes, shoved rags down his throat, and then cut his arms open from the wrist to the elbow and probably made him watch his blood run down his legs along with his piss." If nothing else, I had got their attention. "Now you can sit with your 'Fuck the Guards' expression, Johnny," I went on, years of frustration at people as stupid and intractable as Johnny Cashell finally boiling over, "but at some point in all that, Ratsy lived up to *his* name and gave out yours and Seamus Boyle's to whoever did him in. Hey presto, two weeks later, your innocent daughter is lying cold in a field, while you sit in the pub talking about what a big man you are. I'm sure you're very proud of your husband, Sadie. You got a real catch."

I knew I had gone too far. Sadie's eyes had welled and were red, while Johnny stared at me ashen-faced, a cigarette suspended midway to his mouth. The eldest Cashell girl, Christine, was standing in the hallway, staring at me. I immediately regretted what I had said. A sweat broke on my forehead and the room became unbearably close.

"I think you better wait outside, Inspector," Williams said, glaring at me.

"I'm . . . I'm sorry, Sadie. Jesus, Johnny — I'm sorry."

Sadie looked up at me with eyes empty of any feeling. "You're the lowest bastard I've ever met. Get out of my home," she said. She wiped a tear from her cheek and stared across the table at Williams until I left the kitchen.

■ ■ ■ ■

I stood in the tiny patch of garden at the front of the house and lit a cigarette, drawing as deeply as I could so that it would burn my lungs. I was aware of someone to my right and I turned to see Christine Cashell standing, her arms folded, a cigarette clenched in her right hand.

"Was there any need for that?" she asked, her face lacking the defiance she had presented when we last met. It was almost as though I had confirmed for her all that she believed. We may talk of equality and serving the community, but sometimes, despite ourselves, we treat people badly because we can, because we tell ourselves that we do it in the name of justice or virtue, or whatever excuse we use to hide the fact that we want to hurt someone, to get at them in any way we can to compensate for their total lack of respect for our job and all that we have sacrificed to do it.

"No," I said, seeing no point in sharing my thoughts with her. "I was out of line, Miss Cashell."

"Jesus, don't start calling me Miss Cashell. Christine'll do." She dragged on her cigarette and blew the smoke upwards, holding her face towards the strengthening sun. She sniffed. "Do you think it'll be enough for Mum to leave him?" she asked, without looking at me.

"Maybe. That wasn't my intention, Christine."

"I know. Still, clouds and silver linings, eh? You never know." She stood with one arm wrapped in front of her, the other one, which held her cigarette, hung at her side. She twisted the toe of one shoe into the grass. "Looks like you screwed up with McKelvey."

"Yep. Seems that way." I flicked my cigarette over the hedge in the vain hope that their nosey neighbour would still be lurking there.

"You were told she'd have nothing to do with him. She got into drugs. That was McKelvey's thing. They weren't going out."

"Who was she going out with, Christine?" I asked. "Muire mentioned Angela was going to see someone the night she died."

"Muire didn't know what was going on."

"About McKelvey?"

"You've McKelvey on the brain. Angie was going out with someone, but it wasn't McKelvey. In fact, it wasn't even a boy. Our Angie found herself a girlfriend before she died. Someone to support her habit."

"Who?"

"Some nurse called Yvonne, from Strabane."

"Yvonne Coyle?"

"Sounds about right, aye," Christine said, then turned at the sound of voices from inside. Her parents came out with Williams, who shook hands with each, nodded to me, and strode down towards the car. I smiled gently towards Christine, who replied with her eyes at the same instant that she set the rest of her face into its familiar expression of defiance against the world. I turned to apologize to her parents again, but they only looked at me, ushered Christine inside, and closed the door softly.

"Feeling better?" Williams asked when I got into the car. Then, before I could answer she continued, "Jesus, sir."

"Cashell is a criminal," I replied, a little haughtily.

"Not when you're talking about his daughter's death. He's still a father."

"Well, he shouldn't be. His other daughter was outside hoping this would finally force Sadie to leave him. It's hardly family life at its most idyllic, is it?"

"It's more than some of us have," she snapped, and I stopped arguing.

Neither of us spoke as Williams started up the car.

"What else did the girl say?" she asked finally.

I stared out the side window at the hedge-rows sliding past, the sunlight filtering through the thickets. "Not much of use. Says that McKelvey was a dead end, as if we hadn't worked that out. Seemed to suggest that Angela was a bit of a double-adapter."

"Meaning?" Williams said, glancing over at me.

"Meaning Christine seemed to think Angela was having a fling with Yvonne Coyle."

"Really. Should we bring her in?"

"Certainly worth taking a closer look, I suppose. Though having an affair, even a lesbian one, isn't a criminal offence. She already admitted that Angela stayed with her the night before she died. Said she went out with McKelvey on the night in question." Then I remembered something. "Although, now I think of it, she said she'd seen McKelvey on the Thursday night: in fact she was our only witness. What if she was lying?"

"Maybe we should bring her in, then."

"I'll ask Hendry. She's in his jurisdiction."

I paused. "What did the Cashells have to say about things?"

"Cashell admitted knowing Donaghey and Boyle in the late '70s. Said Donaghey managed a bar where he and Boyle worked as bouncers. Did the odd favour for him. That was it. Knew nothing about Knox or the ring. Or why someone would want to leave it on the body of his dead daughter."

"Did you believe him?" I asked.

"God, no. He was lying through his teeth. He seemed particularly uneasy when I told him that Knox had kids. He didn't seem to know. Though obviously he claimed it was nothing to him, since he didn't know the woman."

"Did you say Ratsy Donaghey was a manager of a bar?"

"Apparently so."

"That's worth taking a closer look at as well. Look, when we get back to the station, I want to call Hendry about Yvonne Coyle. Can you pull me anything you can find on Donaghey? Then I want you to start checking for this neighbour of Mary Knox, Joanne Duffy, living somewhere in Derry. I suspect she knows where the kids ended up."

"You think the kids are involved?"

"I don't know," I said, honestly, "but it's

the only thing we have for now."

As it transpired, I didn't get to carry out my plans quite as quickly as I had hoped, for when we returned to the station Mark Anderson was standing at the front desk, while Burgess tried desperately to shift him.

"Ah, Inspector Devlin," he shouted, the moment I came through the door. "A Mr Anderson here for you. Perhaps you'd be so kind as to assist him." Then he added under his breath, "And take the smell of pig shit out of my station."

Anderson was not for shifting. He took something from his pocket, a skein of brown velvet material darkened at the edges with crusted blood. He let it drop onto the main counter. "That were in my field, where that animal were shot."

"What has that to do with me?" I asked, my head spinning as I spoke. The rag of torn skin was both sickening and strangely pitiful.

"Powell won't give me the reward. He says that ain't no cat. He says that's part of a hound. Where's your dog?"

"He's at home, Mark. That's not part of a dog. That could be part of anything. Powell's just trying to renege on his part of the deal. Makes good TV offering rewards, so long as you don't have to follow it through."

Anderson eyed me suspiciously, his face puckered in concentration. He rubbed a callused fingertip along the white stubble of his chin. "All I know is that I ain't seen your dog since the hunt and nothing's been near my sheep since. If I find your dog's been hurt in some way, I got a right to put a bullet in him. Reward or not, I'll protect my sheep."

"And I'll protect my daughter's pet, Mark," I replied.

"Best thing for you to do is put a bullet in it yourself, before someone else has to," Anderson said and walked out.

Regardless of my annoyance at Anderson, I knew he was right about Frank. I resolved to take my gun home with me that night. I had decided when Penny was just a baby that I would not keep a gun in the house, and so it stayed in a special locker in the station. Guns are quite often a final option for Gardai; generally we do not carry them, as it seems to contravene the very name of An Garda Siochana — the Guardians of the Peace.

I went into the back lock-up, behind Costello's room, where the station safe was located. Above it was a strong box with a padlock. I opened it and removed my .38 revolver and a box of bullets, wrapped both in the oilcloth that had been around the gun, and tucked the parcel into my inside coat-pocket.

I phoned Strabane station and left a message for Hendry to call me. The desk sergeant assured me that Hendry would get back to me when he could. While I was on the phone, Williams came into the office and flopped onto the chair, a thick manila folder in her lap.

"Ratsy Donaghey, this is your life," she said. She placed the file on the table between us and we both read through it carefully.

Donaghey had first appeared on police files at the age of eleven, when he was caught stealing from a local shop whose owner wanted the matter dealt with seriously. He was arrested with some regularity from then on in, for drinking or vandalism or stealing. At fourteen he was sent to a borstal for nine months for beating up an elderly neighbour for the contents of her purse, which amounted to about thirteen euros nowadays. He was quiet for the duration of his stay there, but his name surfaced again afterwards.

His first adult arrest was for aggravated assault and GBH, when he beat the ex-boyfriend of a girl he was dating with a broken beer bottle and a brick until he was unconscious. The case went as far as court but, somehow, Ratsy got off with a suspended sentence despite his earlier record. I made a note of the date, deducing that the court records for it would be found in a newspaper from the period.

Forty minutes later my faith in librarians was repaid once more as we read the court report for the case. According to the papers from the time, Donaghey was shown leniency because of his important position in something called "IID" and his role as an ambassador for the area. The chairman of IID, Joseph Cauley, interceded on Ratsy's behalf, describing the attack as a single regrettable blemish on an otherwise impressive character. The magistrate at the time was Gordon Fullerton, who had since spent three years in jail himself, having being found guilty of taking bribes in a case over land ownership. As neither of us knew what IID was, we set off again to a building a little closer to home.

In the centre of Lifford, almost opposite the Garda station, is the Seat of Power, a museum dedicated to Lifford's history as the administrative centre of Donegal. The museum also houses the original courthouse and cells from the old jail and mental asylum. More importantly, however, the building houses a number of individuals who know more about Lifford and Donegal than is perhaps healthy. One such person is Mary Deeney. Mary is a woman in her late thirties with straight copper-tinted hair, which occasionally reveals glimpses of grey. She was able to give us the rundown on IID in fifteen minutes.

"Invest in Donegal," she explained, pushing her pink-framed glasses up the bridge of her nose, only for them to slide back down almost immediately. "One of these things set up in the '70s to try to bring bigger companies into Donegal. It actually had a few big successes in the late '70s, early '80s with a textile company and an IT firm. Offered incentives, tax breaks, grants and so on; performed feasibility studies; handled contracts for building. Folded up in 1984 — no, 1985 — when Cauley died. Possibly just as well, actually; rumour had it that the Fraud Squad was taking an interest in it by that stage."

"Do you remember a man by the name of Tony Donaghey being involved?" Williams asked. "I think he was quite important to it."

Mary thought about it as she absentmindedly twirled a few loose strands of her hair around her fingers. "No, the name doesn't mean anything. Of course, I'm the wrong person to be taking to. Tommy Powell's the man you'd really want to see."

"Why Powell?" I asked.

"Well he started it. IID was his brainchild. He raised millions through the Dail for it."

"We thought Cauley ran IID," Williams said, and I nodded agreement.

"Cauley ran it alright," Mary said, as if explaining something to very slow children, "but Powell *owned* it. Cauley was just a manager."

Williams and I stood outside the museum while I had a smoke. Across the street we could see Costello moving around in his office, his blinds pulled back to let in the December sun. At one point he walked over to the window and stared across at us, then moved into the shadows of his room again.

"So, what now?" I said.

"Try to track the kids, I suppose," Williams said. "And Coyle. What about Powell? Are you going to speak to him?"

"Maybe," I said. "But not quite yet. Costello said this morning about bringing the Investigation Bureau in on this."

"Are you going to?" Williams asked, looking a little surprised.

"No. But I think they can help us with one thing."

As well as the local Garda stations around the country, An Garda has a centralised Criminal Investigation Bureau which helps in serious-crime cases. It is just one, however, of a number of support systems. We had already called on the Water Unit. I decided that perhaps it was time to contact the Research Unit as well. The Research Unit does exactly what its name suggests. Over years it has collated information passed on from all the other strands of the Garda system and filed it for future reference. No other section of An Garda could access information on companies or national initiatives as quickly. Or so I hoped.

I returned to our office and phoned through to the Command and Control Centre in Harcourt Street in Dublin and asked to be transferred to Research. I was put through to an Officer Armstrong, and asked him to find whatever he could on Ratsy Donaghey in connection with IID. I decided not to mention Tommy Powell just yet, assuming that the name would turn up anyway once IID was researched. I also mentioned the rumour about the fraud investigation and the chairman, Joseph Cauley. Armstrong told me it might take a few days.

I then tried contacting Hendry again about Yvonne Coyle, but he was still not available. I sat in the storeroom, watching Williams scan phone directories and electoral registers for Derry in an attempt to locate Joanne Duffy, Mary Knox's friend. Then I sat beside Williams and helped her. After a number of false leads, three coffees and a shared tuna sandwich, we found her.

CHAPTER FOURTEEN

Monday, 30th December
Duffy had moved from Strabane to Derry in 1983, marrying a man called Edgar van Roost, a Belgian political analyst who was lecturing in Peace and Conflict Studies at a local university. They met at a political rally at which van Roost spoke, comparing the conflict in Northern Ireland with the conflict in the Middle East, while Duffy sold copies of *Socialist Worker* to an indifferent crowd.

They now lived in an area of Derry known as Foyle Springs, in a modest semi-detached house which required painting. However, inside, the house was far from what we had expected from a socialist. The plush-carpeted hallway, despite being quite narrow, was dominated by a huge chandelier which hung so low I had to walk around rather than under it.

Duffy had clearly aged gracefully, though,

perhaps aided by a little surgery, for her eyes were unnaturally free of wrinkles or laughter lines and her lips were full and perfectly pink. Her cheeks were accentuated with blusher and her hair was a steely blonde, set high in a bun.

She smoked a long, slim, brown cigarette, drawing lightly on it and releasing the smoke in a single puff, as if unaccustomed to smoking.

"I can't inhale," she explained, noting my curiosity, and gesturing vaguely with the cigarette, "because of my asthma. I shouldn't smoke at all, but I can't help it."

Williams nodded with understanding. "Ms Duffy, as I explained to you on the phone, we're trying to trace the family of Mary Knox."

Duffy nodded, her bun tottering on her head. "Mary, God rest her. Have you found her? Is that it?" She leaned forward a little in her seat as an indication of concern.

"No, Ms Duffy," I said. "We're re-examining her case. Do you have any idea what happened to her?"

"Oh, Mary's dead," Duffy said in a matter-of-fact tone. "Mary was dead the day she disappeared. I've always known that."

"How?" Williams asked, smiling uncertainly.

"You just do. We were very good friends. I would watch her children for her when she was . . . you know, when she was working." She broke the tip off her cigarette and laid the unsmoked half in the ashtray beside her. "Would you like to see her?" she asked, standing up before we had a chance to answer. She went over to a heavy mahogany cabinet in the corner of the room and opened it to reveal shelves packed with books and photo albums. Duffy flicked through one or two, then located the picture she wanted, removed it from the album and gave it to Williams, who looked at it and passed it to me. "That's her and the children," Duffy said, standing above me, her head tilted to see the picture in my hand.

The picture was clearly from the same batch as the one we had already seen. In the background, grey clouds had massed, but it did not detract from the sunny disposition of the three figures. Mary Knox was still sitting on the concrete steps to the beach, but in this shot her children were on either side of her. She had obviously been an attractive woman. A black swimsuit was visible through the large white T-shirt she wore. Her hands rested demurely on her bare knees, which were pressed together. Clearly visible on her left hand was the moonstone ring.

To her left was a boy of about eight, his blonde hair cut bowl-fashion. He wore nothing but green shorts. His ribs stood out a little through his skin, and he was grinning so much that his eyes were little more than slits. He had one arm around his mother's neck, the other jauntily resting on his hip. Small bruises were visible on his legs and shins.

On the other side of Mary Knox sat her daughter. She too smiled into the camera, but her body was closed, her hands clasped in front of her. She retained a tiny distance from her mother. Her face was thin and her skin light, contrasting with the darkness of her hair, which hung in curls around her face and shoulders. She was wearing a blue swimsuit with a beach towel around her shoulders like a shawl. Something about her expression was familiar and strangely sad. Perhaps it was just that I knew how this family would turn out.

"When was this taken?" I asked.

"Should be written on the back," Duffy replied. "Around Halloween, before she disappeared. The weather was beautiful for so late in the year and we all went to Bundoran for a day out. We had a great day." The dates certainly fitted with Costello's buying the ring.

"That's a nice ring she's wearing," I said. "Looks expensive."

"It was. Didn't stop it breaking, though. In fact on the way home that night she noticed one of the stones had fallen out. Had to send it back to be fixed."

"Where did she get it?" I asked, trying to make the question sound as casual as possible. Still Duffy viewed me with suspicion.

Finally she decided to answer. "I suppose you know anyway. Mary had a lot of men. Made a bit for herself on the back of it. One of her men bought it for her."

"Do you know who?" Williams asked.

"Someone with money. Someone important. One of the important people."

"What do you mean, 'one of'?" I asked.

"There were several," Duffy replied, and smiled coyly, as if to suggest she had gone as far as she could.

"Who were they?" Williams asked, reading my thoughts.

"I don't remember names. Some businessmen, important people. The owner of the Three Rivers Hotel was the biggest of them, though."

"Who was that?" I asked. The Three Rivers was derelict now, and had been for as long as I could recall.

"I don't remember," Duffy said, averting her eyes from my mine. "As for the children, I haven't seen them in twenty-five years."

"Do you know what happened to them?" Williams asked. Duffy looked at her and her face reddened. Her eyes began to moisten and she bit lightly at her lip in a vain attempt to stop the tears.

"I took them," she said, finally, as she wiped carefully at her tears. "I know it was wrong, but I took them to Dublin. Left them in an orphanage in South Circular Road — St Augustine's. I gave them a photograph each of their mother from that same batch you're looking at."

"That was it? You just decided to take them away, for no reason?" I asked incredulously. "What if she'd come back?"

"Someone told me to do it — someone who was very fond of Mary. He gave me money to take them. Gave me a hundred punts to give to them. He told me to do it."

"This man told you to give someone else's children away to an orphanage and you did it?" Williams's voice rose so quickly it cracked and she had to swallow back her last words.

"Yes. He told me she wouldn't be back. Said it would be better for the children if they were kept away from Strabane for a while. I thought they might be in some danger. I couldn't look after two children. I did what he said. It wasn't my fault," she said.

"Who was he, Ms Duffy? We need a name."

"I can't tell you."

"Ms Duffy," I said, as reasonably as possible. "Whoever told you to take those children away probably knows what happened to their mother. In fact, he may have been responsible for what happened to her. Now, please, who told you to take them?"

She looked from Williams to me and back again. Then she looked at her hands, clasped in her lap, and finally back at me, a note of defiance clear in her voice and in her eyes. "Costello, his name was," she said, then preened herself slightly in vindication at her reluctance to speak, as we struggled to make sense of what she had told us.

On the journey home, we tried to examine all the pieces of the case as objectively as possible. Costello had been having an affair with a prostitute with two children. She vanishes and he pays a neighbour to have the children taken to Dublin and left in an orphanage. Twenty-five years later a hood's daughter is killed and her body is dumped wearing the ring Costello had given to the prostitute.

"Costello seems to be fitting the frame more and more," Williams said grimly, though neither of us wanted to consider what would happen if we proved decisively that he was responsible for Knox's disappearance.

"It looks that way," I said resignedly, and decided on one final stalling measure. "The best thing for us to do is to try to locate those children: it's the only solution."

"Are you going to speak to him about this?" Williams asked, as we drove through Porthall, approaching Lifford from the east.

"Not yet," I said, though I knew that eventually I would have to face Costello, as surely as I would have to deal with Frank and the attacks on Anderson's livestock. "What are you doing now?" I asked.

The sky was darkening, although it was only just after four o'clock. The moon hung low in the sky, still little more than a sliver of ice. Three or four stars stood out in the navy sky; a bulkhead of cloud building in the west promised snow by morning. We had already overtaken a number of the local farmers out spreading salt on the minor roads.

"No plans. I'm meeting Jason later for

dinner. In fact, he's cooking."

"Fancy doing one last thing for us before you shoot home? Check out who owned the Three Rivers when Knox was about. I'll try this St Augustine's place and see what I can find."

The only St Augustine's in the book was a church, though the priest was able to give me a number for a nun named Sister Perpetua, who had worked in the orphanage until 1995 when it had closed down. Sister Perpetua, or Sister P as she announced herself on the phone, was a northerner and proved to be as voluble as her memory was remarkable.

"I remember the Knox children, Inspector, yes," she said, her Fermanagh accent mixed with just a hint of the shorter Dublin twang. "Sean and Aoibhinn." She pronounced the girl's name *Eveen.* "A sad case. They arrived with us just after New Year, 1979. I remember because we took some of the children to see His Holiness in Drogheda that year and the Knox children were among them. From what I recall they arrived with next to nothing. An aunt left them off, I think; gave them fifty punts, which was fairly generous in those days." Though still leaving her with fifty punts profit, I thought, for all her socialist beliefs.

She told me the story of the Knox children. It took many months for them to settle into their new home. Their accents, a mix of English and Northern Irish, stood out vividly against the southern brogue of their peers. The girl was subdued and unwilling to participate in any games. The boy was fiercely protective of her and got into more than one fight with people whom he felt were criticizing her. Finally, in September of that year, they were placed with two foster families, on either side of Dublin. The girl lasted four days, the boy less still. They had both cried inconsolably for the other, and, indeed, the boy had attacked his foster mother when she tried to put an arm round him to comfort him. And so they ended up back together again and became suddenly much more settled and content.

It was agreed by all the staff at St Augustine's that the children were precocious with regard to matters of the body. They frequently used coarse language and sexual slang. The boy had to be reprimanded several times for peeping up girls' skirts and, on one occasion, hiding in the girls' toilets.

The children were placed, unsuccessfully, with a number of foster homes, always returning happily to St Augustine's where, for perhaps the first time in their lives, they experienced some stability. Over the next number of years they drifted in and out of foster homes, running away from them before they had a chance to integrate fully. When Sean turned eighteen he left St Augustine's and rented a flat in Dublin, making money doing odd jobs on building sites. When the girl was seventeen she saw an advertisement for a Garda recruitment drive and entered training for An Garda when she turned eighteen.

"She was a beautiful girl, Inspector," Sister Perpetua said, "but troubled. I think she saw the Garda as a chance to join a new family. They were both awful lonely — apart from each other. So . . . what have they done?"

I was a bit taken aback, and she clearly sensed it. She continued, "They're not dead or you'd have said. I can only guess that one or both of them are in some sort of trouble. Am I right?"

"You should have been a policewoman," I said.

"I notice that you haven't answered my question."

"I know," I said, laughing.

"Fair enough," she replied. "I can take a

317

hint. Do me a favour, though? You'll think I'm some kind of wishy-washy liberal in this, but don't be judging those children too harshly. They were dealt a fairly stinking hand in life, do you see?"

I thanked Sister Perpetua and hung up the phone. I could not easily dismiss her parting words, though I reminded myself that I needed to reserve my sympathy, in the first instance, for Angela Cashell and Terry Boyle, more than anyone else. Still, regardless of where the brother had gone, I now knew that aged eighteen, in 1992, Aoibhinn Knox had joined the Garda.

I looked around the station for Williams but she was nowhere to be seen. It was nearing 5.30 p.m. and I wanted to catch the Garda training centre in Templemore before it closed. I dialled and asked to speak to the recruitment officer. A Sergeant O'Neill introduced himself and listened while I explained that I needed a name from the list of recruits for the 1992 recruitment drive and details of that person's postings. He told me that the college would have details only of the first posting of each trainee, if that would be of any help. He put me on hold but, after a few minutes of piped music, he returned and confirmed that Aoibhinn Knox had joined in that drive and had been stationed in Santry for her first posting.

I thanked him and dialled through to Santry, asking to be put through to the officer in charge of new recruits. Again I was put on hold, before, eventually, Superintendent Kate Mailey introduced herself.

"There can't be too many woman Supers, ma'am," I said, having introduced myself.

"Just the four of us, so far," she replied. "But we're doing the same work as the 170 men in our position."

"I don't doubt it ma'am," I said. "I need information about the posting of one of your starting officers."

"I know," she said. "The sergeant told me. I know everyone who's gone in and out of this station in the past twenty years or so. Who are you looking for?"

"A recruit called Aoibhinn Knox. She would have been posted to you in 1993 probably."

"I remember her — a lovely girl."

"That's quite a memory you have, ma'am," I said jokingly.

Her reply was deadpan. "I can't forget Knox. She married one of my own team members. He was killed in 1997 in a ballsed-up drugs bust. I never forget officers killed in duty."

"No, ma'am," I said. "Of course not. I'm sorry."

"Officer Knox left An Garda soon afterwards, Inspector, though by then she was called Coyle. Oh, and by the way — you're pronouncing her name wrong. She's not Eveen. Her name's *Yvonne:* Yvonne Coyle."

I bumped, quite literally, into Williams in the corridor, hardly able to tell her the news. On our way to the car, I tried Hendry's mobile. When he finally answered, I told him what I had learned and asked him to get to Coyle's home in Glennside and arrest her.

Williams drove across into Strabane and, while overtaking tractors and avoiding traffic islands, she relayed what she had discovered.

"The Three Rivers was originally owned by an Indian businessman named Hassem, but he sold up and developed a chain in the North. Now it gets kind of complicated here, because a consortium bought it over in 1974. Five local businessmen and budding entrepreneurs: Anthony McGonigle, Sean Morris, Gerard McLaughlin, Dermot Keavney and, leaving the best to last, a certain Thomas Powell Senior." She smiled over at me, proud of her efforts, then focused back on the road, someone's horn blaring as we sped past them on the inside.

"Shit! You're kidding me."

"I kid you not, boss. It keeps coming back to the same people. Looks like Knox had a thing going with both Powell and Costello."

"The question is, did one of them have her killed? And why?"

"You don't think Ratsy acted off his own bat?" Williams asked, risking a glance across at me.

"I don't see it. He'd no reason to. Someone paid him."

We pulled into Glennside, though there was no need for me to direct Williams to the house, for a PSNI car was already parked outside, its flickering blue lights intermittently illuminating the trees in Coyle's garden.

The house was in darkness. Two uniformed officers walked around the side, shining torches in the windows, using their gloved hands to minimize glare. I went up to the front window. Her furniture was still in its place but, as best I could see, all books, pictures and ornaments were gone.

Hendry came round the front of the house, alerted to our arrival by one of his officers.

"Come on round, Inspector. She's left the back door unlocked," he said grimly.

I felt a wave of nausea wash through me. A cold sweat broke on my skin, prickling on my arms under the heat of my overcoat. I was sure we would find her hanging inside, or lying on the floor, her body discoloured and stiff, or white and drained in a crimson bath. Yet none of those things awaited us. The house was simply deserted, the rooms stripped of anything personal. In the fridge, milk had begun to sour a little, smelling out the other contents. A bunch of bananas had begun to soften and blacken in the fruit bowl. A few circulars lay on the hall carpet behind the front door. The house itself was chilled from several days without heating.

Hendry sent the uniforms to canvass the neighbours while we sat in the kitchen and had a smoke. Hendry and Williams introduced themselves formally and exchanged pleasantries, then I explained the path that had led us to Coyle. I told Hendry about Cashell, Boyle and Donaghey, and my belief that Ratsy had abducted and killed Knox, with Cashell acting as an accomplice at worst or as driver at best, although we had no proof of this. I did not tell him my suspicions about Costello, nor the fact that Powell's name had appeared more than once during the investigation.

"So you think she killed Cashell and Boyle?" Hendry asked.

"Best guess," I said. "We know the ring belonged to her mother. We know she had a photograph of her mother wearing the ring. As a Garda officer she might have had access to a stolen items list." I knew this point was weak, but continued nonetheless. "She would have had a uniform. Angela Cashell was apparently having an affair with her. My guess is she realized that Donaghey had the ring. He's tortured and killed. Presumably he named the person or people involved in killing Knox, including Johnny Cashell and Seamus Boyle. Coyle befriends Cashell's daughter, who then ends up dead, wearing the ring Whitey McKelvey stole and which he claimed he'd sold to a girl in a bar. And I suspect our eyewitness who spotted Terry Boyle leaving the pub with a girl may well have their memory refreshed if we can show them a photograph of Coyle."

Forty minutes later the uniforms returned to say that none of the neighbours had seen Coyle in a week. In fact, the previous Tuesday was the last time she'd been seen; the day I had visited her. One of the neighbours recalled seeing a car which fitted the description of mine — minus the rust they described — around lunchtime. They also recalled that, later that night, a blue car with a southern registration had been parked outside Coyle's house until morning. The witness didn't see the car leave, though, as she went to listen to *Today* on Radio 4 in her "sun room" and when she looked out afterwards, the vehicle had gone.

"Best we can do is put out a 'be on the lookout' bulletin to all officers, north and south," Hendry said as we walked back out to our cars. "She can't stay hidden forever. Unless, of course, she's done what she set out to do and has vanished, like her mother, *into the night!*" This last phrase he said in a mock spooky voice and Williams laughed despite herself. Hendry flashed a grin at her, then winked at me, his face sober and drawn. I felt my phone vibrating in my pocket. Kathleen Boyle's number flashed on the screen. Her ex-husband had arrived, and wanted to talk.

We were sitting in Boyle's living room again, Seamus Boyle on a hard-backed chair, his elbows on his knees, his face buried in his hands. The man looked shattered. His hair, ginger mixed with grey, was unkempt and straggled over his forehead. His eyes were puffy and red, the whites bloodshot; his skin was sallow and smelt of sweat and cigarettes. Throughout our conversation he stuttered and stopped, catching his breath, swallowing back the pain that must have hit him the moment his wife confronted him about the photograph — the one now sitting on the coffee table in front of him. He must have suspected the identity of the subject when his wife mentioned the photograph. One glance had confirmed it, and he had erupted.

"I can't . . . I can't believe he's not here," Boyle spluttered, incomprehension creasing his face. "And for this. For one stupid fucking . . ." He turned away from us and faced the window, head tilted slightly, as if to stop his tears from running down his cheeks. He sniffed heavily several times, rubbing at his face with the palms of his hands.

"We know who she is, Mr Boyle," I said. "We need you to confirm what happened to her."

"She's dead," he said simply, still not looking at us. "She's dead and buried somewhere — I don't know where."

"Did you kill her, Mr Boyle?" Williams asked.

"I might as well have done," he said, looking at us both. "For what it's done. I might as well have."

It was neither confirmation nor denial. We waited in silence, until he composed himself and spoke again.

"I wasn't the one, if that's what you mean. But I knew about it. They told me afterwards. Got me to burn the clothes she was in."

"We think we know who you mean, Mr Boyle, but we need you to give us their names."

"Ratsy and Johnny Cashell. Ratsy did it. Cashell helped him get rid of the body, I think."

"Why did they kill her?" Williams asked.

"Orders. Someone paid them," he stated. "You see, Ratsy and us worked together as bouncers, when I was wee, like — in my twenties. But Ratsy had other things going on. We helped him out when he needed a bit of weight behind him. He was a skittery wee shite. He got us work; we had to help him out. Once you're in, you can't back out again. We were all responsible. Our Terry wasn't, though," he said, and we lost him again to whatever image of his son's last moments he was replaying in his mind. His entire body shuddered with his sobs, his tears spilling unchecked. Across the room from him, perched on the edge of an armchair, Kathleen Boyle watched him with a mixture of pity and horror on her face.

"Why do you think he did it?" Williams asked.

"Someone asked him to, I guess. Ratsy never did anything unless he was getting paid for it."

"Who do you think paid him?" I asked.

He shook his head, then took deep breaths again until his tears subsided. "Could have been anybody," he said, his lips bubbling.

"What's Ratsy's connection with IID?" Williams asked.

Terry Boyle's expression showed us that he had no idea what we were talking about. "Could have been anybody," he repeated, stunned by the direction his life had just taken.

Williams dropped me at the station, which was by now almost in darkness. We pull the blinds at night in the station but leave the lights on inside. That way, it appears to all who pass that the Gardai are ever watchful, when the truth is that we're usually all at home, bathing our kids or having a beer in front of the midweek movie.

I popped into our storeroom/office and lifted a pile of paperwork which had been left for me. I noticed on top of it a fax which I assumed to be from Templemore. There was also a note telling me that two officers from Sligo would be in the station the next day to begin an investigation into the death of Whitey McKelvey; I was to make myself available to be interviewed. I called Debbie and grovelled my excuse for being late for dinner, patted my jacket to make sure I had my gun, and locked up for the night.

As I turned the key in the front door to engage the deadbolt, I became aware of a figure standing watching me. The woman was heavy-set and squat, her blonde hair straggled in rats' tails. She had her hands buried deep in the pockets of a tweed overcoat which would have better suited a man.

"I know your face," she said. "You're that detective."

I smiled a little uncertainly and approached her. "That's right. Can I help you?"

"My name's McKelvey. Liam was my boy."

I stopped walking, caught completely off-guard. "Mrs McKelvey, I'm so sorry. I . . ."

"I saw you on TV, saying you'd visited the families of them what died. How come you didn't visit us? The travellers? Are we not good enough for you, officer?" she said, emphasizing the last word disdainfully.

"No, that's not true. I . . . I'd wanted to visit you. I . . . I felt guilty, I suppose. I'm sorry."

I walked towards her again, my arms outstretched, believing for a second that she would take my hands and, in doing so, would help alleviate the guilt I felt.

Instead, she coughed deep into her chest and spat a globule of phlegm at me before turning and walking off. I could not allow myself to wipe the spit from my face until I reached my car.

As I fumbled in my pockets for my keys, I heard, too late, the rush and rustle of clothing behind me. I spun into the blur of two male figures, arms raised, bearing down on me. Red and green lights exploded in my field of vision with the first blow and I fell forwards, face down, into the gutter. I could feel the dirt and grit scrape my face, taste the mud in my mouth. My head thudded, a sudden coldness spreading from the area where I had been hit. I put my hand to the back of my head and examined it in the dullness, though I could feel the stickiness of the blood without even looking. A glass bottle clattered to the ground beside me and I tried to shield my face with my arms as boots thudded off my trunk and legs. I felt one of the kicks connect with the back of my head, where the skull and spine meet; I felt the bones grating against each other and my stomach heaved. Eventually, the night sky started to spin, then everything slid into darkness.

Chapter Fifteen

Tuesday, 31st December

I drifted in and out of consciousness, and remembered seeing a pair of denim-clad legs running away. I thought I saw an old blue car drive past. The streetlamps danced about me, the snowfall, thick and oppressive, flickered on the edges of my vision. I dry-heaved onto the street, spitting my mouth clean. Finally, slipping and skidding off the pavement more than once, I managed to make it to the nearest row of houses, built on the site of the old asylum at the end of the road.

Forty minutes later, I lay in the Community Hospital next to Finnside Nursing Home, receiving medical attention for the second time that week. Not long after, Debbie arrived and put her arms around me, scolding me because, though she knew it was not my fault, she had no one else to scold.

The doctor told me she thought I should stay in overnight, just in case I had suffered concussion. I asked her for a dose of painkillers so I could go home. Eventually she relented, wrapping a thick bandage around my ribs, which were flowering with welts and bruises, reddish-purple like twilit snow clouds. As I pressed tentatively at my wounds I was reminded of Johnny Cashell and wondered whether the people who had left him in much the same condition were also responsible for the attack on me. After all, my attackers had struck just as I turned from McKelvey's mother. If they were indeed travellers, there would be little prospect of my ever catching them. They would vanish into the fold; pack up and shift to another site for a while. And in a way, I suppose, I believed that I had deserved it. The Catholic in me needed to be punished and, perhaps, now I could forgive myself.

Despite the painkillers, I could not sleep again that night, and fears played continually on my mind. I dozed uneasily until 3.30 a.m., waking several times to pull the blankets up off the ground or from around my feet. Debbie lay curled beside me, blissfully unaware. Even with the tablets, my head thudded dully when I lay down, and my arms and legs ached as though fatigued. Eventually, I got up.

Shane's breathing whistled slightly from the cot at the foot of the bed as he slept, arms outstretched, his face turned to the side and his lips pursed. I stood and watched him, wondering, not for the first time, how something so perfect and beautiful could have been the result of any process in which I was involved. And also not for the first time, I found myself resenting a job which kept me away from him and Penny and Debs as often as it did. I wondered if I had chosen the job precisely because it required me to immerse myself as much in it as in real life.

Unwilling to think too deeply about it, I took my cigarettes and lighter and went down to the kitchen for a smoke. I sat in the darkness at the open doorway, trying to blow my smoke outside, able to see clearly by the snow's reflected luminescence. The flakes were falling thick and steady now, a continual, hypnotic pattern.

When I was done, I opened the window to clear the smell of smoke and lit a candle. Then, for the want of anything else to do, I flicked through the documents I had taken from the station.

Sometime after my fourth excursion to

the back door for a smoke and my second cup of coffee, I read through the list of recruits who had joined Templemore Training College in 1992. Of the 150 names, twenty-seven were women. In the midst of all the names, Aoibhinn Knox's name appeared. It was not until I had scanned the list a second time, through sheer boredom, that I recognized a second name on the list and, all at once, I believed I knew for certain how Coyle had learned about the stolen-items list, and I suspected I knew who had helped her kill Donaghey and who had had sex with Cashell before dumping her body. And I realized who had been the driver of the blue car seen at her house. One of Aoibhinn Knox's colleagues in Templemore was Jason Holmes. And what did this mean for Coyle's brother, "Sean Knox"? Was he even involved? Or was Holmes her only accomplice? Could Holmes be her brother? Was it an assumed surname — a biting pun on his upbringing, perhaps? Or were such thoughts and plots the stuff of crime novels?

As I thought over the case, everything seemed to fall disconcertingly into place. Holmes had had inside knowledge of the course our enquiries had taken. He had identified McKelvey in the videotape, turning off the tape before the "McKelvey" in question would be seen entering the female toilets. He had taken statements from the bars. He had spent the night in the station when McKelvey had supposedly taken an overdose. Indeed, through his involvement with the drugs team in Dublin, I guessed, he'd have had access to the drugs which had killed both Cashell and McKelvey. He had made a point of reminding me of my assault on McKelvey and, in doing so, had implicated me in his own beating of the boy. I recalled McKelvey's broken finger. What if Holmes had forced the boy to take the Ecstacy tabs? Holmes was meant to have searched him, yet McKelvey still, apparently, managed to get the Es into his holding-cell. Most worryingly, Holmes had begun a relationship with Williams once he was removed from the murder team, and had presumably asked her about our findings and progress. He could have kept Coyle abreast of our every move, including the fact that we knew the connection with her mother. Suddenly, what I had considered to be poor police work on Holmes' part became more sinister.

I got dressed as quickly as I could and headed out into the snow. It took almost twenty minutes to drive to Holmes' house. When I got there, his car was nowhere to be seen. The house was in darkness, the blinds drawn back. I checked for my gun in my pocket and resolved to wait for Holmes to return. Then I thought better of it, guessing that he might be with Williams. I drove to her house, but only her own car sat in the driveway. Finally, as dawn cracked on the horizon, lending the falling snowflakes a purple tint, I drove back to the station to wait for support.

I was in the station at 8.30 a.m. in time to meet the postman. I flicked through the post as I entered the station, switching on the lights. I found three pieces of mail for myself and, dumping the rest on Burgess's desk, I went down into the murder room, stopping to fill the coffeemaker.

The first piece of mail I opened was from the General Registrar, containing the birth certificates of the two Knox children, which I had forgotten I'd requested. As I scanned the certificates, Tommy Powell's name appeared once again, this time listed as the father of Aoibhinn Knox.

At Finnside I waved to Mrs MacGowan as I passed her glass-walled office, but did not stop. From the corner of my eye I saw her standing up to get my attention, then scrabbling at something on her desk.

Powell was propped up in the bed, his wispy hair the yellow of dirty snow. His face had almost collapsed in on itself, the tissue paper of his skin nearly transparent. His jaw was slack, a line of saliva dribbling down his chin. I watched him silently for a few minutes, waiting to see if his bird-like chest would rise and fall, but there was no discernible movement.

For a second I thought he was dead, but then his eyes rolled spectrally in his skull and turned towards me, his head inclining ever so slightly on his pillow. All my anger and indignation waned at the sight of him. What sort of victory was it, I wondered, for an able-bodied man in his thirties to remind a dying pensioner of his youthful indiscretion? Yet I still felt a need for justice — for something. Powell was involved, somehow, in all of this. I needed to know what his role was.

I held the birth certificate close to his face, so close in fact that I could smell his rancid breath, the smell of something deeper than hunger, like stagnation.

"Did you know she was your daughter? Mary Knox's girl? Did she tell you?"

His eyes rolled away from me, his face tightening, and he stared at the flowered curtains which hung almost to the floor, blocking the brilliant glare of the frozen world outside.

"You let her go to an orphanage," I said. "Does your son know about this? Did you tell him about your prostitute, Mr Powell? And what about Ratsy Donaghey? What was the connection there? Did you know that he killed her?"

He still did not look at me, but I noticed the corners of his eyes redden and a tear slipped down his face. I was growing to realize the futility of my actions. Enraged by my embarrassment, I leaned in close to him.

"If I find you had anything to do with her death, Mr Powell, I can promise you, I'll nail you for it. Politician or not, all the money in the world won't save you."

I turned then to face Miriam Powell, who looked flushed from running. Behind her stood Mrs MacGowan, looking concerned.

"You really have no limits, Benedict, do you?" Miriam said, her face contorted in disgust.

"This is police business, Mrs Powell," I said.

"No, it's not, Ben. It's some sad . . . I don't know what. Some attempt to make up for your inadequacies," she spat.

"Your father-in-law had an affair with a

prostitute, Miriam. He fathered her child, then let that same child be put in an orphanage when his mistress vanished. She was killed by someone whom he employed. He may know something about her death. This is police business," I said, speaking loudly enough that Mrs MacGowan would hear, and I found some small measure of delight in watching her blanche as she realized that civilized people could commit evil acts with the same or even greater impunity than those outside her social circle.

"I'd like you to leave, please," Miriam said. "My husband will be in touch with you when he gets home." She looked away from me, but as I passed I heard her say, "I pity you Benedict, you're pathetic."

I looked at the side of her face, but she simply went over to her father-in-law and sat on the edge of his bed, holding the withered branch of his hand in hers, stroking the hair that clung to his scalp.

I left the home and went down to the river's edge and, as the snow thickened steadily, I looked over to the spot where Angela Cashell had died.

I had handled the case badly from the start. Now I was left with only this: somehow, either Powell or Costello was involved in the murder of Mary Knox. Costello had the motive of revenge or jealousy; he would certainly have known Donaghey and perhaps had some leverage over him as a policeman. Powell was Donaghey's boss in IID and the Three Rivers Hotel. In addition, Powell was Knox's lover, though it wasn't clear that he had any motive for killing her. In fact, I hadn't really considered the possibility until I stood looking at him. He had not looked after Knox's daughter, but that was not a crime.

Quietly, I apologized to Angela Cashell and Terry Boyle; perhaps the wind would carry my words to them. Yet neither the thought nor the words brought any respite from my feeling of failure. I seemed to be so close, and yet what would I achieve in arresting Yvonne Coyle, assuming she could be found? It would punish the murderer of Angela and Terry. But what of Mary Knox? Would she get justice?

I hardly heard the phone ringing in the car, and by the time I reached it, it had stopped. I recognized the missed-call number on the screen as the station and called back to Burgess, expecting something to be said about my visit to Powell. But I was wrong.

"Inspector! You're highly in demand this

morning. You realize you're meant to be in the station for an interview today over the McKelvey death. It's just I left you a note which I don't see on your desk, so I'm assuming you knew. Also, Officer Armstrong has been on the phone twice for you. Said he has information you said was important. Call him back, will you? I'm not your personal secretary!"

"Sure," I said. "Tell me, Burgess, is Williams in yet?"

"Yep. She's down in your 'office'."

"What about Costello?"

"He's going to the Boyle funeral. Would you like the station's full attendance list, Inspector?" Burgess laughed and hung up before I could ask anything more.

I sat back in the car with the heating on and phoned through to Garda Command and Control and asked to be put through to Research. Armstrong answered almost immediately.

"Inspector Devlin here. I wasn't expecting to hear from you so soon," I said, lighting another cigarette.

"Nor me, Inspector. But you gave me an easy one. There was a full case-file on IID so I didn't have much to do, and someone else must have requested it fairly recently. Do you want me to fax the notes to you?"

he asked, clearly enthused by such an easy piece of investigative work.

"That would be great. I'm not actually in the station at the moment. Can you summarize it for me?"

"Well, basically, IID was under a fraud investigation, as you said —"

"Right," I interrupted. "In the 1980s. Joseph Cauley."

"Well, yes and no," came the reply. "There was a fraud investigation then, but that was the second. There was an earlier one started in 1978 . . ." I lost all track of what Armstrong was saying. My hair felt as though it was standing on end, my skin goose-bumped in lumps so rigid I rubbed my arm to make them fall.

"Sorry, what was that?"

"Theft of government grants. Quite clever, apparently. Paper companies were formed to do consultation work for some big players who were looking to move to Donegal. They were directed to these consultancy groups by IID people; paid money up front. Then the consultation group would fold and the money would go with them. Over one million punts vanished."

"Any names?" I asked, although I already suspected the answer.

"The two you gave me: Donaghey and

342

Cauley. And a third named Thomas Powell. Is that *the* Thomas Powell?"

I could hardly form the words to speak. "What . . . why did it not go anywhere?"

"Not enough evidence, it seems. There was a potential witness. A prostitute who offered to give evidence in return for soliciting charges being dropped. But she disappeared; her and her family. The case couldn't be made that time, so it was left on ice until the mid-'80s when it was brought up again."

I did not even wait to say thanks. I cut the connection and called straight through to Burgess.

"Where's Costello?" I asked.

"He isn't here, I told you."

He became even more annoyed when I told him I wanted a car to pick up Jason Holmes on suspicion of murder.

"I need to check that, Inspector," he replied, all smugness gone.

"Just do it, Sergeant," I said. "Costello's not about. That makes me ranking officer. I want Holmes lifted ASAP. Put me through to Williams."

There was a buzz of static, then Williams spoke. "What's this about?" she snapped. "Are you fucking mad?"

"Caroline. I can't tell you everything yet,

343

but I think Holmes is involved in this — he was in Templemore with Yvonne Coyle; he may even be her brother. I think he knows more than he's let on. We have to bring in him."

"I'll phone him and ask him then, instead of sending someone out to arrest him. I mean for Christ's sake, Ben."

"No!" I said, louder than I'd intended. "Listen, Caroline, I'm sorry. I'll explain everything later. I need you to babysit Tommy Powell in Finnside."

"What?" I could understand her anger.

"Look, Powell is Yvonne Coyle's father. He was running a scam that Mary Knox knew about. She was going to testify against him; then she vanished. That puts him top of the suspect list. Which also makes him top of the target list. If Knox's children are going to go after anyone, it'll be him. I want you there in case they try anything," I explained. "Today is the anniversary of their mother's disappearance."

I cut the connection again and tried phoning Costello's house, but the line rang out. Frustrated, I gave up and slid and skidded my way back out onto the main road, stopping several times to wipe snow off the windscreen which the wipers failed to dislodge.

It took me almost thirty minutes to manoeuvre my way to Costello's house. Before I reached the front door I knew something was amiss — no smoke curled up from the chimney, and the curtains had not been drawn. I slipped on the front path, landing on my tailbone and reawakening the searing pain in my ribcage. With some difficulty, I balanced myself, wiping the snow from the back of my coat. I rang the doorbell several times and then tried the door. It was unlocked.

I went into the house, knocking the snow from my boots, and called out. "Sir? Mrs Costello?" My voice carried through the cold of the house, but did not get a reply. I moved down the hallway and pushed open the door into the living room.

Emily Costello lay in front of the fireplace. The purple-red of her headwound stood out against the soft white wisps of her hair. She lay curled on the floor in her nightgown. Her eyes were still open, though they had begun to turn cloudy. Her hands seemed locked together, raised slightly towards her face. Strangely, even in death, her expression was soft and kindly. Beside her lay a poker, the blackened end shiny with congealed blood.

Costello was lying on the kitchen floor,

weeping uncontrollably. There was a telephone in his hand, but I noticed that the wire leading to the wall had been cut.

He looked up at me in bewilderment. "She's gone, Ben," he said. "My Kate's gone."

I checked each room, one by one, slowly making my way around the house. When I was satisfied that neither Emily's killer, nor Kate Costello, were in the house, I used my mobile to call Burgess, requesting support. While I was on the line I asked about Holmes.

"Your sergeant has just left here. Her words were something along the lines of, 'I'll rip his fucking throat out.' "

"Poor Holmes," I said.

"She was talking about you. They haven't found *him* yet."

Costello had crawled back to his wife. He sat on the living-room floor, cradling her in his arms, her blood clotted and thick against his stomach, his breath rattling in his chest.

"I just came back and found her. Forgot my glasses. Just came back for my glasses," he said, then seemed to panic. He patted his pockets, his shirt, his legs, searching for them. "No . . . I forgot them. I came back and . . . and Kate's gone . . . and . . ." He did not, could not, finish the sentence. I had been wrong. Knox wasn't going after Costello. She was going after his children.

I was on my way out of the house when I found the photograph of Mary Knox that her children had left behind, sitting on the hall table in front of a vase of white roses.

I asked myself why they hadn't killed Kate Costello here, in her house. Taking her away suggested that she was still alive, that she was being held somewhere. But I could not think where. And then I realised again the significance of the date: New Year's Eve. The date Knox had disappeared. It could be no coincidence that Kate was taken on this date. And if they chose the date of her death on which to enact their final plan, perhaps the Knox children had also chosen the place of her death. It was tenuous, but I had nothing else to follow, nowhere else to look. If, indeed, they had taken her to Mary Knox's final resting place, it meant that Ratsy had admitted where he had dumped her body. There was only one other person who would know.

Cashell answered the door in his boxer shorts and a T-shirt, squinting against the glare of the snow. His face was drawn, his skin the colour of ash.

"What?" he asked, leaning against the

door jamb so that I was left standing in the falling snow.

"Where did you dump the body? Mary Knox's?"

"Piss off, Devlin," Cashell said, pulling the door behind him as he walked back into his house.

I stuck my foot against the jamb, holding the door ajar, then pushed my way in. "I know what happened, Johnny. I know Powell ordered Ratsy Donaghey to kill her. My guess is you were just a driver. Maybe you didn't even know what was happening; I . . . I don't give a shit. But four people have died in the past weeks over this, and one more will now if you don't help me." He stood looking at me pleading in his hallway, as he might consider a drunk begging for change in the street. "Please, tell me where you dumped the body. Please."

"Have a bad night, Inspector?" he asked.

"What?"

"You look a little worse for wear. Bit of a headache?" Cashell sneered, snorting as he turned and walked away. I felt my hand reach instinctively into my coat pocket for my gun, my fingers tightening around the grip.

"Borderland," a voice above me said.

Cashell spun around, his teeth bared like

an animal. "Shut up!" he hissed. But Sadie Cashell was walking slowly down the stairs now, ignoring her husband, whose foolishness and pride had cost her her daughter.

"Borderland," she repeated, looking only at Cashell. "It's too late, Johnny. Too much has happened." Then she turned to me. "Borderland. That's where Johnny was working. The Three Rivers Hotel. Borderland was a new disco hall they built around the time she vanished. They threw her body in with the foundations. I washed the blood and cement off his trousers," she explained. She stood halfway down the stairs now, and as she spoke something inside her seemed to be extinguished. With the slightest slump of her shoulders, Sadie Cashell seemed to age by twenty years.

"You stupid bitch!" Cashell roared at her, standing in the doorway of the kitchen, a pint of milk in his hand. "You useless fucking bitch."

I removed the gun from my pocket and with preternatural calmness, levelled it at Johnny Cashell. His jaw gaped open and he dropped the milk onto the linoleum floor, the white liquid stippling his legs.

"Don't," I said. "Don't, Johnny. If I come back here and something has happened to Sadie, I will kill you. Understand that. I won't waste time on kickings or petrol, I will gladly put a bullet through your fucking heart."

Then I backed down the hallway and pushed through the doorway, back out into the snow.

The roads were deserted, save for farmers shifting hay between barns and fields. It took me ten minutes to get to the Three Rivers. On the way, I radioed through to Burgess in the station and asked for support at the hotel. I also asked about Holmes and was disappointed to hear that he had still not been found. It meant that Yvonne Coyle might still have an accomplice. That was if she was still in the area and supposing that Kate Costello was still alive.

Just as I negotiated the final twist in the road, my phone rang. I recognized the number as Williams.

"You spineless prick!" she snapped as soon as I answered. "If you think I'm not capable, tell me yourself."

"What?"

"First you send me to babysit a pensioner, then you send someone down to give me a hand. How dare you!"

"What are you talking about?" I snapped.

"Harvey. I'm sitting here in my car, watching him going inside. Do you not think I'm capable of sitting here myself?"

"I didn't send Harvey down there, Caroline," I explained. "Why aren't you inside, with Powell?"

"His daughter-in-law chased me out. I'm sitting outside, watching. Harvey arrived a few minutes ago. He's just gone in." Her tone changed. "I thought maybe you'd sent him to keep an eye on me."

"For Christ's sake, Caroline, I sent you there because I trust you. Go in and see what Harvey's doing," I said, then thought better of it. "In fact, leave him in there and get over to the Three Rivers. I think that's where they are."

There was a period of silence, long enough for me to wonder if my connection had been broken. Then Williams spoke: "Sorry, sir," she said.

"Later, Caroline."

"Yes, sir."

The Three Rivers emerged out of the snow, skeletal and exposed. The windows had long since been smashed, boarded up and ripped open again. I drove up to the front of the hotel and got out of the car. I could just about make out the faintest tracks of tyres leading around the side of the building, though the snow was falling so thickly it was impossible to say how long ago they had been made. Returning to the car I followed the tracks carefully, the snow cracking under the wheels.

I slid to a halt and checked to ensure I had my gun. Treading carefully, I reached a side entrance where I could make out more tyre tracks gradually disappearing under the snow. I approached the side of the hotel. Inside, the wallpaper was falling off and pieces fluttered in the wind like strips of flayed skin. On the exposed walls, graffiti was scrawled on top of the pink paint which someone had once applied as an undercoat.

The carpet was still intact, though it was almost black, matted with dirt and sodden, so that, with each step, water welled up around my feet and my shoes squelched loudly. My eyes were just growing accustomed to the dimness when I turned a corner and walked into a patch of still grey light seeping in through a hole in the ceiling. Through it, stray flakes of snow pirouetted down.

The musty smell of mice and another sharper, cleaner smell were carried on the wind. Beer cans, cigarette packets, used condoms, all lay discarded along the corridors. As I passed each doorway, I jerked my head in and scanned the room with my .38 drawn and cocked.

Finally I came into a central reception area. In the corner was the door to what had once been a cloakroom. I could hear someone shifting in the darkness. I thought I could see a movement.

"Sean? Yvonne?" I shouted. "Yvonne, this is Inspector Devlin. I know you're here. We're all around you, Yvonne. It's over, love. Why not come on out?"

I waited, holding my breath, straining in the half-light to see if anyone would appear. I was about to call out again when I saw the diminutive figure of Yvonne Coyle step out of the shadows of the room, Kate Costello beside her, a Garda revolver pressed against her side. Further back, to her left, I could make out the outline of a man, sitting on the floor, his back against the wall, though it was too dark for me to see who it was.

"It's over, Yvonne," I said, slipping my gun into my pocket. "Where's Holmes?"

"Who?" she said.

"Jason Holmes."

"I have no idea what you're talking about, Inspector. Please. Throw your gun on the floor."

"I don't carry a gun," I said, stretching out my arms.

"I know that's not true. You took one out of your station the other night. Please. Throw your gun on the floor. Now," she added, nudging Kate with her own pistol.

"Where's your brother, Yvonne?" I asked, glancing around in the semi-darkness in case he was hiding. But I began to suspect that I knew where he was. "He's not here, is he?"

"Lie down on the ground, Inspector," Yvonne said. "Please don't make me hurt you."

The figure slumped against the wall behind Coyle looked up. "Is that you, Devlin?" I realized that it was Thomas Powell.

"You don't know who did it, yet, do you?" I said, realizing the significance of both Powell and Kate Costello being here. "You don't know who killed your mother. Ratsy was given away by the ring; I'm guessing he named Cashell and Boyle. But . . . you don't know who gave the order."

"Which is where you can help me, Inspector," Yvonne said through gritted teeth. "Now lie down on the fucking ground."

"Where's your brother, Yvonne? Did he kill Emily Costello? Murder an old woman?"

I heard Kate whimper.

"Keep talking, Inspector," Yvonne said, "and I'll shoot this useless bitch anyway."

Again she prodded Kate with her gun. The girl's eyes flashed with panic, her face drawn in terror.

"You've got the wrong person, Yvonne," I said, as I walked slowly towards her. "The rest of the station is outside now." I could make out Powell's outline, shaking his head. "You got the wrong person. Costello didn't kill your mother. I'm guessing Donaghey told you that, but he lied."

"Then you have the chance to put the record straight, Inspector. One of these two has to die for what was done. You choose. You choose who should live."

"I can't do that, Yvonne," I said, reaching slowly into my coat pocket for my pistol. "You know I can't do that."

"Throw your gun on the floor, Inspector," Yvonne said. Then I heard her click the barrel of her gun into place and Kate Costello screamed. I took out my gun and threw it away from me, my hands raised in appeasement.

"It was Costello," Powell shouted suddenly. "My father told me. We're family, for fuck's sake," he said, his voice cracking into sobs.

"That's not true," I said. "I don't know who did it, Yvonne. Don't you think enough people have died already?"

She moved towards me a little, the gun still held in her hand. "Why would Powell have killed my mother? How do you know it wasn't this . . ." she gestured towards Costello, unable to sum up a word vicious enough to describe her or her father.

"Your mother knew about some fraud he was running on these big companies he was bringing into Donegal. She went to the police. Donaghey worked for Powell. Donaghey lied to you, though. You can't believe anything he said. Yvonne, where's your brother? Please."

"He's finishing things off. Going to see our father."

And then I knew. "It's fucking Harvey, isn't it?" I said, desperately.

She did not answer. The room lit up as if caught in the flash of a camera, and a sound like ice cracking in my eardrum echoed through the building. In that moment of intense light, Powell's face was lit up and I saw his expression of disbelief as a single horsetail of blood spurted from his body onto the wall behind.

Kate Costello screamed hysterically now, while Coyle struggled to keep hold of her.

I scrambled over to the slumped body, smelt the foulness under the cordite. The wetness of the carpet soaked up through my knees. But Powell was beyond help. "Please stop this, Yvonne," I managed to stutter.

She released Kate now, who huddled against the wall, trying to make herself as small as possible, her body heaving with sobs.

"I'm sorry you got involved, Inspector — really I am." Yvonne's voice assumed a singsong quality, as if removed from the squalor and the dead bodies surrounding her. "You remind me of my husband, you know. He's dead, too."

I nodded. "I know, Yvonne. Look, it's not too late. We can sort something out." I knew, though, as I spoke, that my words were meaningless, born from desperation.

"Can we?" She smiled at me, squatting with her gun inches from my skull, her fingers lightly brushing my face and lips. "I don't think so," she said, with the melancholy of a departing lover. "Much as I'd like to leave you here alive, Inspector, I know that you wouldn't let it go. Would you?"

"My name's Benedict," I said. "Ben."

I wanted to say more to her, to tell her that at some level I understood what she had done. I wanted to tell her that things could be salvaged, even though I knew that they were far beyond that point. "I spoke to Sister Perpetua," I said, a little too late.

We both heard the sound of voices approaching along one of the darkened corridors. I thought I recognized Williams's voice, as ephemeral as those inside your head when you are on the cusp of sleep. Coyle turned suddenly and strode over to where Kate Costello lay in a ball on the floor. I heard another sharp crack of the pistol, while I scrabbled about for my own weapon. As the shot hit Costello, I heard a soft grunting, then the sucking noise her body made as she tried to breathe.

I heard Williams shouting now, and other voices, getting nearer. I tried to call out, but my mouth was dry and seized and the words died in my throat. Yvonne Coyle stood above me, her gun in her hands.

"I'm sorry, Inspector," she said, then raised the gun.

I would like to say that I looked death squarely in the face. I would like to say that I faced it bravely. But I did not. Instead I squeezed my eyes tight shut, already flinching as I waited for the shot, the searing heat of the bullet entering my body. In that last moment, it was not my life that flashed before my eyes, despite what people popularly claim. Rather, I grew intensely sad at the thought that I would never again see Penny smile, nor ever feel the softness of my son's hand as he touched my face while I bottle-fed him. I would not see again my wife, my rock, Debbie, whose touch alone conveyed more generosity of spirit than I could ever express. I felt tears burst from me, and then I heard the shot.

When I opened my eyes, Williams and three uniforms were running up the corridor towards us, torchlights bouncing along the walls and ceiling. Beside me, her face as close as a lover's, her final breath dying on her lips like a parting kiss, lay Yvonne Coyle, her short blonde hair matted with her blood, her body still twitching. Part of her temple was missing, the white bone of her skull just visible amongst the blood. For a second I saw the ghost of something tug at the corners of her mouth, nothing more than a fleeting shadow, and then all was still.

I reached over and placed my fingers against her face. Her skin was still warm and soft. I laid the palm of my hand flat against her cheek and whispered an Act of Contrition for her soul. In spite of myself, in sympathy for all that had happened to drive her to this, I leaned over and placed a single, light kiss on her forehead. Her skin yielded under my touch even as her colour faded.

CHAPTER SIXTEEN

Tuesday, 31st December

Tommy Powell Sr had never really been in danger. Harvey had simply gone to Finnside to deliver the photograph of his mother. Unaware that everything was unravelling in the Three Rivers, he had quietly slipped out again. By then, Williams had left a note on his windshield telling him she had gone to the hotel to provide backup. Needless to say, he did not follow — if he had, he would only have seen his sister being carried out of the derelict building in a black body-bag, like the one Angela Cashell had been wrapped in just a fortnight previous. It was assumed that he had fled across the border, and patrols were set up, north and south.

It transpired that I could have learnt his identity earlier that day from Armstrong. He had told me the IID file had recently been requested. If I had only asked, I would have been told that it was Harvey who had requested it and I could have warned Williams to arrest him when she saw him going into Finnside. On the other hand, had that happened, she would not have made it to the Three Rivers — and how different things might have been then.

Kate Costello was taken to hospital in Letterkenny where she underwent emergency surgery. Jason Holmes reappeared just after one o'clock and was immediately arrested, though by that time I already knew that he had nothing to do with Yvonne Coyle or the killings. He did, however, confess to having a girlfriend over the border, with whom he had spent the night; someone he had met during one of his official canvassing visits to the clubs in Strabane. It transpired that he had been seeing her for almost the duration of his relationship with Caroline Williams. Williams sat in the interview room opposite him, listened to his confession silently, then went home.

Yet again, I found myself in hospital being attended by the same harried registrar who had treated me the night before. This time she insisted that I stay in overnight, and Debbie agreed. Reluctantly, I sat alone and waited while Debbie went home to get me an overnight bag and to collect the kids from her mother.

By 7.30 p.m. she had still not returned. I phoned the house several times and got no reply. I lifted my clothes, which were still dirty and damp, and checked that my pistol was in my coat, having retrieved it from the Three Rivers when the SOCO team had finished. Then, as unobtrusively as possible, I sneaked out, avoiding the nurses who were under orders to keep me confined to bed.

I managed to snag a taxi at the bus stop ahead of a group of four revellers, replete with party hats and champagne bottles, celebrating the New Year. The village looked heartachingly picturesque, yet I could not shake the sense of emptiness with which the day's events had left me, nor the growing doubts about my family's safety. I tried phoning the station, but there was no answer and I guessed that those who weren't looking for Harvey had gone home for the festivities.

The snow was falling faster now, leaving the hills bright. Both our village and Strabane were haloed with the reflected orange glow of the streetlamps. All around us, the world was white and crisp and cold. As the driver attempted the final incline up the hill towards my house, the car slid on the road, turning at a ninety-degree angle. He tried as best he could to correct our position and make the hill again, but this time the car would not move while he accelerated and, when he stopped, began to slide down towards the level again. Finally, the driver admitted defeat and told me he could take me no further.

As he manoeuvred his way back onto the main road, I began to trudge up the hill. I attempted to run but the snow was too thick and my body too sore to make much headway. I should probably have considered conserving my strength, but I had a father's shortsightedness and the only thought in my mind was the possibility that my children were in danger.

When I was perhaps a quarter of a mile from my house, I heard the sound of an engine shuddering through the gently falling snow. A single weak light sparkled through the haze and the lumbering outline of a tractor appeared. I waved my arms, shouting for the driver to stop, a new hope flickering in my chest against the rawness of the winter wind on my lungs. Then, as the silhouette took form and substance, I saw Mark Anderson, perched high up in the cab of his old Ford. He slowed as he drew level with me and I called to him for help. He laughed, spat out the open window, then shunted into gear again and drove on, skittering snow over me.

I screamed profanities in his wake, and pulled my pistol from my jacket, but it was an empty gesture. My screams, such as they were, were blanketed by the snow.

I struggled onward, my ribcage feeling as if it would explode, my head throbbing. At one point I took a fit of coughing so hard that I spat blood onto the snow. Then, amongst the whispering of the snowfall, I heard a familiar yelping which I recognized as Frank's and I realized how close I was to home. As his barking continued I also had to acknowledge that Debbie would have brought him into the house by now, had she been able. I tried in vain to disregard what scene would be waiting for me when I finally reached my house.

The house was in darkness when I finally got there, yet I could see thin skeins of smoke drifting from the chimney. I went around the back of the house, where Frank sat on the doorstep, his bandages bright against the brown of his fur. He whimpered slightly and limped towards me, his eyes mournful. His coat was matted and heavy with moisture; he had clearly been outside for some time.

I opened the back door as softly as I

could. Any element of surprise was lost, though, for Frank shoved his way through my legs and bolted into the kitchen, thudding against the chairs with enough force to knock one over. Almost immediately I heard Penny scream, a shout muffled quickly, and I knew that she, at least, was alive. I also knew that Harvey was here — waiting for me.

Frank scrabbled at the door to the living room. Underneath it, I could see the flickering of the fire. I could wait for back-up, but it would simply turn this into a situation from which my family had no chance of escape. Besides, I couldn't stand out here, waiting for someone to help. I pushed the door open with my foot, my gun in my hand.

Debbie and Shane were sitting on the sofa, Shane squirming restlessly. Debbie had clearly been crying, her eyes wide and red.

Harvey was sitting in the armchair closest to the fire, Penny held in front of him as a shield. His gun was held by her head, though it was pointing at me. When he saw my pistol, he held the gun tight against her skin, her beautiful soft skin. Frank, who had run to Debbie, now turned his attention to Harvey, growling and baring his teeth.

"Drop the gun, Devlin," Harvey said, his own gun steady.

"Give it up, John. I'm not going to let you out of here, you must know that," I said, though the quaver in my voice revealed my lack of conviction.

Frank barked, while Debbie tried to pull at his collar to restrain him. Harvey's attention flickered towards the dog, then back to me.

"Drop it," he snapped.

"Let Penny go," I said, inching closer to him.

Frank barked again, then twisted and tugged so hard that his collar slipped over his ears and he lunged towards Harvey. In turn Harvey kicked out at the him. Penny, seemingly more concerned about Frank than herself, flailed against Harvey and slid off his knee onto the hearth. I fired one shot, indiscriminately, while I grabbed at Penny. The edge of her dress was burning when I lifted her away, and I thumped at the flames with my bandaged hand until they were smothered.

She scrabbled into my arms, sobbing. When I looked up, Harvey lay sprawled in my armchair, a single small bullet-hole in his left cheek, his eyes wide with disbelief. I did not feel sorrow for him, as I had with Yvonne. I did not even close his eyes when he exhaled his final, weak sigh. I simply gathered my family and we stood outside while we waited for the Guards to arrive. I hoped the snow would fall thickly enough to bury all transgressions and make the world fresh and clean with the dawn.

EPILOGUE

20th March 2003

In the days that followed, and in my absence, the NCIB were drafted in to piece together what had happened. They eventually discovered that, having fled her house in Strabane, Yvonne had joined her brother in a rented farmhouse in Ballindrait.

Presumably, Sean Knox, or John Harvey as he had become, recognized the ring belonging to his mother on the list of stolen goods he had been given to check. Perhaps he had waited years for some sign of her life — and death — to emerge. Or perhaps it simply happened unexpectedly, setting in motion a chain of events which would culminate in the Three Rivers Hotel and, later, in my own home. Either way, once he got a hit in the second-hand jewellers, it mustn't have been too hard for him to identify Whitey McKelvey from the description given of a young traveller boy with big ears and hair so blond it was almost white.

Working backwards, they traced Ratsy Donaghey to Bundoran and, there, killed him, having established at least that Johnny Cashell and Seamus Boyle had aided him in their mother's murder.

Yvonne had begun a friendship and ultimately a relationship with Angela Cashell, another woman's arms presumably the perfect refuge from a voyeuristic father and a drug-pushing boyfriend like McKelvey. Using McKelvey as their fall-guy, Yvonne and her brother drugged Cashell. It can only be assumed that Harvey then had sex with her before she died and that Yvonne knelt on her chest as the life drained from her.

Later, Yvonne would pick up Terry Boyle, out for a celebratory pint on his return from university. She directed him to a lay-by on Gallows Lane and Harvey followed. The fact that Boyle's window had apparently been wound down at the time of his death suggested that Harvey had approached Boyle's car in uniform.

It was assumed that Ratsy Donaghey had told them something about Costello's involvement with their mother. Either that, or Joanne Duffy had told them something — though she denied having had any contact with them since she had abandoned them in Dublin twenty-five years previous.

However they learnt of his involvement, the outcome remained the same: on the morning of New Year's Eve, they broke into Costello's house. One of them, probably Harvey, hit Emily with a poker, though they may not have intended to kill her. Then they took Kate Costello to the Three Rivers. At the same time, Yvonne managed to lure Thomas Powell there. It transpired that Miriam was correct in her suspicion that her husband was having an affair with a nurse. Again, it was assumed that Ratsy had named Powell Sr as he died. In each case, they decided on transferring the punishment for the sins of the father onto the children. Harvey went to Finnside to deliver the photograph of Mary Knox, which was found amongst a pile of Christmas cards lying on Powell's bedside cabinet later that day.

Finally, they waited for me to find them and make their decision for them with regard to whether Costello's or Powell's child should die. I was to be their arbitrator and become complicit in their plan. In the end, Yvonne shot Powell, then Kate Costello, and finally herself. And her revenge was complete. Her brother, however, with no one else left to blame, turned to my family.

I was interviewed as part of the investigation into the death of Liam McKelvey. During the interview I admitted to my attack on the boy and accepted responsibility for the various breaks in procedure I had made during the preceding weeks. I was suspended with pay for two weeks for negligence. I have not yet decided if I will make the break permanent. Jason Holmes was likewise suspended for his role in the McKelvey affair. But someone higher up than either of us had evidently decided that it was better to pin the whole lot on Harvey rather than tarnish the reputation of the force further by implicating the man who had solved the murders of Angela Cashell, Terry Boyle, Emily Costello, Thomas Powell and, at last, Mary Knox.

I met Christine Cashell several days later. She was serving in the local chemist's, where I was buying painkillers. She smiled at me when I approached the counter. I asked her how her parents were doing.

"Mum's great. Never better," she said. "I couldn't tell you about Dad. He and Mum had a row about something and she threw him out. Again," she added, rolling her eyes in mock exasperation.

"Will he be back?" I asked, suspecting that her father's departure had affected her more deeply than she was prepared to admit.

"Maybe," she shrugged.

Kate Costello was in hospital for several days. On 4th January, Debbie drove me to Letterkenny General to visit her. Afterwards, I sat in the hospital café with her father for twenty-five minutes, talking of the weather, which had begun to improve. I asked about Emily and he told me that the funeral arrangements were being postponed until Kate was out of hospital. He did not mention the events in the hotel until I got up to leave.

"Thanks, Benedict," he said, as I signalled my intention to go.

"No problem. Doing my job, sir."

"No. Thanks for what you told her. Kate told me. About Powell. I don't know how you made that up on the spur of the moment; it was . . . it was inspired." He smiled lightly, almost apologetically. "I won't forget it; it goes no further than us."

For a moment I wanted to pursue what he had said, to tease out the meaning and be sure I understood it. I looked at him, alone now without his wife, and wondered what I could say. In the end, I simply straightened up, pulled my coat around me, and walked down the echoing corridor, out into the freshening air.

The following day, I visited Thomas Powell in Finnside. I sat in the room, a bunch of flowers in my hand, and watched him sleep. He had suffered another stroke, late on the evening he was told of his son's death, and had hardly recovered any strength since. The blankets on his bed were so heavy that they disguised the movement of his ribcage as he breathed. His room smelt stale and cold, like a crypt. The only movement discernible in the man was a continual twitching of his eyelids which, though shut, fluttered endlessly.

Miriam Powell walked into the room just before I left. Seeing me sitting beside the bed, she went and stood outside, her back against the wall, and waited for me to leave. As I did so, she passed me, so closely that my hand accidentally touched the exposed skin of her arm. I inhaled the air in her wake, but could not smell the scent of coconut. She wore a new, stronger perfume. I believe she intends to continue building on the political career her late husband began.

■ ■ ■ ■

Early on the morning of 3rd March, unable to sleep, I sat in the kitchen watching with horrified fascination as the US policy of "shock and awe" was finally unveiled and Baghdad burned. Eventually, sick to the stomach, I flicked off the TV and sat in the kitchen in darkness, listening to the noise of thaw-water dripping from the eaves outside. I gradually became aware that Frank was whining and yelping from the shed. The thought of what had to be done had lain heavy on my mind since New Year and I knew that the stay of execution he had received was almost over. I ate a bowl of cereal slowly. Then I loaded one bullet in my gun, and rolled up an old towel with which to muffle the shot.

Unlocking the back door, I stepped out into the coldness of the dawn. All around me was the sound of water dripping, from the eaves of the house, from the hedge and trees.

Frank had somehow escaped from the shed once again. Now he lay at the back door of the house, his body flat against the ground, the fur on his back raised, his single long ear under his snout. But he was not looking at me. I followed his gaze to his food dish, and there, in the shadows of the cherry tree near the top of the garden, stood a wild cat.

It was nearly the size of a collie, its body compact and hard, its dark fur sleek and shining in the morning light. It was poised to flee, muscles tensed, legs bent, its hard golden eyes trained on me. It considered me for a moment, raising its head slightly to sniff the air. Then it dipped its head again into Frank's food bowl and ate the remains of his dinner from the previous night.

I shifted my gun from one hand to the other, considering whether I had any chance of firing a shot. The cat lifted its head again and looked at me with disdain. The dawn sun was spreading slowly across the lawn now. The animal snarled once, lightly, baring its teeth, then it turned and padded up through the hedgerow and into the field beyond.

During that month, it hunted freely both in the North and the Republic, eluding naturalist and hunter alike, slaughtering livestock with impunity, making the borderland its own.

Then, in the early spring, it disappeared.

ACKNOWLEDGMENTS

I wish to acknowledge the support of my friends and colleagues in St Columb's College, particularly Bob McKimm, Tom Costigan, Ruth Byrne and Nuala McGonagle, who read early drafts of the novel. Thanks also to Sister Perpetua McNulty, Patricia Hughes, Jude Collins, Paul Wilkins, Martin Meenan and Alex Mullan, who each encouraged my writing in his or her own way.

During the writing of this novel, I received wonderful advice and encouragement from Peter Buckman of The Ampersand Agency. Also, thanks to Billy Patton, Gerard McGirr and Lifford Gardai for their assistance with various aspects of this book. Finally, thanks to David Torrans of No Alibis Bookshop.

I owe a massive debt of gratitude to all involved with Macmillan New Writing: Mike Barnard, Sophie Portas and, most particularly, Will Atkins for his editorial work and his tremendous efforts on my behalf.

Thanks to my family: Carmel and Michael, Joe and Susan, Dermot and Lynda, and the girls: Catherine, Ciara, Ellen, Anna and Elena. Thanks also to Paul, Rosaleen and the O'Neill family.

Special thanks to my parents, Laurence and Katrina McGilloway, for more than I could list. And last, but certainly not least, this book is for my sons, Ben and Tom, who make it all worthwhile, and my wife and best friend, Tanya, with love and immense gratitude.

ABOUT THE AUTHOR

Brian McGilloway was born in Derry, Northern Ireland, in 1974 and teaches at St. Columb's College, Derry. Previously he has written plays and short stories. *Borderlands* is his first novel, and was shortlisted for the 2007 New Blood Dagger award. He lives near the Borderlands, with his wife and their two sons.

The employees of Thorndike Press hope you have enjoyed this Large Print book. All our Thorndike and Wheeler Large Print titles are designed for easy reading, and all our books are made to last. Other Thorndike Press Large Print books are available at your library, through selected bookstores, or directly from us.

For information about titles, please call:
(800) 223-1244

or visit our Web site at:
http://gale.cengage.com/thorndike

To share your comments, please write:
Publisher
Thorndike Press
295 Kennedy Memorial Drive
Waterville, ME 04901